Rose pushed op ⟨…⟩ ',
windowless roo⟨…⟩ s
desk, she noticed that the woman's position was oddly out of the ordinary; her limbs stretched unnaturally and her neck twisted away to the side. The desk itself was covered in a flurry of papers and every drawer had been pulled and left open. A mug of spilled coffee puddled down one side of the desk. Written on the mug was the word Boss.

Rose fought panic as she moved in and surveyed the surreal scene before her. Principal Wendy Storme had not moved. The face on the twisted neck was frozen in an ugly grimace of terror—with mouth and eyes wider than normal. Her swollen jaws and neck had darkened to a macabre blue. A thin stream of drool crept down Wendy's chin and her eyes stared unseeing at the wall beyond. Without notice, Wendy's body flopped to the floor with a flaccid thud, virtually at Rose's feet. Principal Wendy Storme was dead.

Praise for Susan Coryell

"*A MURDER OF PRINCIPLE* is a piercing overview in Susan Coryell's characteristically confident hands.

"Narrative is very engaging, offering true insight into the rigors and joys of teaching. The gritty chores, time constraints, efforts and thankless teenage responses are good. A blend of dialogue and documentary lends depth to characters.

"Coryell's characters expand beyond themselves— educators, townspeople, families.

"Plot, character-driven, gives voice to comradeship, compassion, animosity, across age and ethnicity. Ultimately, bad decisions result in a disgruntled community capable of murder.

"Chapter endings lend to the complexity; threats are unbelievably widespread, compelling. *A Murder of Principle* is the proverbial page-turner."

~Mark Anderson

A Murder
of Principle

by

Susan Coryell

This is a work of fiction. Names, characters, places, and incidents are either the product of the author's imagination or are used fictitiously, and any resemblance to actual persons living or dead, business establishments, events, or locales, is entirely coincidental.

A Murder of Principle

Cover Art by *Kim Mendoza*

The Wild Rose Press, Inc.
PO Box 708
Adams Basin, NY 14410-0708
Visit us at www.thewildrosepress.com

Publishing History
First Mainstream Mystery Edition, 2018
Print ISBN 978-1-5092-1969-8
Digital ISBN 978-1-5092-1970-4

Published in the United States of America

Dedication

I dedicate this work of fiction to my colleagues
in the educational field who daily face
the real-life challenges of teaching
in today's fraught world.

Acknowledgments

My heartfelt thanks to those who contributed to the creation of *A Murder of Principle*.

I am indebted to my long-time friend and colleague, Caryl Porte, who generously shared her knowledge of the Juvenile Detention system.

Nancee Costello, retired nurse and active EMT worker, acquainted me with life-saving procedures health professionals utilize when death seems eminent.

My family of writers, including brother Tom and daughter Heidi, offered valuable editing advice and teen-aged grandson Jack Coryell was an invaluable source of help and inspiration for setting, characters, and conflict.

As always, I am thankful for husband Ned's willingness to listen and critique as I talk out my stories.

Prologue

June—The end of the school year

Wendy Storme was a tornado of a woman.

The thought startled Rose Lane wide awake a full hour before her usual time to rise. No sense trying to shut out the dark reminder of today's meeting with the boss; it was no surprise that Principal Wendy Storme would eventually get around to confronting Rose. After all, she must have discerned that Rose was her nemesis—or, perhaps, her chief nemesis, since it would be hard to find anyone on the faculty or administration of Harding High School who held their principal in much esteem.

Rose stretched, peered at the clock and fumbled for her glasses, thinking, in a way, it was a miracle that she had made it almost all the way through the tumultuous school year without a major clash with Ms. Storme. As English Department chair and a vocal member of the Faculty Advisory Council, Rose had endured many negative interactions with her principal, but she had managed to keep quiet and hold her temper in check pretty much since September when Wendy first blustered into the high school, leaving a path of destruction wherever she went. Now it was just a few weeks until graduation. Whatever the reason for the called meeting, Wendy's full fury was bound to fall squarely on Rose's shoulders. Just as it had on so many of her colleagues. Wendy may have simply toted up the many ways Rose had managed to thwart her over the entire year. It was quite possible the principal suspected Rose to be the chief architect of a plan that landed Wendy in hot water with upper management. Whatever Wendy Storme had in mind for Rose this afternoon she knew this meeting would not end well for her.

As usual, Penny Bright, the doe-eyed intern to the English Department, met Rose for her before-school caffeine fix at the community coffee pot in the English workroom. Energetic no matter how early or late the hour, Penny exuded youthful optimism as she handed Rose her mug with a cow on it, and the printed words: Crazy Old Woman—a gift from the English department. "Chin up, Rose," she chirped. "We're all counting on you to take her by storm." Penny's brown eyes expanded almost to her bow-shaped brows and her ready smile always caused Rose to think of the teacher-in-training as a Bright Penny. What resilience. The girl had surely had more than the typical induction into the reality-show machinations of a big suburban high school. Principal Storme had seen to that.

Other colleagues clustered around the coffee pot, speaking in lowered voices. One never knew when a mole might pass by the workroom—a snitch who would report back to the principal about faculty sniping, gossip centered on the unpopular principal. They all knew about Rose's command appearance in Wendy Storme's office set for after school, and they lavished her with their support. Corina Collins slung a sympathetic arm around Rose's shoulder. "Ah, Mama Rose. I'll never forget the way you stood up for me against that angry parent. Remember? Ms. Storme couldn't be bothered?" She squeezed Rose's arm.

"That witch took credit for the rise in test scores for my students," the Transitional English teacher said. "Seventeen kids who spoke nine different languages, not including English, all scored in the passing range. But, she never even stepped inside my room to observe, much less help the kids. And who wrote the grant for materials not in the annual budget? Naturally it was you, Rose."

Everyone talked at once.

"The lies Storme tells," Burt Boyd growled.

"Remember what she did to Lyn Leeson— bumping her out of a job when she was on medical leave?"

"When I taught up North, we always knew we could take along our union rep for a confrontational meeting with administration," Barbara Zander said. "It's too bad we reside in a 'right-to-work' state which really means 'we don't need no stinkin' unions to support us.' "

Rose shrugged, sighed, and accepted the cow cup. "'To the crack of doom,' as Shakespeare would say." She raised her cup in a toast to her colleagues. She was not surprised that the entire department, all twenty-three teachers, by now knew of her meeting that afternoon. That was one sure result of a draconian leader: collegiality. Bunker mentality. Survival technique. They were all huddled against the onslaught but they stood united in one belief: Principal Wendy Storme was a deplorable poser they would weather together. Word traveled quickly whenever tornado warnings loomed.

"Working with me in first block today?" Rose

asked the intern. "We're decompressing now that the AP exams are over. Anything to keep senioritis from setting in, you know."

"Fun projects?" Penny filled her own mug, the one with Bambi pictured on it. Her liquid brown eyes glowed with youthful enthusiasm. Penny was a compact package, part pep squad and part kitten, alternating between cheers and purrs. Rose had come to depend on her never-ending spirit and warmth, both professionally and as a friend. Together they formed a perfect contrast of jaded pro and dew-eyed rookie.

"Actually hilarious," Rose told the intern. "Each group has to demonstrate the character of five literary figures from books read over the year in some coherent original drama." Rose sipped her coffee. "Too bad you missed the one they did yesterday. Gregor, you know the man-sized beetle from Kafka's *Metamorphosis*? One of the kids dressed up with antennae and all and meeped around the rest of the characters who were on some kind of an all-nighter. Hamlet forever debating suicide, Oedipus Rex lusting after his mother…well you can imagine," Rose said.

"I guess now that the pressure's off with the Advance Placement Literature exam, the kids can just have some fun."

"Likewise the teacher." Rose drained her coffee cup. "Now, let me get my stuff ready for class." She moved to the tiny cubicle where her desk resided. The workroom itself had been aptly designed as a multi-purpose facility. The school housed a similar space for each of the academic disciplines. The English workroom was equipped with two dozen individual desk carrels, a long table for eating lunch, two computers, a microwave and refrigerator and a bathroom, along with a small room for private telephone conversations. A white board for announcements and a metal stand designed for coffee service completed the picture. It was a copious and practical facility which the teachers utilized on a daily basis. But it could never take the place of a permanent classroom to call one's own.

Principal Storme, ever wise in her own mind, had given all of the math teachers one fixed classroom while marching many of the English teachers around all day to different locations in the multi-story building. Especially the older teachers. Especially Rose Lane, who taught three distinctly different preparations. Anyone with a modicum of intelligence would realize English teachers exist in piles of materials—cartloads—videos, portfolios, folders, class sets of paperbacks and stacks of papers for grading. Math teachers? Maybe a calculator. Rose took her kidding from her colleagues in the English workroom. "Creeping Virus," they liked to call her as her twenty-five years' accumulation of teaching materials billowed to the top of her study carrel and dribbled down the aisles, infecting other desks in the room. Rose's carrel was like a spin-off from a Dr. Seuss book:

Room-less Rose
Could reach her toes
But not her desk.
Stuff piled so high
Up to the sky—
Oh what a mess!

With no stationary classroom to call her own, this was Rose's only recourse for storage. Her colleagues knew they could thank Principal Storme for the situation.

Rose rummaged through a precariously stacked hodgepodge of folders. "Where the heck…where's the AP projects file?" Tossing around papers and books, she settled at length on a bright yellow folder. "Oh yes. Color coded. How could I forget?" Scrabbling again, she came up with a box of portfolios. "And here are their graded portfolios." She handed the box to the intern. "Okay. Guess I'm ready. Let's go. Thank God my first room of the day is on this hall."

Laughing with Penny over the creativity of the senior skits, Rose almost forgot that with every click, every bell tone, the clock pushed her closer and closer to her doom—her command appearance in Principal Wendy Storme's office. One 90-minute block done; two to go—until—what? Off with her head? Rose shuddered as she considered the number of faculty and staff of Harding High whom Principal Storme had summarily demoted, harassed or forced into transferring to another school. And, there were any number of incidents the administrator could dredge up against her. This Rose knew. Then, again, Ms. Storme had proven herself adept at fabricating her own reasons for disrespecting staff. No evidence necessary.

As the day wore on, one thought kept Rose sane. She had made up her mind to stand up to the principal, spit in her face, if necessary. Penny Bright had not been far from the truth in her morning comment, "We're counting on you to take her by storm." Yes. Rose was prepared, and she had been repeating her mantra all day: *Stand Strong.* Still, the situation called for concern. A direct hit from a tornado was not to be taken lightly.

And, Rose Lane hated confrontation. If at all possible, she preferred to problem-solve through diplomacy. She had a tendency to clench her fists whenever she knew that a confrontation was inevitable.

"Is she ready for me?" Rose asked the secretary who sat at the big desk in the middle of the main office.

The young, cheery administrative assistant glanced up at the wall clock. "Oh glory. It's almost quittin' time. What a busy day this has been." She drew her gaze back to Rose. "You're the last in a train-length of appointments today—the caboose. Go on in," the woman said with a wave of her hand. "I'll be prayin' for you," she added in an undertone.

The door to the principal's office was slightly ajar. This was unusual. Storme always kept her door firmly closed lest anyone violate her inner sanctum without formal admittance. No open-door policy for this tyrant; it threw Rose off a bit. Her first planned move was to knock authoritatively and enter with an air of confidence far beyond her real feeling. Now what? Balling up her fists and peering furtively through the narrow opening, Rose's gaze aligned with the island coffee bar the principal had installed. A caffeine addict, Storme was known to drink the brew all day. The bar was stocked with all sorts of coffee paraphernalia as well as a fancy latte machine. A strong scent of fresh, dark coffee wafted toward her.

Holding the door steady with her left hand, Rose knocked with her right. There was no answer. Though she leaned an ear toward the aperture, Rose could discern no sound at all in the principal's office.

With a blast of nerves, Rose pushed open the door and moved inside the large, windowless room. Settling her eyes on the principal's desk, she noticed that the woman's position was oddly out of the ordinary; her limbs stretched unnaturally and her neck twisted away to the side. The desk itself was covered in a flurry of papers and every drawer had been pulled and left open. A mug of spilled coffee puddled down one side of the desk. Written on the mug was the word Boss.

Rose fought panic as she moved in and surveyed the surreal scene before her. Principal Wendy Storme had not moved. The face on the twisted neck was frozen in an ugly grimace of terror—with mouth and eyes wider than normal. Her swollen jaws and neck had darkened to a macabre blue. A thin stream of drool crept down Wendy's chin and her eyes stared unseeing at the wall beyond. Without notice, Wendy's body flopped to the floor with a flaccid thud, virtually at Rose's feet. Principal Wendy Storme was dead.

Chapter One

September—Nine months earlier, the beginning of the school year

Penelope Bright, Penny to her friends, bubbled with excitement over her internship at Harding High, a large suburban facility with a top-notch academic rating. Only five years in existence as a secondary school in a huge, diverse county, Harding already boasted numerous local, state, and national awards in everything from sports to music, drama, and forensics. The debate team had maintained its top standing in the nation for five straight years. School spirit! Harding High Hawks rule! Rah, Rah, Rah! And the facility itself was a stunning show of modern architecture. Three stories in height, floor to ceiling windows, attractive open spaces for common use, and even an eco-garden in the courtyard for the Agriculture Studies program. Harding High was an intern's dream high school.

Penny's summer interview with Principal Carter Thompson had left the intern giddy with expectation; Thompson evidently loved Penny's enthusiasm and Penny knew, just knew, the earnest, caring leadership of such a principal would see her through her first real job in education. How quickly she had dismissed Mr. Thompson's reminder that he was retiring before the school year began in September. Carter Thompson had opened Harding High, bringing along with him the brightest and best from his own staff at his previous school and hiring all other staff members himself from schools all over the county. From the reading resource teacher to the director of guidance, the secretaries to the assistant principals, every department chair and every teacher and every coach had been personally vetted by Principal Thompson; they were a spectacular assemblage of educational professionals. What could possibly go wrong, Penny thought.

What, indeed.

Wendy Storme.

Storme could fool a lot of people, it seemed. After Carter Thompson's retirement, the county educational leaders hired her, didn't they? Perhaps it was because she talked as smoothly as a moderator on a cable television show. Glib, though the woman was, it did not take the faculty and staff of Harding High long to realize her actual forte was lying. Though she said she had taught several different high school subjects, what she had actually done was serve in a quasi-administrative capacity for elementary school English as a Second Language on the county level. No classroom experience at all. The biggest lie? "I'm a people person," she crooned at the very first faculty meeting at the beginning of the school year where she was introduced as the new principal. Wendy Storme most definitely cared about people for one reason and one reason only: to further her own career. It was apparent early-on that she wanted to move up in the county hierarchy already top heavy with over two dozen "assistant deputy superintendents," whatever that job entailed. Most of all, Wendy Storme had no time for a lowly *intern.* Which she made very clear to Penny directly after that first faculty meeting. "Oh. You're the intern. I'm sure you'll find someone to help you here."

That was it. *You're on your own, little chickie,* was what Penny heard. Well, she was resourceful enough. She'd paid her own way through college, with help from hard-won scholarships and grants. The internship, which combined a graduate degree with high school field and teaching experience in her chosen discipline, also provided a squeak-by stipend just big enough to cover living expenses. Still, a little guidance from her leader would have been welcome.

Penny had taken a good look at her new boss as she spoke to the faculty. Probably in her mid-forties, the principal wore a nice suit—jacket tailored in dark gray, pin-striped pants. Sensible shoes with a small, chunky heel. Professional as her outfit was, it could not disguise Wendy Storme's flabby jowls and her decisively un-athletic stance in front of the faculty. Penny's bet was this woman spent zero time at the gym. Permed, graying hair frizzed like Brillo around chipmunk cheeks and somehow accentuated her beak of a nose. When she smiled, a space between her front teeth gave her the comical look of a ventriloquist's dummy. When she spoke quickly, her pronunciation of *s* whistled through the space.

Absorbed in her observations, Penny jumped when she felt a hand on her shoulder. Turning, she faced a slim, middle-aged woman with glasses perched on her head and a no-nonsense expression on her pleasant face. Short, frosted hair framed cheeks that remained smooth and unwrinkled, though tiny lines of crow's feet sneaked from the corners of her intelligent, jade-colored eyes.

"I'm Rose Lane," she said. "English Department chair, Miss Bright. I just wanted to let you know that every teacher in my department is eager to help you find your strengths and work through your weaknesses."

Even if she was too green to know it, this was exactly what Penny needed to hear. She had found her mentor.

"My name is Penny. Where can I start?"

"We have a scant four work days to get our rooms ready for the students to begin the school year." Rose gave a slight shrug. "Principal Thompson always gave us as much 'free' time as possible, knowing the extent of our tasks. We'll see how Ms. Storme handles it. We're all hoping there will be a minimum of faculty meetings to take up our time." Rose grunted. "First I have to sort out the three different rooms I've been assigned to this year."

Loading paperback books onto a cart in the book room while Rose directed, Penny lifted her head from her task and wiped sweat from her brow.

Rose chuckled. "You might as well get used to doing all the leg work of teaching yourself, Penny. Need a worksheet? Type it, print it, collate it, hole-punch it. You may even have to do a bit of maintenance work on the printer. The secretaries are all assigned to administrators and they have no time to help the teachers. Supplies? Your department chair will order them for you, budget allowing, of course. You'll have to find a way to transport them to wherever they're needed. Ditto for furniture. Most of us get willing students to do the heavy lifting—computers, file cabinets, you know what I mean?"

Penny nodded. "Yeah. I get it. Guess I never thought about this part of a teaching career, the nuts and bolts."

"Oh, there are many more surprises in store, dear child. Just wait until you deal with bus duty, hall duty, cafeteria duty, bathroom duty—don't raise your eyebrows at me—yes, we all are assigned our IPRs, Individual Professional Responsibilities, though we refer to them as IURs. Unprofessional responsibilities. Any of your education courses in college prep you to monitor toilet stalls?"

"I'm at your mercy, Rose. I see that I need to experience it all. Use me any way you like."

"Duly noted. And remembered." Rose grunted. "Just wait until you see how you will utilize your 'lunch hour,' and I'm not referring to cafeteria duty."

Before Penny could comment, a figure arrived at the door to the book room.

"Finally. I found you, Rose!" Penny stared at the best looking hunk of male humanity she had seen since graduating from college.

"Brad, have you met our intern yet?" Rose tilted her head, evidently observing Penny's visceral reaction to the handsome intruder whose gray-blue eyes laser-locked onto the intern. "Brad's our head football coach. Last year he took the boys to the state playoffs."

Penny stretched out her hand for a shake. "Penny Bright. Nice to meet you...Brad..."

"McIver. Brad McIver."

McIver did not fit Penny's stereotype of football coach. The guy was over six feet tall and lanky and long-armed as a basketball player. None of the usual heft and brawn associated with football. Penny liked what she saw: a full head of sandy hair, angular, clean-shaven Irish-ruddy jaw and a ready smile.

"When he's not coaching the Hawks on to another victory, Brad is leading his high-level math students through the mysteries of logarithms, sines, cosines and such." Rose gave Brad an approving look. "He's the senior class advisor, elected by students year after year. And my guess is he's here now to discuss the AP schedule since he's also the Advance Placement Coordinator for Harding High."

With a sidelong glance at Penny, Brad addressed Rose. "So, when can we meet, Rose? Will this afternoon be okay? After the faculty meeting Ms. Storme has called and before football practice. I know everybody has so much work to do to get ready for classes next week. Never enough time, is there? But we have some new guidelines for AP programs across the board, and all AP teachers need to know about them. I'll keep the meeting as short and to the point as possible."

Rose turned to Penny. "Care to tag along for this one?"

Penny tried to hide her eagerness. "Sure. I have a lot to learn about football." She blushed. "I mean about the AP program."

Seated beside Brad McIver in the auditorium, Penny paid as much attention to Principal Storme's talk as possible, what with the distraction of her companion's proximity. Every now and then Brad would roll his eyes toward her along with a *humpf* or a twitch of his lips. Penny got it. Ms. Storme talked way too much about herself—oddly irrelevant snippets that would appear to elevate her erudition. She went on and on about brain synapses and county policy for textbook purchases and tedious topics far from the minds of teachers prepping for students' imminent arrival. Inexperienced as Penny was, even she could see that this was a colossal waste of teachers' precious time. The woman had not covered a single topic that was useful, helpful or relevant to opening school. It was easy just to sit and bask in the warm presence next to her, Coach Brad McIver. *Damn. He even smells good.*

Penny leaned in and whispered, "Who is this 'Sparky' guy she keeps citing?"

Brad made a sour face. "Milton Sparkman, our illustrious Superintendent of Schools. Only his best buds refer to him as 'Sparky.' Ms. Storme is doing a terrific job of name-dropping."

As the meeting broke up, Brad stood, stretched, and yawned with exaggeration, then turned to Rose sitting on the other side of him. "Gotta call off today's AP meeting, I'm afraid. The boys are probably already waiting for me on the practice field." He flapped his fingers and tossed his head in the direction of the principal. "Yap, yap, yap," he muttered. "Maybe the AP teachers can meet early tomorrow. Before she has a chance to call another useless, time-consuming meeting?"

Rose pursed her lips and nodded curtly. "I'll tell the others. Say 7:30?"

"I'll bring donuts," Brad said. He glanced at Penny and grinned. "We'll meet in my classroom. Y' know, I'm a math teacher. I get to have my own classroom. See you tomorrow?"

Penny smiled. "Make mine Bavarian cream." She

sincerely hoped there was no significant other in Brad McIver's life.

****

Rose, Penny, and several other teachers stood outside Brad McIver's door on the math hall.

"He said 7:30 a.m., right?" one of them commented. "So, where's Brad?"

"Brad's usually so prompt," Rose said, checking her watch. "Oh, look, there's Jose Mendoza. I'll get him to unlock Brad's door for us."

"Glad to help you out, Ms. Lane," Jose flashed a bright smile at Rose as he wielded his master key. "Ms. Lane was my English teacher a dozen years ago," he told Penny. "At the old high school. She's the reason I got hired here at Harding High. She recommended me to Mr. Thompson."

"It's always good to have a custodian on your side, Penny," Rose laughed. "Jose was a hard-working student when he entered my class, only recently completing the English as a Second Language program. Excellent progress due to his determination." She patted the custodian's shoulder. "Thanks, Jose. Having you work here makes my life so much easier."

The teachers filed into the empty room and gathered chairs. Introducing Penny to the teachers assembled, Rose commented, "These are the folks who teach Advanced Placement courses across the disciplines."

"So where's our AP coordinator and where are the donuts?" the psychology teacher grumbled.

They engaged in small talk until Brad arrived, looking shaken and upset. His healthy complexion had gone ashen.

"My God. What's happened?" Rose exclaimed, standing up and holding out her hands. "Were you involved in an accident?"

"No accident," Brad got out through gritted teeth. "You are looking at the survivor of an F-4 tornado. A deliberate hit, in my opinion."

Brad sat heavily in his desk chair. "Ms. Storme just relieved me of my duties as football coach. Right after she demoted three of our esteemed colleagues from their department chair positions. Math, science, and history chairs. I watched them file out of her office one-by-one."

"But, but...why?" Rose sputtered. "What possible reasons..."

"She cited a parent accusation on me from last year," Brad shook his head. "A parent complained that I wouldn't let her son participate on the practice field because a teacher had told me the kid wasn't keeping up with his homework. It's always been standard operating procedure, as you know. Schoolwork comes before sports. It's how we keep the kids focused on academics."

"And a wonderful policy it is. I always consider the coaches my strongest allies for shoring up any and all slack-off athletes." Rose was incensed.

"Of course, I knew all about the incident. I guess it had to go in my file, as an administrative requirement about documenting parent complaints, you know. But Carter Thompson and I had a good laugh over the whole thing when the parent later came to school, at the end of football season, and thanked me for turning around her kid's academic performance." Brad pressed his lips into a thin smile. "I believe you were the teacher responsible for that, Rose. You were the one who reported the student's behavior to me."

"So...so that's why the principal fired you?" Penny was aghast. "Even though the parent said later that it was a positive thing? Wasn't that in the file, too?"

"There's a good chance Principal Storme chose to ignore that part of the issue. She latched on to what she could use as justification for bumping me out of the coaching position." Brad swiped at his hair in agitation.

"And, there may be another wrinkle. After I left her office, the cross-country coach collared me and whispered on the QT that the head football coaching job is going to a guy by the name of Grant. Grant Sparkman."

"Sparkman...you mean...isn't that the same name as Superintendent Sparkman?" Penny asked.

"Quick learner," Brad gestured at Penny. "Yes, the same Sparkman. Seems Grant is the Super's nephew. And, somehow he lost his coaching job at his school." Brad gave a mirthless chuckle. "Goodview High, where he had quite a reputation."

"Reputation?" Penny's eyes widened.

"Grant Sparkman is widely known as a dumb jock." Brad grunted. "And a lousy coach. His team win-loss record is in the toilet."

Brad let this sink in before announcing, "As for the three demoted department chairs? I figured that one out pretty fast." He looked around the room. "Think about it. Those three have PhD degrees. Ms. Storme does not."

"Holy crap," Rose fumed. "So, what's the takeout? What will the...demoted chairs do, I wonder?"

"I had a chance to talk briefly with them. The

science chair is heading off to the science and technology magnet school across town. They've been asking him to chair their robotics department since the school opened. They're getting his papers in order for the transfer as we speak." Brad shook his head. "Carter was delighted when he talked the guy into teaching at Harding—such a brilliant scientist and a fine teacher. Now he's gone."

"History chair plans to stick around to help out the new leader—says she was getting tired of all the extra department work, anyway. And the thought of having to coordinate frequently, as department chair, with the new principal is reason enough to gladly turn the leadership over to someone else in the department." Brad made a face. "Still, it's a big loss. Besides a prestigious degree, she has so much experience."

"Jeez," Rose said. "What a shake-up. What about math?"

"Well, the math chair says if something good comes up, she'll be out of here. The university has some interesting openings for folks with a PhD in math."

The AP teachers sat in shocked silence. "I'd say our new leader is off to a...a stormy start." Rose cupped her chin in her hand. "Maybe now I'm glad I didn't pursue that PhD degree after all."

"The whole thing is a lose-lose for Harding," Brad ground out. "Can you believe Storme is driving out...driving down our most qualified teachers because her ego can't stand an academic degree higher than hers?" He smacked the table and cursed under his breath.

"How about you, Brad," Penny asked, her voice

hesitant. "Will you stay at Harding?"

Brad looked at Penny, then the others. "I'll continue to teach math, continue to oversee the school AP program, even though I won't be coaching any more. At least not here." He snorted. "I have had some coaching offers from other high schools which I might consider." He smacked the table again "I just hate leaving the team in the lurch like that."

"This news will rip through the school, not to mention the entire Harding community, like a California wildfire. Our boys are going to be devastated," Rose murmured. "And the parents..."

Brad's eyes hardened. "Yeah. I know. And that sucks the worst of all." He lowered his chin to his chest. "I could kill that witch," he breathed.

Penny was stunned. It was simply too much to comprehend in her short career. She'd had no idea how much power the principal of a school wielded. She could feel the bubbles of enthusiasm evaporating at a rapid rate.

Chapter Two

The opening weeks of school had always been Rose Lane's favorite. Pristine white boards and fresh text books and binders waiting to be filled exuded the fragrant smell of expectation. Students filed in eager to greet old friends and make new ones, their minds open to whatever instructors had to offer. New school clothes, fall sports, election for class officers and the homecoming court. If only the vibe could last all year.

For the first time in her career, Rose felt deflated rather than exuberated as school opened. The new principal had dropped a dead weight on Harding's most respected colleagues; Rose could not dismiss her misgivings. Her gut and her long experience warned that this was only the beginning of a catastrophic year. Call it academic climate change.

In a way, she felt bad about Penny having to experience such negativity, which is toxic for any educator of any status. On the one hand, she might as well see how bad things could be; on the other, why squelch an eager neophyte who could potentially contribute much to the field? Rose hoped to walk the balance beam without teetering too far into unrealistic expectations on one side or dire reality on the other.

She was not off to a good start. Stopped in the hall on her way to her desk in the workroom before school started, Rose was sucked into a dialog about the Faculty

Advisory Council with the principal.

"I am considering abolishing the FAC, Rose." Wendy Storme's hair looked electrified, standing on end like Medusa's snakes made of wire. "I see no purpose in the council. Frankly, I consider it a waste of time."

Rose thought for a moment. From the opening of Harding High, she had served on the Faculty Advisory Council. The FAC was the only recourse for teacher worries involving classroom issues beyond their control. Once a month the council representative selected by each discipline would meet with the principal to share concerns voiced in their department. Some issues were mundane—for example, why is there no hot water in the teachers' bathrooms? Some were pricklier—how do I handle the kid with Tourettes who spews obscenities in third period class? Rose knew how important the council was, for teacher morale, if nothing else. Wendy, apparently, had zero interest in teacher morale, or in their concerns or complaints, especially if they expected her to listen, respect and react in a positive way. She had more important things on her agenda, like her position on the county architectural committee with Superintendent Sparkman, for example.

Rose stifled the impulse to tell her boss it would be a big mistake to dismantle the FAC. "Why, Wendy, I am surprised to hear you say that. You do realize, don't you, that the council is a wonderful opportunity for you to meet with elected department leaders to disseminate your own ideas to improve school culture. You, alone, can solidify the group and encourage the reps to take back to their departments all the exciting innovations you have in store for Harding High."

The principal stared at Rose. "I hadn't considered that aspect." She chewed her lip.

"After all, you are the *head* of the Faculty Advisory Council; the teachers are simply there to coordinate with you as our leader." Rose knew it was complete BS, but Wendy, though skeptical, seemed to soften to Rose's points, intrigued with the idea that she could wield her power through the group, no doubt.

"I will have to think the matter through. For the time being, the FAC can continue to meet." Turning, Wendy whirled off toward her office.

Rose came away from the encounter tasting bile. Any reasonable administrator should want to get a feel for her staff; Storme's desire to disband the main channel for teacher grievances smacked of a power-grab. This, too, did not bode well for the faculty and staff of Harding High.

Fresh from a verbal tiff with the principal over this, Rose's blood pressure had not yet settled when Penny, unaware of the confrontation, asked a simple question, "An experienced teacher like you, Rose. You must have a daily objective. Mind sharing your goal for today?"

"Not to say *shit* before my first class," Rose said, feeling instantly guilty for the jaded response.

Penny flinched.

"Sorry, Penny. I'll tell you about it later." She patted the intern's hand. They'd opened school only two weeks ago.

****

Rose and Penny conferred in Rose's special hiding place, a spot no one had yet discovered in Rose's five years at Harding—the reference room of the library.

Rarely used, a small, windowless, isolated square of quiet, the room contained a dozen wooden desks, each with a small brass lamp, the kind with a little green shade and a pull-chain to turn it on and off. Books that could not be checked out such as encyclopedias, atlases and other reference materials lined the shelves on two walls. The librarians, close allies of all teachers, but of Rose, in particular, had always maintained sealed lips whenever someone came looking for Rose. Especially administrators. And now, especially Wendy Storme. Here Rose and Penny could discuss classes, curriculum and teaching styles and techniques without interruption.

Penny opened their talk. "There's an issue with Devin Giovani, you know, in English Eleven. Two tardies already. Aren't we supposed to write them up and send some form to the assistant principals after two late attendances?" Penny cocked her head. "And then what happens?"

Rose had cheerfully turned over attendance issues to her intern. "Ugh. Tardies are such a bear, for teachers as well as students. And the administrators love to do their 'hall sweeps,' usually after lunch periods when kids dawdle at their lockers or rush out of restrooms. Then they can assign detentions, which we teachers end up monitoring."

"After-school detention?" Penny shook her head. "Sorry. I am such a newbie. I haven't learned all the finer points of high school discipline yet."

"Let me talk to Devin," Rose said. "I taught him last year when he was a sophomore. Dealt with some family problems. We have a good rapport."

Penny gave her a pensive look. "Rapport. I guess every teacher strives for that, with every student. I get the feeling Devin doesn't believe I'm a real teacher, or something. He gives me a bit of attitude occasionally. When I confronted him about the tardy attendance situation, he acted as if I have no authority to do so."

Rose gave Penny a sympathetic look. "I have some background information on Devin that makes him, oh I don't know...makes him trust me, perhaps. As I said, I'll pull him in for a chat."

"Are you comfortable sharing that 'background information'?" Penny asked.

"It's a somewhat delicate situation. Last year, with the help of his guidance counselor, Christine Yamada, we worked through some problems Devin was having at home. You've met Ms. Yamada, right?"

"Oh yes. Lovely lady. So patient, so kind..."

"And thorough. Follow-through is her forte. We have a solid counseling staff; I'd say Christine Yamada is the top of the chart." Rose nodded for emphasis. "Don't let her warm, comforting counselor personality fool you. 'Though she be small, yet she is full of fight.' A character right out of a Shakespearean play." Rose chuckled. "I've seen Christine in action and she can be as fierce as a mother hen protecting her chicks."

"I instantly liked her; I knew she was the type a kid could confide in." A wistful look crossed Penny's face. "It takes a special professional to counsel high school kids."

"So, as I said, last year there were some issues impacting Devin's school performance, which he confided to me. I sense the student's...let's call it *unrest* again this year. I do hope he's already working with his counselor." Rose gave Penny a thoughtful look. "Rapport and responsibility. A fine line there."

What Penny did not know and what Rose couldn't tell her without breaching confidentiality of a student, was that Devin Giovani's mother had left the family last year. Upset at having to live with an overbearing father, Devin assumed responsibility for protecting his younger sister whom he felt his father mistreated.

"My dad has always had trouble controlling his temper," Devin told her. A handsome lad, stocky and muscular with curly, dark hair and black eyes, he spoke with strained effort. "Dad tries to excuse his behavior sometimes by blaming his Italian heritage. 'It's-a my hot-blooded Italiano ancestry,' he jokes. My mom and sister and I have never thought it was funny, though."

Devin's unhappy, unstable situation at home had affected his academic progress in every class over his soph year. Ms. Yamada had arranged for family counseling that seemed to help. But Rose could already see the signs of recurring anxiety in Devin this school year. It worried Rose. She had her own reasons for understanding the jarring psychological results when a parent breaks with the family.

Rose thought about Devin Giovani and his little sister all the way home, barely listening to the beach music she'd programmed into the car radio. Devin had brought his sibling to introduce to Rose after school one day last spring. A diminutive ten-year-old with huge, dark eyes, Gabby Giovani belied her name by barely uttering a word as her brother poured out their plight to Rose. The child's eyes darted nervously around the classroom and when Rose reached for her hand in an effort to pull her into the conversation, she flinched as though she had been struck. The little girl is missing her mother, was Rose's first thought. She needs protection from her father was what she later learned from Devin. Rose often found herself concerned about a student's personal problems, but this situation with Devin Giovani and his sister was particularly worrisome. She'd seen so many cases of broken families and how they impacted a kid's life. It was a familiar pattern: withdrawal, failure to engage in class discussions, loner behavior with his peers. And now the tardy class attendance. She would find time to talk to Devin. Soon. But it was hard to stop worrying. She turned into her driveway with no recollection of her route home.

Kicking off her shoes, Rose placed the mail and newspaper on the kitchen counter and rummaged in the pantry for a snack. Bananas. Good choice. Granola bar. And a tall glass of iced tea. Lunch had consisted of an orange, nothing else. She was famished. She'd made the mistake of taking an unpeeled orange for lunch, along with a half sandwich, forgetting that there would not be time to both peel and eat the fruit and consume anything else. A scant thirty minutes comprised the teachers' lunch period. It was never sufficient to cover what must be accomplished. Breaking out of the classroom from students who needed to confer on something or other was the first hurdle. Then a dash to the bathroom, possibly the only chance in the entire day, took up more minutes. Sitting at the computer to check for emails from parents and administrators that had to be answered immediately could easily suck up the remaining minutes for "lunch." Every teacher Rose had ever met had learned either to fast all day or to chew lunch so rapidly as to defy digestion. It was the exact opposite of the three-martini lunch as she imagined it.

Settling into her favorite armchair, she began checking her personal phone messages. There was never time to do so at school. Another text from her ex-husband, Max. Knowing it would only be the same plea he repeatedly offered, she deleted the message without reading. Would he ever give up? She had blocked him from her email and Facebook, stopped using her Twitter account and refused to answer his phone messages and texts. After all, he was the one who wanted out. He'd left Rose and their daughter Margo and hooked up with his *true love*, the one he'd met at an office function, but it hadn't taken long before he wanted Rose back. Begging her to forgive him, trying to get to her through Margo. Turned out the other woman was a full-on femme fatale adept at seducing naïve males and moving on to the next victim.

Luckily, Rose had pressed for ownership of the house in the divorce agreement. Max lived in a nearby apartment now, and, since they both worked locally, Rose was always wary of seeing him unexpectedly around town. As far as she was concerned, the separation and subsequent divorce had turned out to be a good thing; she was much happier staying out of Max's periphery. She'd even changed the locks on the doors. The fact that Max worked as a personal banker at the credit union where so many of her friends and colleagues did business made her situation a bit dicey. So far, since they'd been apart, they'd only met up in person a handful of times.

Rose had no interest in letting Max back into her life. He could try to influence their daughter Margo all he liked; Rose was done with the marriage—with any relationship other than that of co-parent to their daughter. Margo could raise only a twinge of remorse in her when she cried and fought for Max's pleas to repair their family split. Lately, now that Margo was well into her college studies, Rose had noted a heightened awareness on her daughter's part. Had Margo learned what it was like to feel used? Had a male friend taken her for granted? Had her daughter turned to feminism? Rose couldn't be sure, not that it mattered. Margo was maturing into a beautiful, savvy and smart young lady who was learning what it meant to be an independent female in the modern world, a woman comfortable being herself, perfection not required. Rose felt she'd had some influence on that transformation. She harbored no interest whatsoever in Max's texts. Whiney. Let him cry on somebody else's shoulder. The divorce was final.

Rose checked her other phone messages. There was a text from Cliff: "Meet me for a drink and dinner tonight? I'm teaching 5 PM class. Town Bar and Grill at 7:00?"

Sure. Perfect, in fact. It would give her time for a nice soak in the jetted tub, a chance to wash off the detritus of the work day. She texted her reply and headed for the bathroom. Cliff, the professor she'd met while working on her master's degree after Max had deserted. Cliff, like her, left by a spouse with too little commitment. Rose had momentarily forgotten about Devin and his little sister.

Chapter Three

Penny huddled closer to Brad on the top tier of the stadium bleachers. The shivering October air penetrated her Harding High Hawks hoodie as if it were made of Swiss cheese. Under a clear, crisp starry sky, she welcomed an excuse to cuddle with the former head football coach.

"I don't know, Penny," Brad had confessed when she'd proposed attending the Friday night game. "You say watching the team play under the new coach might help me overcome my...what did you call it...my separation anxiety?"

"I guess that was a poor choice of words." Penny flinched. "I was just trying to help. You're a brilliant teacher. The kids love you, the parents love you. Heck, the AP Board loves you! There's so much more to Brad McIver than coaching high school football. But you seem...completely undone by what Ms. Storme did to you—relieving you of your coaching position like that."

"The *way* she did it." Brad made a face. "'Your behavior as a coach was unprofessional.'" He lisped the *s* sounds in imitation of the principal's speech impediment. "She knew damn well it was untrue. Not that she cares about truth. Or football, for that matter."

"I understand why you might not want to be seen at a home game. We can sit way up high, to the side of the press box, out of sight. And, if it's too painful, we can just ease our way out of the stands and leave already." Somehow Penny had convinced Brad to view his old team from the perspective of a fan rather than a coach. She'd really hoped it would work to jolt him out of the doldrums. Though they'd only met at the beginning of the school year, Penny instinctively knew Brad was not normally so morose. In fact, Rose had corroborated her intuition, saying, "Ms. Storme has really done a number on our man Brad. He was a jokester, optimistic, always planning ways to energize his boys on the team. Now he walks around with his chin dragging the floor." She cast an appraising gaze at Penny. "I can tell Brad is taken with you. Think you could find a way to cheer him up?"

Well, Penny's football strategy was not working. Part of the problem was the way the team was performing. Though Penny knew only the rudiments of the game—when we're in the huddle we have the ball, when the referee points one hand it's a first down, and when the ref throws two hands to the sky it's a touchdown—even she could tell how badly the boys were playing. Brad spent much of the time muttering under his breath about mistakes, primarily caused, evidently, by the coach. "No, no! Bad play, coach," he'd blurted out before clamping his hand over his mouth. Every other play elicited either a cringe or a groan. "The idiot coach has benched the best quarterback," he confided to Penny at one point.

The reaction of the hometown crowd did not help. Despite the upbeat efforts of the cheerleaders, pep band and color guard, the mood of the stands was dark. Where, they wanted to know, was their championship team? After all, only a handful of the stand-out players had graduated last year. A solid squad remained, but the new coach seemed to have no idea how to utilize his talent. More than one disgruntled fan had voiced disdain for Coach Sparkman without taking pains to speak softly, Penny observed. "Where's coach McIver? We need McIver!" rumbled like thunder over the stadium planks. It reminded Penny that numerous letters to the editor had been published in the local paper complaining about Brad's firing and his replacement. It seemed nobody was happy about the situation.

Penny was afraid to peek at Brad to see his reaction to the crowd, but she felt him stiffen when his own name wafted their way on the breeze. "We need McIver?" Penny thought. McIver needed them. Attending the game had been a big mistake.

"Let's go get coffee." Penny stood. "I know the game's not over but I'm freezing."

"At the concession stand?" Brad looked surprised.

"No. At the coffee shop on the corner near my apartment. You know, the one with the original name: Ground to Please."

Brad rose from the wooden bench. "I've had enough. A cup of Joe might boost my spirits."

"I know nothing about football, Brad. But even I could see tonight's game was a disaster."

"Half way into the season, it doesn't look hopeful for the boys."

Penny linked her arm with Brad's. "So much for my idea of psychology. Sorry I dragged you to the game."

They entered the warm and fragrant space and slid into a corner booth out of the direct light. It was never a good idea to be seen together by students. Who knew what rumors they'd start on Snapchat or Facebook or some other social network so readily available via the phones glued constantly to their hands. Not to mention the camera apps just a fingertip away.

"I haven't told anybody this," Brad began. He tapped the table. "I've been getting phone calls. Lots of phone calls. Texts. Emails."

"From...from...?"

"Parents, mostly. Some from students and former students who've gone on to play college ball."

"All with a similar message?" Penny picked up the menu and pretended to read it. "They want you back as coach, eh?"

"Well, yeah. Pretty much that." Brad smiled for the first time that evening. "But a good many of them broaden the theme."

Penny closed the menu and placed it on the table. "How so?"

"Here, let me show you." Brad pulled his phone from his pocket and scrolled down to a text message. "This one came in while we were at the game a few minutes ago. I heard it beep, but I haven't read it yet. Let's see."

Penny stared at the screen. "Somebody ought to kill that witch," it read.

Penny did not try to hide her shock. "It's just high school football, Brad. You mean...somebody is mad enough to murder over this?"

"They're pissed. Their kids aren't getting to play. College scouts won't see the best players in a good light, whether they're sitting the bench or looking like clumsy fools because the coach is a moron." He shook his head. "And then there's the rabid fan base. After five years of winning seasons, they are ready to kill the cause of the change, as they see it."

Somebody ought to kill that witch. Wow, Penny wondered. Are they serious?

Brad walked Penny to her apartment. "Come in for a while? I have a nice bottle of red wine," she said.

Brad hesitated. "Why not. It might take the edge off of...the coffee. Let me get a good night's sleep for a change."

"Do you want to talk about it? Your anger, or whatever it is?" Penny settled into the couch beside Brad, relishing his arm around her.

"More psychology, Dr. Bright?" he teased.

"Seriously, Brad. This whole thing. It's obviously eating away at you."

"I suppose you're right. It was just so unexpected. The team and...we were psyched for another winning season. The spirit, the camaraderie, the concentration, and effort. I did not realize how much I would miss it all." He reached for his glass. "You know, as a coach I always felt I could influence the kids on the team in ways no teacher or principal or guidance counselor, no other mentor can. Because it happened that way for me."

"You grew up with football?"

"Not exactly. In high school I was a bit of a lost soul. Not many friends, a slacker when it came to my studies. My mom was raising my sister and me single-handedly since my dad's death and there wasn't money for anything extra like county sports." He sipped his wine. "Then when I got to high school, a teacher reached out to me. I still don't know why. I was skinny and gawky and klutzy. Not your typical athletic build or anything."

"Please go on," Penny encouraged. She could feel Brad loosening up. Was it the wine? Or the talk therapy she so firmly believed in.

"My ninth grade math teacher, Mr. Haines, who also happened to be the football coach. Maybe it was a lean year for recruits. Who knows? Anyway, he encouraged me to go out for the junior varsity team and I fell happily into the whole football aura. For the first time I had friends and direction, a secure place to go." He pulled Penny closer. "The biggest surprise of all? I turned out to be pretty darn good at the game. Coach Haines put me at wide-out where I could use my speed, my only natural athletic plus." He chuckled. "I think I was hooked the first time I blocked the safety and our halfback ran for a touchdown that won the game for my team."

"Interesting that the coach was also your math teacher." Penny curled her fingers around her glass.

"Yes. I have to admit, football led me to math, my only other natural ability, it seems. The football scholarship paid my way through college where I got the chance to dive deep into numbers. Teaching and coaching were forever sealed in my psyche." He paused. "Or so I thought."

Brad placed his glass on the coffee table and encircled Penny with both arms.

"Enough about my brilliant past, dear Penny. Do you know how well your name matches your gorgeous hair? In the lamp light it is like burnished copper." He leaned in for a long, soft kiss which Penny returned warmly. How long they remained entwined, Penny could not say, but it was long enough for her to wonder, would he want to spend the night?

Brad answered her unvoiced question. "It's late and I still have to retrieve my car from the school parking lot." He pulled away. "See you again. Soon?"

"I'd love that, Brad. "Just no more football dates. Right?"

He kissed her again. "Right."

Chapter Four

Rose was surprised, make that shocked, to discover that Gwen Rogers, who had served as the principal's secretary since the opening of Harding High, had quit. Presiding over the main office was of top importance for a variety of reasons. PR, for one. Facilitating communication with students, teachers and parents and following through with administrative needs for another. Carter Thompson, who'd opened Harding High, had joked about stealing Gwen Rogers from Superintendent Sparkman's office. "Gwen is the best secretary I've ever had. The woman could type like a maniac," Carter mimicked Sparkman's praise of his secretary. But Gwen had willingly left the Superintendent's office to open Harding High with Carter Thompson. Now Gwen was gone, vanished, without even giving the usual two-weeks' notice. Rose sought the details on good authority from Jose Mendoza, her custodian friend who'd been hired at the same time as Gwen.

Jose had stopped by her first room of the day to show Rose a picture of his new baby.

"What a sweet little face," Rose told him. "Congratulations, Jose. Now you're a family man without a doubt."

Jose grinned. "Well, with the baby here, my wife, she's not working, so I'm picking up odd jobs after hours." He looked fondly at the picture before returning it to his wallet. "This little bambino is worth the extra work, believe me." He made to leave.

Rose stopped him. "Jose, do you have a minute? I wanted to ask you about Gwen Rogers. I know you were good friends and I just found out she's left. Do you know why? What happened? Gwen was such a fixture here at Harding. I mean, she was the archive of everything. Need contact info for a county official? Gwen had it in an instant. Date for the next school board meeting? She knew it. How to conquer the fax machine or ply the copier with toner? Gwen was your go-to gal. Central-central intelligence."

Jose shook his head. "I tell you, Ms. Lane, but you cannot repeat. Okay?"

"You have my word."

"Gwen, she tell me she cannot stand working for the new principal, Ms. Storme. She say something wrong with that lady, like she got a screw loose maybe. Crazy stuff like, 'Do this, Gwen,' then hour later, 'Why you do *that*, Gwen?'" Jose rolled his eyes. "'Can't do nothing right. Acts like she know it all but don't know nothing about being principal.' I gotta say, I already notice some crazy stuff myself." He scratched his chin. "But, thank God, I no have to work with her all day every day like my friend Gwen."

Rose squeezed the man's arm. "Thanks for telling me. I have to say I sympathize. Understand, Ms. Storme is not the easiest woman to work with sometimes." She made eye contact with Jose. "I guess we'll all have to be careful. Walk on eggshells, as the expression goes." She hoped Jose got her meaning. The young father could not afford a run-in with the temperamental

Storme who obviously had a penchant for firing folks or driving them off one way or another.

As Jose left, Penny entered, balancing her Bambi cup and Rose's cup atop a stack of folders. "I graded the sophomore essays," she said, placing the items carefully on the teacher's desk. "I must say, I feel dumber for having done so."

Rose chuckled. "The Sweat Hog Sophomores. By and large they're a sweet group. Just a PITA here and there."

"PITA?" Penny waved a hand over her coffee to cool it. "What's a PITA?"

"It's an acronym for Pain In The Ass," Rose snorted. "Teacher jargon. You might as well learn it."

Penny smiled. "Well, the class is certainly a mixed bag. Some in reading resource. A couple of repeaters. Several really hard workers. And, as you say, the PITAs." She pointed to the folder of corrected essays. "But not a one of them can write a coherent paragraph, I'm afraid." She sipped her coffee. "I'm going to stay after school tomorrow, conduct a little writing workshop. What do you think?"

"After-school help is a good way to remediate kids who are willing to put in the extra time. Of course, the two repeaters are on the football team and they'll have to be at practice after school so they won't be able to take advantage of your offer." Rose picked up her coffee cup. "Speaking of football, how did the date with Brad go?"

"He's still conflicted. He just can't seem to get over Wendy's actions, and he misses coaching terribly. You know, Rose, we went out to brunch on Sunday and I asked him why he doesn't think about transferring to another high school mid-semester, maybe applying for a football coaching position there for the fall season. Certainly his reputation in the county would help him land a good job."

Rose lifted her brows.

"Know what he said?" Penny dashed on without waiting for an answer. "He said, 'Well, I've thought of that. But, no. I've decided to stay right here at Harding.'"

"Because he wants to teach with you?" Rose asked hopefully.

"Hardly that. What he said was, 'I can't leave now, Penny. I have to get back at Wendy Storme.'"

The two were silent for a moment. "What do suppose he means?" Penny asked.

"I guess we'll find out," Rose said with the lightest tone she could muster. "Oh, I have Faculty Advisory Council this afternoon. I'm compiling a list of departmental concerns. Do you have anything to add?"

Penny thought for a moment. "Advisory Council meeting with Principal Storme, eh? Talk about a PITA!"

****

Rose made it her job to check with every department member before an Advisory meeting. Most of the teachers' beefs were routine. For example: A request for fire drills to be administered at different times on different days instead of B-block, 6th period over and over again. It was possible to miss some twenty-five minutes of class what with the emptying out and filling back up for such a large school during a drill, so it would make sense to spread fire drills around at different times. That should've been a no-brainer,

40

but, then again, Wendy Storme was rarely sensitive to academic needs. Even the students realized the fire drill scheduling was taking too much time away from one specific class period. A cheeky senior in Rose's B-block, 6th period class had looked up at the speaker box on the wall as the announcement for yet another fire drill came on: "This had better be a *real* fire!" he grumbled, with a gesture aimed at the speaker.

As Rose made her way to the conference room for the FAC meeting, she couldn't stop thinking about what her colleague and best friend Corina Collins had told her. Corina had been born and raised in Jamaica where her father was a clergyman. Coffee-colored like a brewed dark roast, with languid eyes and coal-black hair, Corina dressed daily as if she were a fashion model. Tall and curvy as a Greek urn, she made the halls her runway, always clad in the latest style with accompanying jewelry and other accessories and perfectly coordinated, drop-dead-expensive shoes. Rose liked to kid Corina, suggesting her underwear must surely match her outfit. But her friend's most striking feature was her poise. Calm, confident, Corina rose above the brawls that so often mired the rest of them down. Even the most recalcitrant student would pause to consider when Ms. Collins locked their eyes with hers, and, in the most dignified Caribbean lilt, intoned, "Excuse me, but that is *not* appropriate."

"Mama Rose," Corina's cadence was melodic. "I do have a concern for our new principal. But I fear it would not be suitable for the FAC meeting."

Corina wore a bright lavender sweater, belted with a silver cinch. Encircling her throat was a multi-colored scarf perfectly highlighting the purple hues. Her silver earrings gleamed in contrast to her jet-black hair. As always, Rose stood in awe of her glamorous friend.

"Corina, Corina," Rose sang. "Surely you're going to let me know your 'concern,' even if it is not suitable."

Corina rolled her expressive eyes and sighed. "Yesterday Ms. Storme pulled me aside. I thought perhaps she would comment on my students' *Canterbury Tales* projects adorning the halls. Some are quite clever. Artistic. But, oh my dear, that was not her intention at all."

What now, ran through Rose's thoughts as she nodded her friend on.

"Ms. Storme asked me if I ever moonlighted, her word, cleaning houses. Barring that, she wondered if any of my family might be available to serve as a housekeeper for her home."

Rose flinched. "The nerve! Unbelievable. Crass as Wendy can be, this beats all. What in the world did you say to her?"

"I simply said that I spend too much time on my teaching, what with lesson plans, grading papers, taking professional courses, to have any hours for extra jobs." Corina's lips curved into a sly smile. "And as for others in my family, I said, 'You see, Ms. Storme, both of my parents have advanced degrees from Oxford University. I don't believe you could afford them.' I also told her about my sister, the lawyer, whose hourly fee is in three figures." Corina chuckled. "I stopped short of acquainting Ms. Storme with my uncle, a brain surgeon with Doctors Without Borders and my cousin who is a missionary in Africa."

Rose snorted. "The perfect rejoinder. I expect she

will try to mend her fences with you, Corina."

"Not if I can help it," Corina lilted.

****

"The FAC meeting wasn't a total bust," Rose said. It was late. Rose and Penny conferred over the lunch table in the deserted English workroom.

"I can't believe Principal Storme never showed up. You mean she left all those reps just sitting and waiting?"

"Well, Garrett Barnes, you know, the Assistant Principal for Instruction. He came dashing in about ten minutes late. Seems Wendy had just texted him to fill in for her. She was busy with…something more important, as Garrett said. He let it be known that Ms. Storme has her aspirations set on moving on up from principal to upper administration in the county." Rose made a wry face. "Garrett is nice, quite supportive when he wants to be, but he's way too weak to withstand a tornado like Wendy. She'll bend him whichever way she wants."

"So, the department reps got to have their say? Read out their lists of grievances?"

Rose frowned. "Garrett took notes and promised to pass it all on to Wendy." She shook her head. "I give that zero chance of success. What an excuse for her to ignore our concerns."

"But, you said it wasn't a total bust." Penny said.

"As we sat there, waiting, we all talked with each other. The English Department is not the only group that's pissed off. Believe me, it's universal." Rose cupped her chin in her hands and looked thoughtful. "There's really something going on with ESL, that's English as a Second Language, you know. They're running scared; the whole department is afraid of Wendy's mandate that they bring up their kids' scores on the spring standardized tests."

"Doesn't the principal know how difficult that is? I mean every professional article about mandatory public school testing points out how the tests themselves favor the native speaker. And, Harding has a large population of these non-native-speaking kids, right?"

Rose nodded. "Our new principal either doesn't know or she doesn't care...or both. I suspect she's only concerned with how a lot of low test scores might make *her* look." She paused. "Anyway, the teachers are scrambling frantically to find staff and extra instructional time to prep the students. It's a shame, really. There's so much more to moving immigrant students into the mainstream curriculum, school life itself, than teaching to the test."

"I can sure understand those teachers' concern," Penny said. "Did you learn anything else?"

"The three departments whose chairs were demoted are struggling, too. The new chairs are trying their best to settle textbook and curriculum issues, standards of learning and such, but it's hard to attend to while teaching full time. Usually the chairs work over the summer to establish goals and bench marks and plan strategies. Now they're scrambling to hone their departments while teaching and planning for their own classes, an unbelievable time crunch."

"The math department?" Penny tried not to sound too eager to hear Rose's take on Brad's situation.

"Those math teachers are probably the angriest of all. Their brilliant former leader snagged a solid position at the state college and she was gone in a week.

So, not only has the department lost a valuable colleague, but the new chair has no one to confer with on a day-to-day basis. And there are so many new county and state requirements and regulations to be considered." Rose gave Penny a questioning look. "What does Brad say?"

"Funny thing…he almost seems excited about the chaos. That's what he calls it: chaos. You know, he said he wants payback for Wendy's stealing his coaching job. His own department in shambles? He'd be happy about that? Hard to believe in a professional like Brad." Penny did not know what to make of it.

Rose shook her head. "It's a new side to my friend Brad McIver. The man is a brilliant teacher, but…"

The door to the workroom opened. "Ms. Lane?"

It was custodian Jose Mendoza.

Rose gestured. "Come on in, Jose. We're just chatting. You're not interrupting anything."

Penny stood. "I have to run, folks. I'm due at the university for my night class. See ya." She waved and hurried off, leaving Rose and Jose alone.

Jose shuffled his feet, looking at the floor. "I gotta ask your advice, Ms. Lane. Not sure what I should do."

Rose indicated a chair across from her. Seated, he continued. "Ms. Storme, she want me to do some construction work. Moonlighting, she calls it. At her house. I need the money, but…"

"What's the problem, Jose?"

"Well, I build a coffee bar for her office here at school. She want me to build another one for her house, in her basement room, using left-over material from the coffee bar I build for her office at school. When she pays me, she say, don't tell nobody about using free materials." Jose shifted nervously. "I tell her that sounds like cheating to me."

"I see your point. It *is* cheating if those left over materials could be used for other county-financed projects."

"See, I think she ordered twice the wood and granite and hardware she needed for that bar in her office. So there would be left-over for the one in her house." Jose looked miserable. "I think I maybe should tell my supervisor, but I don't want no trouble." He pulled at his shirt collar. "When I tell Ms. Storme is not right using free materials for her own house, she say, 'Don't worry. Our secret.' Then, she hint at more jobs for me at her house. For moonlighting."

"I can tell you feel bad about this, Jose." Rose thought for a moment. "What if you got the work order from your supervisor. To prove what Ms. Storme did?"

Jose gulped. "Ms. Storme, she is one very smart woman. Before I even think of it, she tell me, 'I've already taken care of the work order, Jose. No problem.' "

Rose exhaled. "She's put you in a moral bind. A pickle. For now, my advice would be to lay low. And don't take her up on any more offers to moonlight. If there's no proof of illegality, maybe you'll be safe." She tried to project a reassuring smile. "I certainly hope so."

Jose stood. "Thanks, Ms. Lane. You are a good friend. I didn't know nobody else to tell about this."

"Give that baby an extra hug for me," Rose watched the young custodian make his way out. *Dammit. This tornado is wreaking havoc all over the place.*

Chapter Five

The professor who taught Penny's night class had emphasized that all the interns in the program needed to branch out now to observe and shadow others in their respective departments, not just their mentors. He also instructed the interns to start teaching some mini-lessons. Where to begin? The English Department was the largest at Harding High. Why not observe the other AP Literature class, whose teacher, Barbara Zander, was a crusty thirty-year veteran. Brilliant, yet down-to-earth, Zander knew her subject and she knew how to teach it. Every summer she went to Texas to score the AP Literature exams from all over the country. She joined experts there who were responsible for grading the open-ended essay that was the capstone of the exam.

Adept at sarcasm, Barbara Zander became known for her barbs. Any slacker caught without preparation for class got her acerbic epithet: "Eat dirt and die." Though Ms. Zander might deliver the barb with a twinkle in her eye, the student, nonetheless, comprehended the message: Get serious about your studies or plan to slide back to a regular English class where you undoubtedly belong.

Zander's barbs were not confined to recalcitrant students. She'd been known to hurl sharp retorts to any deserving individual, regardless of age. Her concern sent via Rose to one of the FAC meetings was delivered thus: "If Ms. Storme really thinks the English Department is full of shit, she should see to it that the custodians supply our workroom toilet with sufficient paper products." Rose had confided to Penny that Barb Zander often reminded her of barbed wire: prickly and capable of emitting electric shock to anyone within range.

Cautiously opening the door to the classroom, Penny spotted a student standing at the podium, leading an enthusiastic classroom discussion about existential elements in "Rosencrantz and Guildenstern are Dead." The class pulsed on high-level octane. Penny finally located Ms. Zander sitting at a student desk in the back of the room, participating occasionally herself. A tiny splinter of a woman, smaller than every student in the class, Ms. Zander would have been hard to locate except for her white-haired pixie cut. She liked to describe herself as a Q-tip. The teacher patted an empty seat beside her without taking her eyes off the student leader. "SLD," she whispered to Penny. "Student-led-discussion. Each kid signs up for two a quarter." She nodded. "They love post-modernism." She laughed. "So do I…and so do the folks who make up the AP exams each year."

After an hour, the SLD ended and Ms. Zander called for students to move into their novel groups for the remainder of the block time. Penny realized that each group comprised of five students was discussing a different book; the room was a one-floor tower of babel, but, again, the students appeared to be engaged in high gear. They sprawled all over the floor in loosely-arranged circles sharing ideas.

"This is amazing," Penny exclaimed as she and the teacher worked their way around the room, tuning in on the various discussions. "How does it work? Why does it work might be a better question."

"Many teachers find this type of activity daunting. It looks disorganized to them. They prefer to teach one book at a time to the entire class." The two stepped gingerly over a student lying prone, chin cupped in his hands as he listened to a fellow student. "I, myself, prefer teaching novels with similar themes in this fashion," Ms. Zander said. They continued moving from group to group. "The real pay-off comes when the groups process out and share their findings with the whole class. Suddenly you've got a room full of kids who can't wait to read the other four or five books!"

As the bell tone sounded for the end of the period, Penny noticed the students were still involved in their discussions, some reluctant to leave and others taking their talk out the door and down the hall.

"Thanks for letting me observe unannounced," Penny told the teacher. "Awesome class dynamics. Are your students always so actively engaged?"

"Oh, I'd say the good days definitely outnumber the bad ones. Though the majority of the kids really dread the in-class timed writings which are key to their being able to max out the open-ended essay question at the end of the national exam."

Penny grimaced. "I clearly remember my own experience with timed-writings when I was in high school, and in college, too. You gotta learn how to do them; it's an acquired skill."

Next stop, English Eleven, Honors. American Literature, Penny's own specialty as an English major.

The class had just finished a short-story unit, according to the teacher, a fresh-faced young man who appeared not much older than Penny.

"Each group is tasked with telling the class one of the short stories we studied, telling it any way they like, but using only the 'props' within the classroom, such as chairs, tables, books, whatever is at hand."

Penny watched in fascination as the first group turned Nathaniel Hawthorne's "The Minister's Black Veil" into a marionette show during which only one student narrated the story as the 'puppets' jerked their limbs portraying the actions.

Another group used five chairs placed in front of the room, four turned with backs to the audience and just one facing forward. Each student spoke a part of the story from the front-facing chair, then turned their back as another student revolved to face front to continue the story. It was an oddly effective telling of Shirley Jackson's chilling short story "The Lottery."

And what a creative way to include speech and drama and story-telling skills into literature studies. Penny was happily adding layer after layer to her file of good teaching strategies. She considered herself quasi-staff and, as such, she could float above the current of rancor from Principal Storme the others were forced to endure. She was a free-floating observation balloon, drifting miles above the constant storm clouds that hovered over Harding High. The practical part of her knew that when she began actual teaching, even short lessons, her feelings would, no doubt, change. She could hit the ground with a jarring, resounding thud.

For her last observation of the day, Penny decided to revisit Rose's Sweat Hog Sophomore class. She'd seen two upper-level courses; now for some contrast. Anyway, she'd grown fond of this motley crew and was curious to see how they were getting along with *Macbeth*. If Shakespeare was difficult for the best of students, it was a real challenge to convey the Bard's spirit to the RKs , the "Regular Kids."

Penny found all of the students standing in a circle in a cleared area near the front of the room. Clapping, snapping their fingers, grooving, and chanting. At first their actions were a blur of sound and movement, until Penny at last discerned the words:

"Bubble, bubble, toil and trouble
Fire burn and cauldron bubble
In the cauldron, boil and bake
Eye of newt and toe of frog
Wool of bat and tongue of dog."

The students were performing a group rap rendition of the witches in Shakespeare's *Macbeth.*

Brilliant! *Meet the kids on their own terms and let the genius of Shakespeare sink in.* Rose never ceased to amaze her; the versatile teacher could relate to just about every kind of student she faced. She wondered if Wendy Storme had an inkling of the talent residing in this department, as well as in all the other departments of Harding High. Talent she was willing to sacrifice for what? For her own ego? For her own career advancement? Thoughts of Brad and his highly successful math students flickered across Penny's mind's eye.

Wondering where she should begin teaching her first mini-lesson, Penny found Rose at the desk in her third classroom for the day.

"Why don't you begin your teaching experience

with Lyn Leeson's English Nine classes?" Rose suggested. "I've placed Lyn in charge of curriculum for the grade level. She has a firm grasp on where the kids are coming from in middle school and where they're going next in high school. Though the other teachers of frosh are also strong, Lyn is phenomenal. She just gets it, you know?" Rose leaned back in her chair. "I'll check with her right away and set you up for the week before Thanksgiving break. How's that sound?"

"Exciting!" Penny enthused with a little shiver. "I can't wait!" She helped Rose gather her materials and load them onto her cart. Wheeling down the hall to the workroom, the two talked as students threaded the halls and stopped at lockers before heading to their after-school activities.

Rose lowered her voice. "Do you realize the principal's secretary, the new one, has already absconded? She lasted, what? Three weeks?" Rose waited while Penny held the door to the workroom so she could squeeze in the bulky cart.

Barely inside, Corina Collins accosted them. "Mama Rose," Corina cooed. "You aren't going to believe what I'm about to tell you."

"Another principal's secretary has flown the coop," Rose blurted out. "I just heard."

"No surprise there." Corina said. "But this time the escape involves upper management. Here, let me help you park this cart before we sit down."

Settled at the table where the teachers ate lunch, Rose and Penny looked expectantly at Corina. "Out with it!" Rose demanded. "What's up?"

"Garrett Barnes. He slipped out, evidently in the middle of the night. Cleared out his desk, removed his diplomas from the wall, and vamoosed!" Corina made a sweeping gesture with her arm.

"Garrett Barnes?" Penny gasped. "You mean the Assistant Principal for Instruction? The one in charge of our department?"

"The very same. I'm good friends with his secretary. She was the only one who knew what he was planning to do. He's moving into an administrative job with the county, a notch or two below his Assistant Principal status here." Corina's lips twisted into a sardonic smile.

"So...you mean he didn't let on to Wendy that he was leaving?" Rose frowned. "That's weird." She paused. "Although, I had noticed Garrett looking frazzled lately. Unusual for him. He's always appeared so laid back."

"According to his secretary, he was afraid to say anything to Ms. Storme about leaving Harding," Corina said. "Garrett feels that the principal's behavior suggests borderline personality disorder. She's all sweet and smooth, 'I trust you to do this for me, since you have so much experience,' and then, no warning, she's screaming at him, throwing things, calling him names. Loves to send Garrett off to county meetings in her place without any prior notice or preparation, so he's playing the fool, damaging his own reputation in front of the uppity-ups in the central office." Corina shook her head. "Evidently, Garret was convinced that Storme would do something drastic if she found out he was working on a transfer. Thus, he absconds in the middle of the night...never to be seen again."

Penny and Rose were too stunned to speak. "Know what Garrett told his secretary, just days before he sneaked out?" Corina straightened her shoulders. "I do not usually resort to such language, Mama Rose, but for the sake of truth, I shall quote him verbatim." She paused for dramatic effect. "'Wendy Storme is bat-shit crazy. I stick around long enough...I'd have to kill that witch.'"

****

"Rose, we need to talk. About Devin Giovani," Penny plopped the folder of graded journals onto Rose's disheveled workroom desk.

Rose looked up from her lesson plan book. She had to move piles of materials around to make room for Penny's contribution to the chaos. "What's up with Devin? More attitude? More tardy slips?"

"Worse. Reading his journal, you know. I think the boy needs help. Our help, maybe, if he'll let me in." Penny sifted through the journals she had graded until she found Devin's. "You know how we tell the kids to turn down any page they don't want us to read if it's too personal? Well, Devin's made no attempt to conceal his worries here." She tapped the journal. "Let me read it to you, Rose."

Penny cleared her throat and read out loud. "'I'm doing something I know is bad. Wrong. I could get in big shit over this. But it's all for Gabby. I have to save my sister. I have to get her away from my dad.'" Penny looked up at Rose. "I know you're worried about a student confidentiality issue when it comes to Devin's personal problems and what he shared with you last year. But, look. Devin knew I was the one grading the journals. I'm in on it now. Can you please tell me what's going on?"

"First, we need to alert Christine Yamada, Devin's

guidance counselor." Rose pulled out her mobile phone. "Let me text her now. See if she can see us right away. We'll take the journal to show her. In the meantime, I'll fill you in."

Rose picked up her phone again as the return text beeped. "Christine can see us now. She says she's been concerned about Devin for weeks."

"I know there was a divorce last year and that Devin and the sister are living with their father. No surprise that they're having a hard time adjusting to the divorce." Penny collected the journal and her purse.

Rose sighed. "Yes, but, unfortunately, there's more to the story. I'll tell you about it as we walk down to guidance. Maybe Christine knows additional information."

Penny pursed her lips. "Our showing the journal to his counselor. Won't Devin be upset, maybe consider it a violation of trust or something?"

"The students know we're required to follow up any time they write about certain situations: suicidal thoughts, feelings of rage, threats of violence. Devin's comments 'I'm doing something wrong, bad,' and, 'I have to save my sister,' qualify; I am quite sure he knows that. In fact, I suspect it's the reason he wrote about his situation and didn't turn down the page, making sure we would see." Rose placed a hand on Penny's arm. "You did exactly the right thing in showing the journal to me. And we are doing exactly the right thing in following up with his counselor. As you suspected, Devin is crying for help."

As the two entered the guidance hall, Wendy Storme lashed out of her office waving a sheet of paper in Penny's face. "I just received this from your university intern program director." The coils of her hair quivered like tightening wires.

Penny flinched and stepped back. "Wh-what is it? I don't know what you're talking about."

The principal flapped the paper just below Penny's nose. "A copy of a questionnaire you filled out and submitted to the university, that's what, Miss Bright." Storme's breath was wet with anger. "And I am most unhappy about the way you answered number seventeen, here." Wendy's s-sounds whistled through the space in her front teeth and her beak-nose quivered, nostrils flared.

Before Penny could look at the paper, the woman whisked it back and barked out, "To the question, 'How helpful has the principal been with your internship?' you answered, 'Not at all. She has spoken to me only one time and that was after an all-faculty meeting at the beginning of the year.' "

Penny straightened her spine. "Well, Ms. Storme. That happens to be the truth."

Wendy fumed a moment before speaking. "I am a very busy person, running a large, difficult school. Do you really expect me to have time to waste on an *intern*?" Though she didn't voice it, her tone said *lowly* intern.

"Are you suggesting that Penny lie on the questionnaire, Wendy?" Rose's voice was calm and firm, though her fingers were tightly clenched at her sides. As Wendy glowered silently, Rose added, "She is about to begin teaching some mini-lessons, which is a wonderful opportunity for you to see how Penny handles the material and the students."

The principal's face and neck had shaded into a

mottled red. She turned her eyes on Penny. "Just remember, Miss Bright. Carter Thompson may have approved your internship, but I, I am the one who will write the final evaluation." Turning she hurled herself away.

"Whew!" Penny exhaled. "Thanks for coming to my defense, Rose. But, I must say I'm a bit worried. Will Principal Storme be breathing down my neck every minute, observing me as I begin teaching?"

Rose snorted. "I don't think you need worry about that. I had to bite my lip to keep from adding, 'While you're at it, Ms. Principal Storme, how about visiting some of your established teachers' classrooms to observe. You might learn something about education.' " Rose shook her head. "I fear teachers, students and instruction are low on our eminent leader's list of priorities."

The door to Christine Yamada's office stood open, causing Penny to wonder if she had heard the interaction with the principal in the hall.

One look at the counselor's face told the teachers two things: Christine had heard and she was appalled. "C...come in, Rose. Penny." Christine glanced furtively down the hall before firmly closing her door. She appeared to settle herself before saying, "I'm glad we have this opportunity to confer. I've been so worried about your student, Devin Giovani. I hope we can help him...before it's too late."

Chapter Six

Rose couldn't wait to get home. Margo was due to arrive for her five-day Thanksgiving break from college. Though they frequently emailed, texted, and connected via Facetime, they had not seen each other in the flesh for months.

"What the...?" Rose muttered out loud as she recognized the car in the driveway. "What's Max doing here? And how can he get in the house when I had all the locks changed."

Slamming her car door, Rose strode up the walkway and tried the door. Unlocked. He was inside; she knew that for a fact. Ex-husbands should never take such liberties. He'd finally quit sending those ridiculous texts pleading for a reunion so now he lets himself into the house? Rose could feel the blood rising from her neck to the roots of her hair. Flexing her fingers into fists, she took a deep breath and stepped into the foyer.

"Hi, Mom," Margo ran to Rose and enveloped her in a hug. "I got in early so Dad picked me up from my carpool drop-off point." She kissed her mother's cheek. "I could've waited around for you to get out of school, but I thought...well, I thought it would be okay to call Dad." She looked hopefully at Rose.

Still pulling for a reconciliation Rose suspected, but she didn't want to destroy the moment. "Of course it's all right, Margo. Just because your dad and I are no longer married, it doesn't mean we can't ever be together, especially when our daughter is involved." Not exactly the full truth, but Margo brought out Rose's mothering instinct to soften the world for her child.

Rose hung her coat in the closet. "Where is the old bear, anyway?"

"The old bear is in the living room," Max called out. "Sitting in what used to be his favorite chair."

Rose peeked around the corner and waved. "Don't get up. I'll join you as soon as I wiggle out of these school clothes." She disappeared into the bedroom where she changed into jeans and a sweat shirt. As she approached the living room, she had to admit that seeing Margo and Max together looked like any natural father-daughter family scene. Max still had the athletic good looks that had drawn Rose to him when they'd met at college. Sitting in his old chair with his long legs stretched out in front of him, he seemed to belong there. But he didn't. His cheating on their marriage had jerked Rose out of matrimonial bliss, destroyed her blind trust and made her realize she'd been living a naive sham-life based on a false commitment. Though still wounded, she felt each passing day added a thin layer of healing over the scars Max had inflicted, leaving just a prickle of pain. She was moving on, even if he was not.

But here was Margo. So animated, perched on the arm of the wing chair, gesturing as she talked to her father, skin glowing and eyes fired up with life. By lucky karma she had inherited the best features from both parents: her slim, athletic frame and big hazel eyes from Max and her infectious smile and pert nose from Rose. However failed her marriage to Max had been,

Margo was the reward they could both appreciate.

"How's it going at the credit union, Dad?"

Max sat up straighter. "I know that you..." He gave Rose a sidelong look. "You and your mother both think banking has got to be the most boring job on the planet. And I admit it often can be routine, mundane, unexciting..."

"Uncreative, Dad? Is that the word you're searching for?" Margo laughed. "All my friends in the business department try to defend their major as *practical*, say as opposed to my humanities studies. I try to tell them how satisfying it is to dig into the culture and lives of humankind. The conflicts, sorrows, rewards and recoveries."

Max slowly shook his head. "Just look at you, so philosophical at such a young age." He chuckled. "Now I am going to burst your little college-induced bubble, my dear erudite daughter. Life at the credit union right now has all the characteristics of your humanities studies and then some. It's humanity of Americana in a microcosm."

Margo lifted her chin. "Awesome, Dad! Let's hear it. Maybe I can go back to college and give heart to my friends, the business and computer majors. Tell them there is a life after technology."

Savoring her daughter's maturity and poise, Rose almost missed Max's startling statement.

"There's a huge brouhaha in the community over the new principal at Harding High. You wouldn't believe how it spills over into the credit union."

Rose was suddenly listening with both ears. "What do you mean, Max?"

"Well, as you know, lots of teachers belong to the

credit union. As do so many others in the community whose kids attend the high school. And they talk. Many of them know, of course, that you, Rose, teach at Harding. After all, you are a fixture. I guess that makes me some kind of kindred spirit, even if I am the *ex*-husband of the highly-respected English chair." Max twisted his lips into a wry smile. "Hey, they don't call me a 'personal banker' for no reason."

"So, what's being said about the new principal? Her name's Wendy Storme, by the way."

"Oh, believe me, I know her name. I hear it a dozen times a day. And during football season? Holy cow. The booster club keeps their money in our bank, you know. The treasurer is beside himself. He can't quit talking about how the principal fired the best coach in the state and replaced him with the worst. Also, the cheerleading sponsor who buys the squad's uniforms and the pep band and marching band parents, even the crew at the local radio station that broadcasts the games. They come in to deposit or withdraw funds for school functions and they grouse about Wendy Storme." Max shook his head. "And I haven't even mentioned the teachers who trade with the credit union. They alternate between anger and frustration and despair. I'm afraid to ask them how their school year is going."

Rose looked thoughtful. "Interesting. Very interesting, in fact. You know, the staff by and large either fear Principal Storme or despise her for making so many abrupt decisions that impact negatively on instruction, on teachers and students alike. She has a few supporters, though, but they are mostly new hires to replace the staff that jump ship. It seems she has her toadies, the moles she uses to spy on the rest of us. The kids are feeling the trickle-down effect, but I understand some of them have their own issues with the new principal. She didn't bother to attend the fall convocation for the honor students, for example. And then there was the whole football thing. Plus, she plays favorites. While ignoring violations of the dress code for some kids, she tries to turn others into a public example."

Rose looked at Margo. "Talk about your 'conflicts'! The epic battle between the female soccer star and Wendy Storme was one to behold. The star had worn yoga pants the day of a big game, covered modestly by a long t-shirt, mind you. But that didn't stop the cyclone from striking. 'Go and change. Immediately,' Storme barked in front of the girl's entire class. So, that's what the student did. She went out to her car in the student parking lot and waited until the last bell of the day sounded, and then returned to the building wearing her soccer shorts, which, by the way, are much more revealing than yoga pants. Since the game was to occur within the hour, the principal couldn't say a thing, except, 'You'll be marked down for an unexcused absence. Report for Saturday detention.'"

"How did it end, Mom?" Margo had slid off the arm to the cushion of the chair, listening.

"Want to guess what the girl wore to detention that Saturday?"

"Yoga pants," Margo and Max said at the same time.

"Yep. And every kid there applauded her. Seems the story raced around the school like an F-5 weather warning so that they all had heard about Storme's edict. Topping it off? The teacher in charge of detention happens to have been burned by our leader enough times that he secretly enjoyed the act of defiance and allowed the girl to stay for the entire detention without changing her clothes, despite her defiance of the dress code."

"All I can say, Rose, is the community is ready to do battle with Principal Wendy Storme," Max said.

Rose bit her lip. "You know, when a new school is built and consolidated with an old one, it's very difficult to try to meld the re-districted kids and their parents into enthusiastic acceptance. The process is a delicate operation, requiring finesse. These folks have spent generations supporting their old familiar community school, and, suddenly they're asked to refocus their loyalties onto a whole new venue. There's disappointment, fear, really, and a lot of negative push back." She directed her gaze to Margo. "Talk about culture! The staff at Harding High? Every one gave Carter Thompson, the principal who opened the school, kudos for his handling of the new-school shock. A month before school began, he invited the entire community to meetings and receptions where he introduced the teachers and counselors and administrators. He organized tours, opened the building on weekends for use of the gym and auditorium and lecture hall, and even offered up the availability of computer labs and library. By the time school opened, the families from all the merged districts welcomed their new community center—Harding High."

"Wow, Mom. That guy sounds like a genius."

Rose frowned. "Yes. Carter was a genius who

believed in collaborative work, dedication, and collegiality. And look at how Wendy Storme is single-handedly destroying everything in her path, all that Principal Thompson worked so hard to produce." Her look was strained. "There's a good-sized group of staff who stand opposed to Wendy Storme. But the tendency in the face of an onslaught is to dive for the corners, to seek shelter for oneself. So, we have to work on keeping up the spirit of mass resistance."

Max had been following Rose's words. "I have to say I've heard more than one of my clients vow to call the Superintendent on her. Register their complaints and ask him to fire her or send her to some other unfortunate school."

"A lot of good that'll do," Rose harrumphed. "First of all, The Super has to recommend the firing to the Board of Trustees. Secondly, Storme and the Super are very chummy, at least according to her."

"Maybe there will be no need for the Superintendent's action." Max leaned forward and lowered his voice for dramatic effect. "I've actually heard more than one of my clients say, 'Somebody ought to kill that witch.' "

****

Thinking about the wonderful Thanksgiving break with Margo, Rose opened the door to the main office to check her mailbox. Looking around, she was surprised to see all new office furniture, including upholstered chairs set around a low wooden table, brass lamps perched on new side stands and a colorful area rug. A nice first impression for visiting dignitaries and parents. But the old furniture was not too shabby. She'd wondered why it had been removed several weeks ago and the space left empty until now.

The secretary du jour sat at her big central desk looking bewildered. Apparently in her early thirties, nicely groomed and attractive, she wore a stripe between her brows. "Anything I can help you with?" Rose asked, knowing it must be hard adjusting to the new job, thrown into the middle of the school year like this, and following the latest secretary who'd only lasted weeks.

"Ms. Storme asked me to look for the arrival of the new long-term substitute, but I don't know enough teachers yet; I can't tell who's permanent and who's subbing. I've only been here a week. I don't see how she can expect me to follow through..." The woman looked ready to burst into tears.

"Did the principal let you know which teacher the substitute is in for?"

The young woman continued to look distraught. "No. Yes. Maybe. Oh, I don't know. She blasted out a dozen directives and left me without anything in writing. But I do remember she said it was for an English teacher."

"That's my department," Rose said. "I'm the chair and I should have been notified if one of my teachers needs a long-term sub." This seemed to distress the secretary even more.

"It's not your fault, dear," Rose said kindly.

"I was a school secretary for five years at the elementary here in town. Then I stayed home to have my kids. I've taken courses to rejuvenate my skills, but nobody prepared me for...for..."

For foul weather, Rose thought. "Any idea where Ms. Storme is at the moment? I need to talk to her about this."

The secretary flinched. "She's in her office. But, please don't disturb her. She gave me strict orders and…and she gets really mad when I screw up." The woman shook her head. "It makes no sense. I mean, she asked me to alert her when the substitute arrives, and then tells me she's not to be interrupted."

"I'll be sure to let her know you told me not to interrupt her. But I'm going to go knock on her door anyway. This is too important. I'll have to orient the substitute, give them the texts for classes to be covered, and take care of lots of other details. Plus, I want to know what's happened to whichever colleague the sub will be replacing." Picking up her book bag, Rose marched down the hall to the principal's office, her fists at the ready. She knocked on the door, then opened it and stepped in, made brave by the principal's neglect of protocol concerning long-term subs.

Wendy Storme stood at the elaborate new coffee bar Jose Mendoza had described to Rose. Turning abruptly at Rose's interruption, she sloshed some coffee onto the granite counter top, uttering a curse under her breath.

"Didn't that numbskull of a secretary tell you I was not to be disturbed?" She wiped up the spill.

Rose ignored Wendy's barb. "I need information about the long-term sub for one of my teachers. It's important to situate him or her before the students arrive in the next half hour." Rose did not add that the courtesy of being informed about the need for a long-term sub in her department should go without saying. Wendy Storme was short on courtesy.

"I do not understand why my administrative

assistants so consistently display their lack of knowledge when it comes to office etiquette," the principal said. Her nostrils flared.

Rose was losing patience. She unclenched her teeth and spoke. "Whenever a long-term substitute is hired, the department chair needs to be informed. Before the fact. Not afterward."

Unperturbed by Rose's demeanor, Wendy took another gulp of coffee. "The sub is for Lyn Leeson. She was in a severe automobile accident over the Thanksgiving holiday. Broken pelvis and some other injuries. She'll be out several months."

"Lyn? Oh my God," Rose exhaled. "That's terrible." She swallowed her despair. "Lyn teaches Freshman English. She knows what she's doing and she's good at it. The students will be devastated."

"I've chosen the best candidate from the long-term sub pool. You'll find Mr. Farcus, Ralph Farcus, to be an excellent replacement. We worked together at…at my last job."

"So, he's had a lot of teaching experience?" Rose couldn't resist asking, as it had become known all over the school that Wendy Storme, plucked out of a county office, had never taught a class in her life.

"He just loves children. That's the most important thing." Wendy dithered about her desk. "He's been vetted for the substitute pool. And he has my personal seal of approval."

Loves children? Her personal seal of approval? Hardly comforting recommendations.

And requirements for the sub pool were little more than absence of a criminal record and the ability to communicate in English. Freshman level English was key to student success. It was where they practiced and honed their critical thinking skills, grammar knowledge, writing basics, and abstract reasoning, which was exactly why Carter Thompson had hand-picked Lyn to captain a steady ship with her firm and capable hands. A substitute teacher taking over for a day or two would not disrupt the program; for months? Better have a competent and hardy soul on deck. One with the flexibility and knowledge base to deal with young adolescents. Rose's thoughts turned to her colleague Lyn. The department would set up a rotation to check on her, take her meals, help her with her two school-age children…whatever she needed to recover and return.

"I'm going back to the office to catch Mr. Farcus. The new secretary can't be expected to recognize who's a sub and who's a teacher when she's only been here a week, Wendy."

Storme glared at Rose, gathering wind to contradict her, but Rose did not give her the chance, turning and marching out with deliberate strides.

Damn. Her warm buzz from her holiday with Margo had dissipated in a nanosecond.

Chapter Seven

Only half-awake, Penny lay savoring a few moments of semi-consciousness before moving into her day. Thoughts of her Thanksgiving holiday wafted in and out of mind. Brad had invited her to dinner with his family, which lived less than an hour away. With only three days off from school, Penny felt she could not justify the airfare to go home half-way across the country. She found Brad's mother to be welcoming and warm; his sister Lizah appeared to be a feminine version of Brad: tall and slim, sandy-haired and sharp-witted, smart, with-it. She worked for an IT firm in the city. As their conversation roamed the world and back, they found they were, for the most part, on the same page politically and intellectually when it came to current events, allowing Penny to relax and enjoy the day.

They sat over their pumpkin pie, talking. "So, how's school going?" Lizah tilted her head toward Penny, though she spoke to her brother. "And the lovely intern. Are you teaching her everything there is to know…about the education profession, I mean?" She all but winked to show she was teasing.

"Penny's doing great with no help from me. My math classes have a ways to go, but they'll get there. The new principal, on the other hand? Let's just say she must have been recently ejected from Oz. Most of us are hoping someone will throw water on her and make her disappear." Brad shuddered.

Lizah nodded sympathetically, making Penny suspect her brother had filled her in on the coaching debacle, if not other grueling details of working under a living tornado. "I don't understand how you teachers can continue to do the arduous job required of you...I mean it must be hard enough disciplining the students, keeping them on task while respecting their numerous individual needs. I realize it's a lot to ask even when you have a supportive and caring boss..." she drifted off. "In the IT business, we can always go to HR to report unfair practices. Or we can transfer to another department. Another company. What recourse do you teachers have?" She looked from face to face as if expecting an answer.

Brad pushed back his chair. "I hate to leave with such an unanswered question hanging midair, sister dear. The short answer is we can always apply for a transfer, a process wound tightly in red tape. The thing about teaching at Harding is that we love the school, the students and the community. It would make much more sense to simply get rid of the principal. If only we knew how." He stood. "Now, Penny and I must be on our way." He turned to his mother. "Thanks for a fantastic feast, Mom."

"And for the opportunity to share in a wonderful family get-together," Penny added, offering a hand to Lizah and then to Brad's mother. "It's been perfect for a Thanksgiving orphan like me." She felt unexpectedly gratified when Mrs. McIver enfolded her in a warm hug.

Brad and Penny said their goodbyes and headed for

Penny's apartment. Overloaded with holiday carbs and warmed with a bottle of wine, almost without realizing it, they found themselves in Penny's bed wrapped in each other's arms. Penny could easily fall in love with Brad. Except for…how to put it into words? Except for an edge, a darkness held within. He hid it, of course. Especially at school; but when his defenses were down, the gloom turned his eyes into flint and locked his jaw in a clinch. The mood swing could be swift. Laughing at some silly thing, he might suddenly pound the table in anger. Other times it was a slow burn building from kindling to flames over several hours. There had to be more to this black periphery than the loss of a coaching job. Until Brad leveled with her, their relationship could never deepen to unconditional love. For either of them.

It was a worry, but, in the meantime, Penny relished the memory of their unflawed night together. His warm kisses on her neck, moving slowly and gently down her body. Though Brad had left to go home after that one night, the pillow still smelled faintly of his shaving lotion. She shivered with pleasure at the sensory memory.

Back to reality, she hopped onto the cold floor and headed for the shower. So much to look forward to! She'd spent the week before the holiday teaching mini-lessons in Lyn Leeson's three ninth grade English classes. Penny admired the way Lyn maintained control. Whenever the class appeared on the verge of chaos, Lyn had simply stood at the lectern and whispered for quiet. Despite the clamor, the students heard and reacted to their teacher's whisper, relaying one to the other, "She's whispering! Get quiet, she's whispering!"

Though all of Lyn's students were ninth graders, each block manifested its own distinct and unique psycho-dynamic. Lyn proved to be a master of tailoring curriculum and instruction to fit the students' needs. The honors class had been working on literature from the Middle Ages. Penny's part in the lessons was to teach "Sir Gawain and the Green Knight" and some of the Arthurian legends. Now they were engaged in a fun project to enhance their study. Each student assumed a knightly name, such as Lady Writes-a-Lot, for example, or Sir Sport the Challenger. Each "knight" then pledged to perform for one week good, chivalrous deeds wherever possible, at home or school or on the playing field, to be written up as a story. The catch was that they had to keep their vow to perform these deeds a secret. Thus far, some of the results had been quite humorous: family members taking advantage and getting the secret knight to clean the whole house; friends backing away, skeptical at the sudden courtesy and helpfulness of the knight who offered to take cafeteria trays to the waste cans or clean out their student desks.

The other two classes also read the literature involved, but, since they needed more time to process, their project was a bit different. Observe good deeds and write about them in a log. It was a different level of learning that Lyn enhanced with choral readings, video clips of knights in action, and individual student conferences for editing their writing. Penny especially liked working one-on-one helping students improve their writing skills. Now that she had her own piles of student papers to correct, she felt like a *real* English teacher.

Stepping from the shower, Penny reflected as she dried and dressed for school. She had never known how much she would enjoy working with the youngest high schoolers. So many of the freshmen were naïve, eager to learn, if nothing else, how to be more like the upper classmen who slouched against their lockers in casual conversation between classes. She loved the way Lyn established rapport with her young charges, encouraging them to stop in any time before or after school to discuss a problem or concern. Lyn often reassured her students, saying, "Some of the teachers don't like to mess with you rookies, but you are my favorite kids to teach."

Penny quickly realized that she was under guidance of another master teacher; she was learning so much about the art and craft of the profession. She couldn't wait to continue. Grabbing her book bag, she hurried out the door.

****

"Penny," the guidance counselor waved at the intern from her office door across the hall. "Got a minute before school?"

Penny glanced at the big hall clock and calculated she'd have a good fifteen minutes before Lyn Leeson's first period Freshman English class began. "Sure, Christine." Maneuvering around the students milling in the corridor, Penny made her way to Christine Yamada's office. Dropping her book bag onto a chair, she loosened her coat and looked expectantly at the petite counselor. "What's up?"

"I intended to share this with Rose first, but she's super busy. It's something about orienting a long-term sub for a teacher in the English Department." Christine indicated a seat facing her desk. "Rose asked me to talk to you, says you can fill her in later, if that's okay. It's about Devin Giovani."

Penny scooted the chair closer to the counselor's desk. "Oh dear. Are you going to tell me the news is not good?" Penny's week with the innocent-appearing ninth graders had temporarily eased her thoughts about the upper classman and his apparent cry for help via his journal. Christine shook her head. "I'm afraid *not good* is an understatement." She pressed her lips into a thin slit. "You see, Wendy Storme has been carrying on an investigation into allegations of a student selling drugs here at Harding."

"Not Devin. Surely not Devin." Penny had to swallow down the sour taste that rose in her throat.

"Well, as Wendy relayed it to me, she suspects Devin but does not have enough concrete evidence to turn him in." Christine sighed. "Devin, of course, denies it. Or so Wendy tells me."

"Let me guess," Penny said. "Wendy wants *you* to ferret out that evidence she needs to accuse Devin. Right?"

"Afraid so." Christine winced. "Ms. Storme doesn't grasp the role of guidance, I'm afraid." She blinked rapidly. "She knows nothing about the journal you and Rose showed me. I consider that privileged information for now. Of course, if Devin is proven the culprit, I'll have to turn over the journal and any other possible evidence to the authorities."

"So...what exactly *is* your role here, Christine? And mine?" Penny wished now that Rose had not been too busy to talk with the counselor before she herself became involved. "I am completely in the dark about such matters."

"I realize you are a green little newbie," Christine smiled. "But you might be surprised to hear how little even the most experienced teachers know about this kind of situation." The counselor lowered her head for a moment before locking eyes with Penny, weighing her words. "I'm also wondering if our…our know-nothing principal has any idea how to proceed." She gave a grim smile. "In fact, I'm counting on that as I work out a plan to help Devin through his…through our difficult situation."

Reaching in her desk drawer, Christine pulled out a copy of Devin's journal the teachers had shared with her. "Let me refresh your memory." She read: "'I'm doing something I know is bad. Wrong. I could get in big shit over this. But it's all for Gabby. I have to save my sister. I have to get her away from my dad.'" She placed the paper on her desk.

"Sounds pretty damning, doesn't it?" Penny gulped. "'Something bad…wrong…big shit…'"

"Here's the rub, Penny. It's the other part of the journal that's actually more important." She looked down at the paper again. "'It's all for Gabby. I have to save my sister. I have to get her away from my dad.'"

Penny looked perplexed. "Not sure I understand what you're getting at."

"After you and Rose showed me Devin's journal, I called him in for a conference, or, more of a chat, at least that's what I told him. I didn't let on I'd read the journal entry. Instead, I asked him how things were going at home."

"And…?"

"He clammed up. No surprise, really. After some

gentle probing, I got him to admit that he and his father do not get along and that tension is escalating. Lots of yelling, arguing over everything, even Devin's new after-school job. I'd say the man is a control freak with anger issues. Devin implied that was a factor in the divorce." Christine tapped the paper on her desk. "When I asked him about his little sister, his body English told me more than his words. He clenched his teeth and a slow flush crept from his neck all the way to his forehead. 'I have to get Gabby out of the house. Take her back to Mom.' And when I asked him why, all he would say was, 'I have my reasons.' Typical male adolescent. Knows he needs help but wants to look strong enough to go it alone."

"I still don't understand, Christine…"

"Sorry. Let me just say, if Devin has a legitimate reason for getting his sister out of the house, there may be an avenue for professional interference that could save not only Gabby, but Devin. From Wendy's accusations. You realize a drug offense could send Devin to the Juvenile Detention Center."

"I'll tell Rose what you've shared. But, I'm not sure what we can do."

"Rose has a special rapport with Devin. He respects her and I think he will listen to her. If she, or you, Penny, can convince Devin to let me help…well, that could be the breakthrough we need." Christine stood. "Now, I expect you need to be off to your duties. Are you teaching yet or still observing?"

"I've been teaching alongside Lyn Leeson. What a role model!" Penny gathered her purse and book bag.

"Oh my, yes. She certainly knows how to handle the frosh, doesn't she? I always enjoy working with her kids." Christine walked Penny to the door. "Thanks for anything you can do to help Devin. We need to work fast if we're going to save him from...bad weather." The counselor made a sour face.

Penny rushed to Lyn's first period class. There wouldn't be time to check in with Rose as she usually did before school started. Quickly dropping her coat and purse in the teacher workroom, Penny bolted back into the hall at the sound of the bell tone for first period. Opening the classroom door, she was surprised to see a balding middle-aged man standing at the podium. A substitute? Where was Lyn? Then it hit her. Oh no. The long-term sub Christine had mentioned. For Lyn Leeson? What could have happened to Lyn?

As Penny entered the room, the man turned toward her, his troll face like a knot in an aging tree set larger than normal on his squatty trunk. He wore an unfortunate plaid sport coat, altogether presenting the picture of a reptilian character straight out of the children's book *Frog and Toad Together*.

Students stood about the room clattering and chattering, testing the boundaries of the sub.

"Sit down!" the man yelled over the din. "Quiet! I said sit down and be quiet!"

Eying Penny, the students gradually drifted to their seats, but the buzz of conversation continued. This would never happen with Lyn at the helm.

"Want me to settle the class?" she asked the man. "I'm Penny Bright, an intern. I've been working with Ms. Leeson."

He glared at her. "I believe I am supposed to be in charge," he spat out. "I said quiet!" he yelled again.

Penny was grateful Lyn was not there to observe

such unprofessional behavior in her place. Sighing, she took a seat at the teacher's desk in the corner. She had to talk to Rose.

Chapter Eight

Chin cupped in her hand, Rose sat secluded in her hiding place, the library reference room. The week after Thanksgiving had turned out to be a briar patch. She'd given Substitute Farcus lesson plans culled from Lyn Leeson's files and handed him the teacher's edition to the literature text. Ordinarily, Rose felt confident her department substitutes would learn and adjust once she had apprised them of routine procedures. But, a knot of concern twisted her stomach. The man had appeared clueless as she'd led him through the usual drill: hall passes, tardy slips, attendance folder, lunch shifts, bell and block schedules. She had the uneasy feeling Mr. Ralph Farcus had never taught a class in his life. And he was to replace the most valuable member of her ninth grade team for…how long? Maybe months. Penny had related her horror with his class management style which consisted mainly of yelling over the din and banishing the worst offenders to sit in the hallway outside class, where they would, most certainly, not learn anything. Rose would have her work cut out for her with Sub Farcus. She had an appointment with him to go over the curriculum requirements and she was already dreading it. Was there any way to replace him, what with Wendy's strong endorsement of the guy?

And then, there was the case of Devin Giovani. Blustering with principal protocol, with or without evidence, Wendy Storme appeared determined to pounce on the kid and turn him over to the narcs for selling drugs. As a show of her control of all things regarding law and order for Harding High? A notch on her belt? Rose and Penny and counselor Yamada were convinced that there were underlying causes for Devin's behavior that needed to be aired and attended to. It was possible their efforts could save the student from the horrors of juvie. Another cyclone to be chased amidst the thorns. A terrible mixed metaphor. Shakespeare said it better: *'Tis an ill wind which blows no man to good*. A perfect description of Principle Storme.

Deep in thought, Rose was slow to respond to the gentle tapping at the door. "Rose? Rose?" One of the librarians poked her head into the room. "Jose Mendoza's out here. He's desperate to talk to you. What should I tell him?"

"Oh, sure, send him in."

Rose was shocked at the custodian's appearance. No longer wearing his standard-issue uniform, Jose was dressed in ratty jeans and a stained t-shirt. Usually well-groomed, the young man stood unshaven and his black hair stuck up in brushy tufts. His eyes were bloodshot. Had he been drinking?

"My God, Jose. What's happened to you?" She led him to a seat.

"Oh, Ms. Lane. I...I...the principal, she fire me."

"What? Why?"

Jose brushed a tear from his cheek. "Is a long story. I tell you now, if you want."

Rose caught a clandestine look at her watch. "Of course. Go on, Jose. How did she come to discharge you?" She spoke quietly, like mother to child when her instinct was to growl her disapproval of Wendy Storme.

"It goes back to the coffee bar I build in her house. You remember? She on purpose ordered twice the material for the office bar so she can have me build her one at home—no charge for wood, granite, and other stuff. When I tell her that is not right, she say not to worry, she will take care of the work order, the proof of what she done." Jose slumped into the chair. "And she remind me she paid me for the home job."

"Go on. Please."

"Well, then Principal Storme, she decide to order new furniture for the main office. I tell her the old furniture look fine to me, and she say, 'That's where you come in, Jose. After the night custodian leave, I want you to beat up all the office furniture so it look bad enough to order new. Don't tell nobody.' "

"What then, Jose?"

He sat up straight. "When I refuse, she remind me about the coffee bar I build at her house. Say she will report me for stealing county materials to build it if I don't bust up the furniture like she want me to. 'Remember, Jose. I kept the work order for the office coffee bar. And I paid you good to build the one at my home. Easy to prove you a thief.' That is what she tell me."

"I've noticed the new furniture; I take it you did her bidding and beat up the old stuff?"

Jose bowed his head. "What choice I have, Ms. Lane? She got me, how you say it? She got me in a basket."

"She had you over a barrel." Rose chewed her lip. "There's more to the story, right?"

"After I bust up the stuff, county officials haul it off and come back saying it look like vandalism, not just wear and tear. They want investigation into why Ms. Storme did not report it."

"So she ratted you out and blamed you for vandalizing?" Rose could not hide her shock. "And then she fired you?"

Tears formed in Jose's eyes. "Ms. Lane, we got a baby at home. My wife, she quit her job. We live on my check." He gulped. "Now I got no job. No check. No money for food for baby."

"This is so unfair, Jose. Unbelievably unfair." A low blow even for an ill wind like Wendy Storme.

"I work so hard for Harding High School. I love my job you help me get even though I learn English after I speak *Espanol*." A sudden flash of anger hardened his features. "She won't give me no good recommendation, either, so I can't work at no other county schools." His eyes flashed his fury. "*La Bruja*," he whispered.

****

"Would you take a look at this, Rose?" Burt Boyd approached her in the workroom. He looked around before lowering his voice. "I don't want anybody else to hear about this until I show you. See what you think about it." He held a small white envelope in his hand.

Pulling her glasses from her head, Rose removed a card from the envelope and read, "You are invited to a special buffet dinner for the best teachers at Harding High, to be held at the home of Wendy Storme." Rose gave Burt a puzzled look. "You just received this?"

Burt nodded. "Can you beat it? I'm wondering who else got one of these swell invites?"

"I haven't heard of anybody else in our department, except you, of course." Rose turned the card over to discover a post script of sorts: "This is an exclusive invitation."

"Is this bullshit, or what?" Burt frowned. "Why me out of all the teachers in our department? Hell, I only teach one English course. The rest is electives, as you know—creative writing and speech and drama. What's she up to, anyway with this 'exclusive' shit?"

Actually, Rose *had* heard about these invitations, on the QT at one of the FAC meetings. This was not the first "best teacher" event Wendy had hosted; she'd held at least one other earlier in the semester. Rose had dismissed it as a silly whim, especially when she found out that most of the invitees were Wendy's own hires, overwhelmingly young and inexperienced replacements for teachers who had transferred to other schools under her so-called leadership. As far as Rose knew, Burt was the first teacher hired by the original principal, Carter Thompson, to be included. And, certainly, the only teacher in the English Department to receive a "best teacher" invitation.

It was well-known throughout the English Department, if not the school, that Burt Boyd was a weak teacher when it came to academics. Those in the know realized why Carter Thompson had hired him in contrast to the stellar academicians he had picked for the opening of the new Harding High. Carter himself had informed Rose that he considered Burt to be extremely well-attuned to the least motivated students. A member of a band that played at weddings and bar mitzvahs on weekends and during summer break, Burt could woo reluctant or failing students with music and lyrics and stanzas when more content-oriented teachers failed. He was known to sing his students into cooperating. The one English Eleven course Burt actually taught always contained a substantial number of strugglers who'd barely made it through English Nine and Ten. There was a place for a teacher like Burt; Carter knew it, Burt knew it and Rose knew it. What did Wendy Storme *think* she knew?

Rose replaced the invitation inside the envelope and handed it back to Burt. "Are you inclined to accept the invitation?"

"Hell no," Burt growled. His mouth turned down like a bad taste.

Rose scratched her chin in thought. "Let me throw something out here, Burt. How about you swallow your gall and take Wendy up on the invitation?"

"And then come back and fill you in on what she's up to?" Burt chuckled "Because, you know she's up to something." He appeared to consider. "Okay, Rose. But only for you would I waste my precious personal time on a blast of foul air like Wendy Storme." Holding the invitation over the trash can, with fingers pinched to his nose, he pantomimed tossing it out before returning it to his pocket. "I'm good at playing dumb," he said, walking away.

Rose watched him go. If the principal was trying to butter up support for herself, she had sadly mistaken Burt Boyd for a toady, a yes-man. Instead, he just might turn out to be an informer…for Rose. And he was damn good at playing dumb. After all, with his class load, Burt was not buried under a daily avalanche of papers to grade like the rest of the department, thus allowing him plenty of personal time for playing with his band, his real passion. *Dumb like a coyote*.

****

Conversing in low tones, Rose and Penny sat in the next-to-last booth in the Ground to Please coffee shop. Both felt the need to seek shelter from the tornado warnings on school grounds where the atmosphere had become too threatening for any thought beyond survival.

"I can't work with Farcus, Rose. The man has no idea how to discipline and the kids are taking gross advantage of that. I know you spent a lot of time trying to acquaint him with the curriculum, but he has no clue there either." Penny stirred cream into her coffee. "And he refuses to take any suggestions from me. His attitude is, 'You're nothing but a brainless young woman.' It's like if my hair were a little lighter I'd be a dumb blonde joke." She sipped her coffee. "The students are having a field day. Lyn would be appalled that her classes have fallen so far so soon under a sub-par sub." Her eyes widened. "Please, please, Rose. Don't tell Lyn. She doesn't need to be any more upset."

Rose twisted her lips and looked pensive. "I agree. Lyn's in pretty bad shape. Her husband is trying to keep up with the house and kids and the neighbors regularly pitch in. Our department and other faculty members are providing dinners for the duration. But, you can't make broken bones knit any faster. The pain and frustration are taking their toll on Lyn, that's evident. You can hear it in her voice and see it in her messages."

"So, I'm leaving Ralph Farcus and Lyn's ninth graders. I feel kinda bad about it, but I know I'll get in trouble with my intern program if I stick around without legitimate teaching experience; believe me,

Farcus is anything but legit. Which teacher should I work with next? Any suggestions?"

Rose started to answer, then paused, placing a finger to her lips and turning her head toward the tall, wooden back that divided their booth with the one behind them, the last nook in the coffee shop. She leaned closer to the separating panel. "Shhhh. I think I recognize that voice," she jerked a thumb over her shoulder."

Penny raised her eyebrows. "Who," she mouthed without sound.

"It's Carter Thompson, who opened Harding High. You know, the principal Wendy replaced."

"Oh, yes. He interviewed me for my internship," Penny said. Both were whispering.

Rose cupped a hand to her ear. "Oh my God! I know that voice, too. It's Garrett Barnes, the assistant principal who deserted in the middle of the night." She paused to listen again. "And Gwen Rogers! Carter's secretary, who also quit because she couldn't stand working for Wendy. They're talking about her. The three of them are talking about Wendy Storme." Rose snorted. "I bet they thought nobody would see or hear them in that last booth, it's so secluded. Ha!"

"They're hiding out, kinda like us, eh?" Penny whispered.

"Let's listen," Rose said. "They're getting heated up and talking louder. Maybe you can hear them, too."

Both women grew silent, straining to catch the subdued conversation barely audible behind them.

"...ruining the school...all we worked so hard to establish at the opening...every time I'm out and about in town someone complains to me..." Carter

Thompson's voice.

"Running off some of the best teachers...driving the other administrators crazy with ridiculous orders..." Garrett Barnes.

"...the community wants to name the stadium after you, Carter. Not so much of an honor with the reputation the school is getting under Storme..." Gwen Rogers. "Can't you do something with the county higher-ups?"

"Believe me, I've tried. Once a principal retires, there's not much clout left with the Superintendent's office," Carter Thompson said. "Not only that... Storme seems to have some kind of 'in' with Superintendent Sparkman. It's almost like she has something on somebody in upper management in the central office."

"Well, you probably don't know it, but Superintendent Sparkman just hired me to be his secretary. Rehired me, as he put it since you, Carter, 'stole' me from him. I'm going to keep my eyes and ears open. See if there's anything going on...with Wendy Storme and the Superintendent." Gwen was silent for a moment. "It's not in my nature to stick my nose into others' business. But I'll do anything to restore Harding's high standards and reputation in the community."

Silence for a moment, then Garret's low growl. "It might be easier just to kill her and get on with it."

Rose waited for the laugh that did not come from the other two in the last booth.

Chapter Nine

Penny's eyes fluttered open. For a tall man, Brad McIver snuggled into a spoon position like a magician. Rousing herself, she rolled to face her bed-mate, loosening his arm as gently as possible. That must have been some nightmare. Over the course of the night, Brad had thrashed and yelled out several times, apparently without awakening. She moved to get up when Brad's arm tightened over her once again.

"What's your hurry?" he mumbled, still half asleep. "It's Saturday, isn't it? No need to get up yet."

Penny snuggled back into Brad's fold. "You had a bit of a bad night. I thought you'd want to sleep in. I, myself, need coffee."

"Bad night, you say? How could any night with Penny Bright be bad?" Wide awake now, Brad gently pulled her with him to a sitting position so that both could lean against the headboard.

"Nightmares would be my guess. Lots of wailing and flailing. Any recollections?"

"Hmmmm. Maybe." Brad's brow creased. "Trying to remember. Somebody chasing me. There was a weapon. No, not a weapon. It was a football and the person grabbed me, tried to mash my face in with the pointed end, an unusually pointed end, sharp like a knife. I could see it coming at me, closer and closer. I fought back." He stroked Penny's shoulder. "You know how in dreams you want to hit something hard and you can only move in slow motion? Maddening! But I was fighting for my life."

Penny shivered and pulled Brad's arm snugly around her. "Whoa! Any idea who he was? Who was trying to harm you?"

Brad pulled back to look her in the eye. "He, you say? Ha! You mean *she*. All I could see was her eyes. Her eyes and her open mouth. There was a space between the front teeth; her breath whistled as it blew on me."

"Jeez. Now, that's what I call one scary dream. I mean, Wendy Storme is menace enough in daylight hours. But to have her visiting in the subconscious of sleep? What would Freud have to say about your mind, Brad? How would he interpret your dream? Didn't the good doctor consider every dream to have sexual elements?"

Brad snorted. "Freud might diagnose me as paranoid." He chuckled. "However, I doubt he'd see any sex symbolism in *that* dream. Ugh. Equating her with sex." He pretended to gag.

"I'm seeing Lady Macbeth." Penny pulled him closer. 'Screw your courage to the sticking post,' as the Lady said. Now, banish that image from your mind, dear. Let's make our own dream."

"No need for Freud to interpret that." Brad enfolded her in an embrace.

****

With winter break looming, Penny felt pressure to wind up her teaching logs and turn them over to her internship advisor at the university. That done, she could plan for her trip home for Christmas. As much as she looked forward to seeing her family again, she knew she would miss being with Brad for a whole week. Their relationship had grown from companionable to…what? Intimate, yes. But, more. And less. She sighed. There was an edge to her boyfriend that surfaced without warning. On weekends when they were out shopping. At night in his dreams. Often at the end of a hard week at school, especially a week when Principal Storme touched down multiple times, churning up whatever lay in her path. Then Brad would become moody. Insular. Pushing her and everyone else away as he brooded.

Penny wanted more than anything for Brad to confide in her about his own churning turmoil. Because, internal agitation was surely at the center of his unrest. If Wendy Storme was the catalyst, what was the origin? Maybe Penny could help him overcome whatever simmered inside.

Deep in thought, she jumped when Rose approached her in the workroom. Looking around to see that they were not observed, Rose spoke in an undertone. "Meet me in the hiding place?"

"Give me five minutes. I'm finishing up this log entry."

Penny found Rose seated at one of the little desks in the library reference room. As usual, except for the two of them, the room was deserted. Her mentor looked cheerful, for a change. "I had a long talk with Christine Yamada this morning. Things are looking better for Devin Giovani."

Penny settled herself across from the older woman. "Oh, thank goodness."

Rose broke into a huge grin. "I tell you, that

90

guidance counselor is a gem. She just won't quit until she knows the students' best interests have been met. This appears to be a true win-win for Devin and his sister Gabby."

"So, tell me, Rose. I love win-wins."

"First, Christine asked me to be sure to relay this to you. She gives us both credit for getting Devin to finally confide in her. They had a long talk where the kid bared his soul."

"Well, I guess we did do some prodding." Penny smiled. "Gentle arm twisting? Like for every journal entry, I'm responding, 'See your counselor, there's help out there if you seek it.' Stuff like that."

"Yeah. And how many little heart-to-hearts did I have with Devin before school. At lunch time. Whenever he looked like a drowning victim in need of CPR." Rose sat back in her chair. "Establishing a strong relationship with Devin last year paved the way for his opening up to me about what's going on in his life now. Poor kid."

"So," Penny crossed her arms on the table and leaned forward. "What's the scoop?"

"The school counselors have a line of communication to an active local community child advocacy council. They've found a foster home that looks excellent where both kids can stay together. They can remain in their same school district and Devin can keep his part-time job. The father has come around after a good bit of counseling from Christine and the advocacy group and it appears he's on board. Evidently, it's only a matter of signing some papers." Rose paused, thinking. "Let me fill you in on some background. This is all strictly confidential, of course."

"The counselor—the family. They're okay with me knowing this?" Penny asked.

"As I said, Christine insisted you and I both be informed. We're considered a part of the team." Rose collected her thoughts. "Let me begin with the breakup of the family. Mrs. Giovani, the mother, had complicated back surgery which required heavy pain meds. Apparently, she became hooked on prescription opioids during the recovery period. She spent weeks in a residential rehab center recovering from both the operation and the drug addiction. That's when the family dynamics began to crumble. Stress, of course, and, from what we can tell, Mr. Giovani wanted the divorce. Because of the mother's condition, the courts awarded him the children."

Penny pursed her lips. "I know Devin and his dad don't get along. And that he is worried about his sister."

"Yes, well, that's another thorny issue, I'm afraid." A ridge wrinkled between Rose's eyes. "Devin intimated that the father had begun making untoward comments to Gabby, about her physical development, the fact that her breasts are budding, for example. And Gabby told her brother about some sexually overt touching from the dad. The girl has taken to locking herself in her room at night and staying with friends until Devin gets home from his job. Devin was trying to save up enough money to buy a bus ticket for both of them to go live with their mother, who is now physically healthy but impoverished."

Penny absorbed the information before asking, "What about Wendy Storme's drug allegations?"

"It seems Devin was approached by another student, one who has a history of drug distribution. The student wondered if Devin could get his hands on his mother's unused opioids. His plan was to sell them and share the profits with Devin. Somehow the student knew Devin needed money. But it never got to that point, thank God. Christine's intervention did the trick." Rose paused. "Devin said he had the drugs his mom left behind. Bottles of them just waiting for him to make the money he'd need for Gabby and him to run away from home. He knew it was wrong and didn't want to get involved with the pusher, but he couldn't find any other way to make enough money for two bus tickets quickly." Rose looked at Penny. "He was that worried about the father's abuse of his sister."

"So, let me get this straight. With the foster home opening up for Devin and Gabby, there's no need for him to find the cash for a quick get-away? Devin feels his sister will be safe away from the dad's control."

Rose nodded. "Right. Now Devin can save up from his after-school job and he and Gabby can travel later, maybe when school lets out. By then, their dad might even be willing to help finance the trip."

"And the mom? What's with her?" Penny asked.

"Mrs. Giovani is living two states to the south of here. She has just gotten a new job and she's working hard for a court settlement for custody of the two children." Rose sat back with a smile of satisfaction. "Merry Christmas to all!"

Penny exhaled with a whoosh. "Whew! So, both kids are going to live with a foster family until their mom can get herself together. Maybe she can actually acquire custody...Devin no longer tempted to get into the drug trade. It settles a host of problems." Breathing easier, she added, "I'd say that was a close call."

"Now Wendy Storme can leave off her narco-investigation of Devin Giavani." Rose's relief was tinged with a dollop of concern. Tornado Woman might not be so easily diverted from her path of fury.

****

The visit to the convalescing Lyn Leeson had not gone as they'd hoped. Sworn to keep quiet about the mess Ralph Farcus was making as Lyn's sub, Penny and Rose were unsettled when Lyn greeted them with a scowl and a question, "What the hell is this Farcus fellow doing to my students?"

Flat on her back in a hospital bed erected in the family room of her small suburban home, Lyn's spirit appeared undaunted, though she was wrapped like a mummy from collar bone to ankle in a plaster cast. A computer keyboard rested on the tray extended over her bed. "I'm sending Farcus lesson plans every day," Lyn said. "Can't sit up enough to see the keyboard, so I use the mirror behind me to view what I'm writing. It's backward of course." She jerked a thumb behind her. "And every day at least one parent calls to complain about what's his name? Farcus. 'My daughter tells me the class is chaotic.' Says one. 'They are learning nothing. Absolutely *nothing*,' says another." She cringed, then mimicked, 'Can't you just come back—get a wheel chair or something?' "

"It's good to see you, too," Rose joked, giving her colleague a gentle hug.

"The kids and their parents aren't the only ones who miss you, Lyn." Penny offered her own hug. "I've moved on to Corina Collins' English Ten for my teaching experience. It's lovely, of course, and she's lovely, but I miss the wonderful programs we worked on together with your classes." Penny could only think about the bond she'd felt with the youngest high schoolers in Lyn's class who were trying hard to grow up even though they were scared to death of their new independence so different from middle school. Kind of like Penny herself, growing and maturing in her new career, venturing out even when she was afraid of what might happen.

Rose placed a casserole she had brought on a side table. "I've tried to instill some principles and practices of teaching in Farcus. I've given him simple, fool-proof discipline suggestions, for example. But he thinks he knows how to conduct class. Refuses to follow my directions. Never a day goes by that he hasn't sent some young fellow to sit outside class with his pipe-stem legs stretched half way across the hall. That's no way to discipline a student."

Penny added a large bowl of green salad to the table. "Today one of the hall sitters said to me as I stepped over him, 'Can't you go in and show him how to teach?' Pretty pitiful." She blinked. "Oh, I am so sorry. Rose and I vowed not to upset you, Lyn. I mean, there's nothing you can do about it."

Trying to sit up straighter, Lyn winced. "Ouch! That hurts." She took a breath before continuing. "I don't suppose there's any hope our esteemed principal can replace this jerk."

Rose thought for a moment. "Well, if you ask the complaining parents to call the principal about the situation, maybe she'd be willing to do something. Unfortunately Farcus was her personal hire, not chosen out of the usual county sub pool, as I understand it."

"Oh, believe me, Rose. I suggest everyone who has

a problem call Wendy Storme and voice it. She's had an earful by now, I'd think." Lyn closed her eyes for a moment, breathing shallow breaths.

"I'll make an appointment to talk to Wendy about that." Rose grasped Lyn's hand. "Just keep sending those good lesson plans in. Now, we don't want to tire you out any further. Don't worry about school. Put all your efforts into knitting up those bones of yours."

"I'm going to put tonight's dinner in your fridge," Penny said, moving into the kitchen with the casserole and salad.

"The dinners provided by faculty have been wonderful," Lyn said. "My husband and children thank you. Especially the children, anticipating their dad's cooking." She smiled for the first time then took a hand from each of her visitors. "Even though I groused the whole time, please know your visit is the best thing that's happened all week! I love you guys."

Driving away, Rose turned to Penny. "I didn't have the heart to tell Lyn I've already spoken to Storme about replacing Farcus."

"And...what'd she say?"

"The short and the long of it? You will be shocked to hear that Wendy lied. She told me about all the compliments for Farcus she's been hearing from parents." Rose bit her lip. "I don't believe a word of it."

"Ha! 'The short and the long of it.' I do love the way you manage to weave Shakespearean quotations into everyday conversations, Rose," Penny said. "Anyway, he's well named, this Ralph Farcus." Penny twisted her lips into a sardonic smile. "Know what the students call him?"

"Yeah. I heard. 'Mr. Fuckus,' " Rose snorted.

Chapter Ten

Winter holiday could not have come at a better time. Rose and every staff member at Harding High that she knew of needed a break from the severe, damaging winds emitted by Principal Storme. She intended to use the two weeks off to renew her spirit and confidence in the goodness of humanity. Having Margo home would certainly help in the effort. She was ready for a taste of the *milk of human kindness* that her friend William Shakespeare wrote about.

"Mom, can we talk about Dad?" Sitting cross-legged on the couch, Margo cradled a huge bowl of popcorn. "Come share this with me. It's slathered in butter, just the way we both like it."

Rose plopped down beside her daughter. "Has Max been bending your ear again, dear? Trying to Ingratiate himself back into the nuclear family?"

"So, I've been home a week already, you know. Dad took me to lunch a couple times, and, yes, he did bring up the subject of reconciliation." Margo scooped up a handful of popcorn. "Gave me all kinds of reasons why you two should get back together. Ever the banker, I suppose, he even brought up the economics of living in one house instead of two." She chewed thoughtfully. "Bottom line, Dad's a slick talker, but he admits he was wrong, so wrong, to get involved with another woman and…I really think he's still in love with you. Wants to make amends for his affair; start over with a clean slate, as he put it."

Rose dipped a hand into the popcorn bowl. "Though, I must admit, it is somewhat gratifying that Max feels his infidelity was a mistake, I'm moving on. And on that note, it's about time I filled you in on all the sordid details. Maybe you'll understand why I am never going back, no matter what your dad promises."

"That's fair. I've sure heard enough from Dad's side. I've wondered if you'd ever share your point of view with me. Go ahead, Mom. I think I'm adult enough to handle it." Margo smiled.

"The affair had been going on for almost a year when I found out. The office Jezebel had tried her luck with several other males she worked with, but she zeroed in on Max because of his good looks and, at the time, he was one of the highest-paid employees at the credit union. I'd met the woman at an office party, way before I knew what she and Max were about. She had an uncanny way of working her wiles on males. I can't begin to tell how she did it, but she appeared to have some kind of antennae attuned to exactly what would turn a guy on: a look, a gesture, a compliment. She instinctively knew how to stroke the old male ego." Rose shifted. "What I discovered later was that your dad was also on the make, for reasons I will never understand. I thought we had a solid marriage. Twenty-plus years, for God's sake." Rose shook her head. "And then there *you* were, our beloved daughter about to head off for college. Evidently, he didn't care enough about me, or you, to consider that his affair would most likely break up our family."

"You said it went on for a year? And you didn't

suspect anything?"

"I trusted Max, you see. Why wouldn't I? In hindsight, I realized he'd begun attending many more out-of-town, overnight seminars with the office staff than usual. Jezebel included, of course. And I wondered about some of the credit card receipts showing elaborate lunches costing way too much just for one person and uncharacteristic for my frugal husband. He had become distant, too. Gradually less involved in family life. To his credit, when I finally put the pieces together and confronted him, he confessed. Told me the other woman was unhappily married and had children of her own." Rose frowned. "Neither of them cared they would be breaking up two families with their shenanigans."

Margo sat silently for several minutes. "What a shock. Like, in the blink of an eye, you discover your lifetime partner has been unfaithful." She looked at Rose. "So, what was your reaction? I can't imagine."

"Like you say, at first it was shock. I thought I'd better call our lawyer, except she was, as I said, *our* lawyer and I knew that wouldn't work. I also considered forgiving him, maybe telling him I'd wait for him to come to his senses. But, he saved the worst for last. I knew then that our relationship could never be the same."

Margo's eyes grew huge. "The worst?"

"Max told me he was in love with this Jezebel. 'Completely in love,' was the way he put it. He did not love me anymore. Did not want to stay married to me and did not care enough about you to stick out your last year of high school. He only came back begging for another chance after Jezebel jilted him for a younger, handsomer, richer guy."

Putting her arm around her mother, Margo murmured. "Okay, Mom. I get it. I promise I won't let Dad try to schmooze his way back into your life." She sighed. "But he's still my father. I do love him."

"For that I am grateful. And there's something else I'm grateful for." Rose returned her daughter's embrace. "I want to tell you about someone I've met."

Margo's brows shot up. "A man, Mom? Oh! Do tell!"

"Actually, I've invited him for dinner tonight so you'll meet him. His name is Cliff Watkins. Dr. Cliff Watkins, an English professor at the university. I met him while I was working on my master's degree." Rose's lips lifted in a smile. "When your father left me, I had to find something to fill my thoughts besides abandonment. Plus, it was time I updated my educational credentials. Graduate school was just the ticket. Cliff was the bonus prize. At first, we were only friends. Now..."

Margo hugged herself and shivered with delight. "How exciting! My mom! Dating again and I get to be a witness. What's he like, this Dr. Watkins?"

"Handsome, in a professorial kind of way. You know, hair graying at the temples, short, neatly-trimmed beard, wire-rimmed glasses. An engaging smile and a ready wit. Intellectual, liberal-minded and informed on every subject imaginable. You'll be able to converse for hours about your humanities degree and just about any other subject." A faint flush crept over Rose's cheeks. "I have to say, I'm smitten. Cliff is such a joy to be with. He loves live theater and poetry readings like me, but he's also into such diverse activities as sailing, wine-tasting and he runs half-marathons. Oh, and he follows college basketball with a vengeance."

"Sounds like the proverbial Renaissance Man," Margo observed.

"Cliff is divorced. No children. He's honestly looking forward to meeting you, getting to know you, Margo. I think the two of you will hit it off. Cliff is right at home with college students."

"What's on the menu for tonight? One of your home-made specialties?"

Rose laughed. "Cliff eats anything and everything. He hates cooking for himself, so whatever I whip up in the kitchen strikes him as gourmet. Mac and cheese is one of his favorites. Ha!"

"Well, I can't wait! A new chapter in my mom's life." Margo hopped up and handed off the popcorn bowl to Rose. "I'm going to make sure I have something suitable to wear."

"Jeans will be fine. I'm betting Cliff will show up in Levis and a flannel shirt."

"Super! I have jeans for every occasion."

****

Rose, Margo and Cliff sat around the table savoring their after-dinner coffee and talking. As Rose had intimated, Cliff proved to be a ready and willing conversant on a wide variety of topics, including some appealing career choices for humanities majors. Margo was obviously enchanted and engaged; her eyes sparkled and her cheeks flushed with animation.

"So," Cliff turned to Rose. "What's going on at Harding High?"

Rose exhaled with a whoosh. "Ugh. I'd almost

forgotten, what with Margo being home...and you two getting to meet and all." She made a face. "I am fervently hoping there will be some New Year's resolutions made at my high school, by our principal, Wendy Storme, that is. Pledging to start all over as our principal and guide rather than the despotic wannabe dictator trying to climb the ladder to the throne."

Cliff's brows arched into bows above his glasses rim. "You've spoken before about some problems when she was first hired, but I assumed things would become smoother after a period of adjustment. What's the principal's name again?"

"Storme. Wendy Storme. And she's aptly named. She tends to blow down everything in her path."

Cliff gave a little start. "Hmmm. I'm thinking your principal might possibly be connected to our Dean of Students. Dean Storme. That's Storme with an 'e.' "

Margo leaned in closer, while Rose stiffened. "Could he be Wendy's husband?" Rose looked skeptical. "It's an odd name, well, an odd spelling, at any rate. Somehow, I cannot picture Wendy married. To anybody."

Cliff smiled. "Well, William Storme gives a whole new meaning to the title *Dean of Students*. If you can believe campus gossip, that is." He paused. "Storme's an ordinary-looking middle-aged fellow, but I suppose there's power in his position...enough to make the coeds amenable to..."

"You mean he's bonking the students?" Margo blurted out. She covered her mouth with her hand. "Sorry. We girls hear similar stories from time to time at my college."

"Wendy, married?" Rose was still in denial. "She's

run off three secretaries and a dozen teachers, not to mention an assistant principal who considers her mentally deranged. Fired a football coach and a custodian and demoted three department chairs. Who in the world could stay married to *that*?"

"Evidently Dean Storme has let it be known, in academic circles only, mind you, that his marriage is, well, *different*." Cliff took a sip of coffee.

"'Different'? What does that mean?" Rose splayed her hands apart and rolled her eyes.

"I am not usually a carrier of rumors and innuendos. And, I'd appreciate it if what I am about to say goes no farther than this room." Cliff looked at the two women, awaiting affirmation. Both nodded vigorously.

Cliff tapped his coffee cup reflectively. "Not long ago, at the water cooler, so to speak, I overheard Dean Storme talking with some colleagues. He said, I believe these were his exact words, 'My wife. Oh yes. I could be cheerfully rid of her, but the bitch makes big bucks. Otherwise, I'd be plotting her demise as we speak.' "

"It sounds as if they are quite a match," Rose said. "You know, principals certainly make bigger salaries than teachers, but all signs point to Storme's wanting to advance her career for even bigger money. She's bucking to move into a more prestigious position, like a Deputy Assistant Superintendent, for example."

"What makes you think that, Rose?" Cliff looked curious.

"For one thing, she spends a lot of time away from school; evidently volunteers to be on every committee possible to get her out of the building and into the inner circle. Then, she's constantly name-dropping the uppity-ups. Plus, all she really seems to care about in terms of Harding High itself is how our scores look, and I'm not talking about sports. She's looking for high test scores to make it seem she's cracking down on academics. Storme tries to project herself as the supreme commander, very tough on student crime, or perceived crime, I might say." Rose paused. "Wendy Storme just wants everything to *look* good. She doesn't give a rat's patootie if it really *is* good."

"You have my sympathy. I've encountered a good bit of ladder-climbing at the university level. It is ugly business." Cliff turned to Margo. "It was wonderful meeting you, Margo. If you like, I can have my administrative assistant gather together some brochures on careers for humanities majors and bring them to you before you return to college."

"Super!" Margo beamed. "I hope to see you again, Cliff." She darted a glance at her mother. "Soon."

Cliff said his goodbyes, leaning in to give Rose a quick kiss on the lips. "Thanks for dinner, Rose. Delicious, as usual!"

As the door shut behind Cliff, Margo pulled her mother close. "Oh, Mom, he's awesome! Amazing! While we're playing 'truth or dare,' tell me, are you two sleeping together?"

Tilting her head, Rose sported a Mona Lisa smile. "Not tonight, dear."

****

"Ready for a walk?" Margo slung a flannel scarf around her neck. "It's cold but sunny out there." She pulled on gloves. "You said you want to get back in shape over your holiday, you know."

"Right behind you, dear." Rose yanked a polar

fleece jacket from the closet. "Cliff's been hinting at my running with him. Five Ks, not half-marathons, thank God. I guess I'm at dual purposes here." She zipped the jacket and flipped the hood over her head. "Didn't you say you've been walking every day with a new neighbor?"

"Oh yes. Clementine Young. She's meeting up with us at the stop sign at the end of the block. She seems like a real sweetheart, Southern-style. We sort of found each other while we were both out walking at the same time. Now our morning walk is kind of a ritual. She's recently moved to the neighborhood and I get the feeling she wants to make some friends in her new digs. I think you'll like her."

As mother and daughter approached the stop sign, a slim figure headed in from the opposite direction and waved a mittened hand. "Margo! Hey! This must be your mom. Hello, Ms. Lane."

"Hello, Clementine. I may look like an old lady to you, but please call me Rose."

Curly blonde strands escaped from under a wool stocking cap, artfully framing the young woman's heart-shaped face. Rosy cheeks highlighted a creamy complexion and bright blue eyes shone like gemstones. Clementine was a very attractive thirty-something, by Rose's estimation. Her drawl fit the picture of a Southern belle blooming in the fresh winter air.

"Margo tells me you're new to the neighborhood," Rose ventured as they took off at a fast clip somewhere between a walk and a jog. Rose struggled to keep up with the other two.

"I have the cutest little apartment in the basement of my step-mother's house. She begged me to come live with her after my dad died because she was lonely. I moved up here from South Carolina a few weeks ago."

Clementine's accent lilted over her vowels and completely missed the *R's*... "Ah have th' cutess li'l apahment...mah stepmotha...moved up heah..."

"That was nice of you," Rose puffed.

"Well, my job folded up on me and I was kinda at loose ends, anyway." Clementine's curls bobbed with her stride.

"What did you do in South Carolina?" Margo asked.

"I was office manager for a lightin' business. Ten years, in all. I started there right out of community college and moved up from bookkeeper to junior accountant to administrative assistant before becomin' office manager." Clementine wasn't even breathing hard, Rose noticed, while she herself struggled to talk and jog at the same time.

"Sounds like a good job," Margo put in. She and Rose flanked Clementine on her right and left sides.

"Oh, I was heart-broken when the company merged and they up and moved to Denver. I would've gone with them, but my daddy was terminally ill and my granddaddy, I call him G-Pop, begged me to stick around to help out with Daddy's care. Bless his heart, G-Pop is your typical Southern patriarch, I'd say. Family is all-important, y' know."

"But...you moved North. Is your G-Pop still living in South Carolina?"

A shadow crossed Clementine's pretty features. "Y'see, G-Pop was senior pastor of a mega-church. He was a televangelist with a huge followin'. And, yes, he's a multi-millionaire, but he's a true believer, not one a' them cheatin' money-grabbers. Retired, now, his heart is failin'. Mind is sharp as ever, but he's moved into an assisted livin' facility. He didn't even fight me when I told him I was headin' north to live with my step mother. Just said, 'Clementine. You stay righteous now. You're my heir, you know. I wouldn't leave a cent to that jail-bird brother of yours. An' your sister is a loose woman, accordin' to everybody in town. I earned my livin' in God's work and I will only bequeath my wealth to the most righteous one in the family. Go ahead an' move, but don't ever lose your moral compass.' G-Pop sees everything in black and white. Take one step over his God-line and you are O.U.T." Rose appreciated the fact that Clementine had not broken stride throughout this entire monologue.

Margo appeared to have no problem keeping up with Clementine. "Are you looking for a job here?" Margo asked.

"I check on-line openin's every day. So far, nothin' appeals to me." Clementine smiled, showing perfect, white teeth. "God will guide me to the right position. I have complete faith."

They had made a three-mile circuit and were back at the stop sign. "Why don't you come home with us," Margo suggested. "Mom has made her famous cinnamon buns and we can heat up some hot chocolate. We've earned it with our three-mile run."

"You had me at cinnamon buns," Clementine laughed. "Hey, I'm usually not such a motor-mouth. I guess I've been cooped up in my apartment too long. It's a new place for me and my step mom keeps to herself much of the time. I guess I just needed to talk."

"No better opportunity for talk than a walk.

Walkie-talkie," Margo quipped.

No sooner had they removed their outerwear, then Rose received a beep from her cell phone. "Oh, it's Corina Collins. A teacher in my department. I'd better see what this is about. I hope there's nothing wrong."

The younger women made their way into the kitchen as Rose continued to work her phone. Minutes later, she joined them. "Clementine, you said God would guide you in finding a job?"

Clementine nodded, her mouth full of the sticky bun.

"I don't know if this is divine action, or not, but I just learned that the principal's secretary at my high school has left the job. They're frantic to fill it over the holidays before school resumes in January. With your credentials, you could probably get hired, at least temporarily. Something to add to your resume, if nothing more. My friend called to see if Margo was interested just for while she's home from college until they can get someone permanent, but it seems more like something in your line of experience. That's at Harding High here in town."

Clementine's blue eyes appeared to deepen in color. "Oh my. That truly was fast, wasn't it?" She chuckled. "I do think I'd like to apply. I absolutely loved my own school years. Bein' back in the hallowed halls might be just what I've been lookin' for. This could surely be an answer to prayer."

Rose poured herself a generous mug of hot chocolate. "I feel I must warn you, Clementine. You would be the fourth secretary for the main office this year. Wendy Storme, the new principal is...let's just say she can be a real challenge to work with."

Clementine flashed a brilliant smile. "I love a challenge, Rose. With God's help, I can get through most anything. I've had a setback what with my old job leavin' town, but I always say setbacks should be viewed for what they are, temporary inconveniences. One door closes and another opens if you have faith."

Rose figured Wendy wanted to save face, to have a new secretary installed before the teachers and students returned after winter break. She wouldn't care if it was a permanent hire or not, her usual effort to make things look good even if they were anything but. Rose dropped a marshmallow on top of her cocoa and watched it melt into a white puddle. She hoped this would not be a huge mistake, getting a new neighbor and potential friend into an untenable situation. On the other hand, maybe Harding High needed someone like Clementine, a Miss Southern Hospitality who might possibly nullify Wendy Storme's evil presence. Someone willing to turn the other cheek. How would God view that?

Chapter Eleven

Penny had flown back to her apartment several days ahead of the return date for students after winter break and the beginning of school. She had lesson plans to make before her next teaching stint and some university class work to do. Plus, she wanted a bit of quality time with Brad before the work week cranked into gear again.

She was relieved to note that Brad seemed refreshed and eager to be reunited as he met her at the airport. He loaded her suitcase into the trunk of his car then folded himself into the driver's seat and pulled her to him for a long kiss. "God, how I missed you," he breathed.

Penny returned the embrace enthusiastically. "Likewise," she murmured into his neck, inhaling his good man-scent hungrily.

"Want to stop for coffee? Unwind a bit after your long trip? Those red-eye flights are the worst." Brad glanced at her. "I have the whole day reserved." He chuckled. "And the night, too, I might add."

"Sure. Coffee might revive me. And we can catch up. It seems I was gone for a month instead of a little more than a week."

They slid into their favorite booth at Ground to Please and ordered. "You look terrific, Brad. Restful break? Did you get home for some of your mom's cooking?"

"Oh yeah. My sister Lizah took time off to come home, too. We had us a big ole family love-in."

Penny smiled. "I do like your family dynamic, especially the way you guys communicate with each other. I'm an only-child myself, always waiting for the sibling who never materialized. It was great seeing Mom and Dad again, but I miss the bustle of school in the quiet of my little hometown world. My folks are so used to not talking to each other, they've forgotten how to talk to me, I'm afraid."

"You don't ever say much about your parents."

Penny stirred cream into her coffee. "Mom has always been a homemaker. Very domestic, sews up a storm, cooks dishes from scratch, and depends on Dad for everything. She doesn't even drive. A real throwback, I'd say. Dad worked a lifetime at a local furniture factory, until all the manufacturing dried up and left half the town unemployed. Including him." Penny bit her lip. "They understood my wild desire to leave the area and attend college, but they had no means of supporting that notion financially. So, I worked my way through undergrad school waiting tables, baby-sitting professors' kids, anything I could do to make a dollar."

"A self-made woman," Brad reached across the table and took her hand. "And now you're working on a master's degree and a career. I admire your drive." He looked sheepish. "I feel like I've wimped out myself. Where's my fighting spirit, I ask. Lizah and Mom and I talked and talked about Tornado Woman—how she made me so damn mad. I must say, I'm feeling better about the situation now." He grinned. "The ladies called it a mini-intervention." He looked beneath lowered lashes at Penny. "I believe you refer to the technique as 'talk therapy.' "

Breathing a sigh of relief, Penny squeezed Brad's hand. "Oh, I am so glad to hear you had a chance to move those dark feelings into the light. I confess I've been worried to distraction sometimes trying to help you...to..."

"To get a grip?" Brad grimaced. "You're not the only one who noticed. But, as I said, my fam helped me sort things out. I guess I had to be reminded of something. When our dad got sick, his employer was a real stinker. Wouldn't ease up restrictions on sick days, dumped him from his employee-based insurance and ultimately fired him. It impacted our whole family, of course. We watched Dad slowly diminish until there was nothing left except resentment for the way he was treated at work."

"Wow. That's harsh," Penny sympathized.

"During Dad's last days, he made Lizah and Mom and me promise we'd never allow something similar to happen to us. 'Don't take it lying down, like I did. Stand up for yourself when injustice pulls you down. I wish I had. Now there's nothing left of me to fight with and I'll die a bitter, wasted old man.' "

Penny looked confused. "I'm not sure I'm following..."

Brad shook his head. "Sorry. I realize I haven't explained my New Year's resolution at all clearly." He paused. "I'm going to follow my dad's dying advice. Although I didn't discuss it with Lizah and Mom, I intend to give Ms. Wendy Storme a taste of her own lousy medicine. It's time I actually did something about it. My resolve has rejuvenated me."

"And just how do you plan to accomplish that?" Penny said, feeling her pulse leap.

"No particulars. For one, my plan is not yet complete. Plus, if it fails, and I've revealed the details, you could be implicated in the..."

"The crime?" Penny's alarmed response brought a tight smile to Brad's lips.

"Just sayin'," was his terse reply.

****

Penny stopped cold as she entered the main office. Another new secretary? Storme must have blown off the last one with all due speed. A pretty blonde with clear blue eyes greeted her in a cheery drawl. "Well, hello, Sugar. Aren't you an early bird! I'm told the students don't come back until tomorrow."

"Penny Bright, intern to the English Department." Penny shook the secretary's hand.

"I'm Clementine Young." The secretary returned the handshake. "My goodness. Things have surely changed since I was in high school. Believe me we had nothin' as fancy as an intern back then."

"Not sure how fancy I am," Penny laughed. "I will say, though, interning here at Harding I've learned a whole lot my education courses never touched. Call it Pollyanna meets real life in the classroom."

This made the secretary smile. "I reckon I could join you there. All my experience is in the business field. I have never worked in a school settin' before now. Could be quite a learnin' curve."

"I think you'll find most of the faculty and staff to be fine to work with. The students, too." She hesitated. How much to tell this neophyte? Penny didn't want to frighten the woman; however, it seemed fair to warn her about her boss. She wasn't sure just how to do so. "Is the principal in?"

"Ms. Storme emailed me. Seems she's caught in some kind of legal situation involvin' a student. She's not sure how long it will take but she expects to be back in school by the end of the week at the latest."

Penny noticed a Bible prominently displayed on the secretary's desk. "I see your Bible there. You know, this is a public school and we're not supposed to show favoritism for any one religion. You might want to put it away."

"I also have some helpful tracts." Clementine opened a desk drawer and drew out a stack of thin booklets, which she fanned in her hand like a deck of cards. "See, here's one that tells you how to pray for guidance when you're stressed, and this one walks you through a bad day with healin' prayers." She plucked a leaflet and handed it to Penny. "This little jewel is a big help when you have to make tough decisions." She beamed a dazzling smile in Penny's direction. "There's God's advice for any and every occasion here."

Penny didn't know what to say. "I feel obligated to tell you, Clementine." She chose her words carefully. "Principal Wendy Storme can be hard to take sometimes." She pointed to one of the tracts entitled *Prayerfully Dealing with a Difficult Boss.* "You might want to take a look at that one before Wendy lights into you for something. She can be quick to criticize."

Clementine replaced the tracts in the desk drawer and looked lovingly at the Bible. "I just feel that God called me to this job. I plan to give it my all, every minute of every day." She smiled sweetly. "With God's help, I can do anything."

She did not remove the Bible from its place on her desk, Penny noticed as she turned to leave, thinking: Storme will mash this little softie into flat bread in short order. Clementine is going to need every one of those religious tracts for her own peace of mind.

"Don't you worry about me, Miss Penny Bright," the secretary chirped, evidently having read Penny's mind. "I can be sweet as vinegar pie. Now, you have a blessed day."

Penny found Rose at her desk in the workroom. "Thanks for agreeing to meet me, Rose," she said, parking her book bag on the adjacent desk. "I'm sure there's a lot you could do on your last day of vacation besides coming into school." Penny sat down. "Is Burt's coming in, too?"

Rose pushed her glasses to the top of her head. "I'm always glad to help a new teacher plan ahead." She looked at her watch. "And, yes, Burt should be here any minute." Rose lowered her voice. "Just between us, I'm not sure you'll gain much in the way of constructive advice from Burt. Actually, the former principal and I vowed never to give him a student teacher for a whole semester, for any length of time, for that matter. His lax attitude could rub off. I'd say take whatever positive there is and mold it to your own good teaching sense."

Penny had been somewhat startled at Burt's laissez faire attitude toward her upcoming stint with him and his English Elevens. She wanted to be prepared, to become familiar with his lesson plans, projects, and requirements for his students. "Don't worry," he'd told her when she approached him, just prior to the winter break, about what she was to teach. "I'm not a stickler for following the curriculum. Just keep them busy enough so they don't give me any trouble. You know?"

Penny did not know. All the other English teachers she had worked with had a firm grip on curricular requirements and goals for student learning. They had tried-and-true techniques and practices that worked. And she had learned so much herself in the bargain. She hated to admit she was actually somewhat scared for the first time in her intern role. Feeling like a rudderless ship, she had requested Rose's collaboration before the students arrived.

"Here's Burt now," Rose announced as the teacher approached. "Thanks for coming in. Sorry to shorten your winter break, but Penny and I would like to get some lesson plans in place, you know, before school starts up again."

"I've run off some worksheets. Vocabulary exercises and such. And we're still under Hawthorne's spell with *The Scarlet Letter*."

"You do realize the other English Eleven teachers finished up the literature of early America long ago, don't you Burt?"

"Well, I've interspersed the readings with some motivating materials," was his mysterious rejoinder.

Rose tapped her desk. "A good opportunity for a breath of fresh air, then. Let's say Penny starts off with some of Poe's works."

Burt looked skeptical. "She can give it a try. At least Poe's poems are not too long." He tapped his head. "Short attention spans in that group you know." His face brightened. "Let's discuss this over lunch. I could do with a cheeseburger and some fries right now."

He stood then looked at Rose. "Would you believe I got another 'best teacher' invitation from Wendy Storme?" He darted a cautious glance at Penny.

"Yeah, I know about her special parties for special teachers," Penny said, her voice mocking. She blushed, "Sorry, Burt. I didn't mean…"

"No problem, girl. We all know by now, I'm sure. Anybody who gets an invitation tries to hide it from others on the faculty. Wendy's looking for spies who will come back to her and inform on their co-workers. She picks teachers she thinks are weak enough to tattle-tale. Which is why I can't figure out her zeroing in on me. I made it quite clear at her last bogus party that I wanted nothing to do with her devious plan." Burt looked confused. "Maybe she's desperate. I do know she thinks the English Department is particularly hard to crack. She looks at us as trouble-makers. Says we have more gripes for the Faculty Advisory Council than all the other departments put together."

"So, you'll do it, right Burt? We could use a double agent, as you well know." Rose slung an arm around him. "Remember what Shakespeare wrote: 'Give the devil her due,' to paraphrase."

"Not only will I go to the next best teacher party. I'll take my guitar and serenade the witch," Burt growled. "And I'll come back and tell you what happened. Tell you which way her broomstick leans."

The three teachers left via a side door off the guidance hall. Rose suddenly stopped. "Hmmmm. That's odd."

"What?" Penny and Burt asked at the same time.

"Christine Yamada's office." She pointed. "Her

name's not on her door. It's been removed, for some reason. Look. All the other counselors' names are still posted on their office doors. I wonder what's going on?"

"Maybe her office is being painted or something," Burt suggested.

"Only Christine's office? None of the others." Rose shook her head. "Doesn't make sense."

Penny's heart fluttered in her chest. She looked at the other two. "Clementine, the new secretary? She told me Wendy is out on a student legal case. You don't think…?"

Rose returned a horrified look. "Oh my God. I hope not."

At Burt's confused look, Rose said, "Just a student case Penny and I have been helping Christine with. Before break it seemed to be working out for the best. Surely this has nothing to do with…" She clamped her lips into a line. "Let me see what I can find out," she finished.

Chapter Twelve

"I've never been so angry in my entire life," Christine Yamada's voice quavered. "I'm too mad to even cry about what *she* has done. Not only to me. To Devin, his sister Gabby, the parents. We had a chance to rehabilitate the family, to ameliorate multiple crises. Drugs, sexual abuse, run-aways, even the possibility for the mother's regaining custody of her children. Storme was willing to throw all of that away for her own ego. I call it criminal."

"Don't forget about yourself, Christine." Rose and Penny sat facing the fraught woman. "What Wendy has done to you."

"Well, yes. That too." Christine stirred sugar into her coffee. "I suppose I'm completely washed up as a guidance counselor. In county schools, if not elsewhere, as well."

They sat in sympathetic silence for a moment. "Can you start at the beginning. Tell us what happened?" Penny ventured.

Christine took a deep breath. "As you know, Wendy was looking to nab a kid selling drugs at school. She had zeroed in on Devin, possibly alerted by the real perp, to save his own ass. I'm talking about the student who approached Devin about selling his mother's pain pills."

Rose and Penny nodded in unison, encouraging

Christine to continue.

"My guess is Wendy wanted this to be a feather in her cap. A tough-on-crime principal. To make her look good at keeping order in *her* school. So that the higher-ups in the county would be impressed enough to elevate her to the central office." Christine gave them a perplexed look. "Hard to believe, isn't it? Like the brave little tailor who killed five with one blow: Devin, Gabby, the parents, and me. It's like, 'Too bad, so sad. I made my point with the Superintendent and that's all that matters.' "

"Not to mention the real drug dealer is still at large, presumably continuing to sell to students," Penny added.

"So, over the winter break, Wendy contacts you?" Rose sipped her coffee.

"My husband answered the phone. We were sitting down to a family meal and we almost let the call go to voice message. We don't often bother with the land line anymore. It was Wendy Storme saying she needed to see me immediately at her office."

"How intimidating," Penny breathed.

"At first, I thought Wendy had good news about Devin and his family. I mean, why else call me in at dinner time over break? But, one look at that storm of a face told me otherwise." Christine shivered. "'You're in real trouble, Ms. Yamada,'" was how she began. "'I've taken immediate action on this.'"

"I remember staring at her, speechless, unable to form a single word. Shocked into silence."

"'I have it all, right here on tape. There's no denying the fact of your inappropriate actions regarding student Devin Giovani.'"

"Finally regaining my senses, I said I didn't understand." Christine shook her head. "That's when she played it to me, the tape. It was Devin's voice all right, clearly saying he had drugs left from his mother's surgery. 'Bottles of them waiting for me to make the money I need to get Gabby and me to our mom.' " She paused. "Wendy didn't bother to tape the rest of my session with Devin that day. The part where Davin said he had never actually gotten involved in drugs, knowing it was wrong. The part where I told him about the foster family wanting to take him and Gabby in. The part about his father ready to cooperate and comply—a matter of signing some papers."

"How'd she do it?" Penny asked. "Did she bug your office?"

"She probably simply reversed the public address system used to make announcements. There's a way to listen in rather than talk on the PA system. I suspect she was just waiting to catch me talking to Devin so she could nail him. And me."

"So that part about bottles of drugs? That's Wendy's evidence against you...against Davin?" Rose was incredulous.

Christine stared at the table; she lifted her head. "There was one other bit on the tape. Very damning. I told Devin I would keep the conference confidential, even though I was supposed to report it because of the severity of the drug issue. Of course, as soon as we got the dad's signature and the kids installed with the foster family, I intended to let the authorities know what had happened. I didn't tell Devin, but I was afraid of how Social Services might handle the problem, not to mention Wendy Storme's reaction."

"Wendy had that on tape, too, then. Your non-compliance with counselor confidentiality limits?" Rose asked.

Christine nodded. "I call it selective taping. She conveniently left out or erased the words that should clear Devin. Where he said he couldn't do it—couldn't go through with the drug deal. It should also exonerate me."

Rose snorted. "Is it legal for a principal to eavesdrop on counselor-student conferences?"

Christine's shoulders slumped. "From the interrogation hearing it was clear that Wendy's 'evidence' was convincing enough for me to lose my job. But I haven't told you the most awful part yet."

"Oh my God," Rose breathed. "What will happen to Devin?"

"It's a done deal, I'm afraid. Devin has been sent to the JDC, the Juvenile Detention Center, where he'll stay until his sentence is completed. As for Gabby, they've called Social Services and she'll be removed from the home, to who-knows-where. I cannot imagine how the mother is coping or the father, who already has psychological issues. It's just too horrible to comprehend, all of it."

Rose swallowed a gulp of coffee. "You've talked to the family about this?"

"Only the father, who's understandably furious about the whole situation. He called me after the hearing, said he doesn't blame me, knows I was trying to work things out for them." Christine's eyes widened. "His last words?" She paused, looking at both Rose and Penny. "'I hope I never set eyes on Ms. Storme again. I'm afraid of what I might do. Right now, I could kill that witch...with my bare hands.'"

Rose was horrified. "Christine...I...I don't know what to say. There must be some recourse. Have you contacted the county lawyer? The one our tort insurance supports?"

Christine nodded. "Apparently our legal services only kick in when there's an issue of physical harm from staff to student. The lawyer expressed her sympathy and suggested I get in touch with my personal attorney. She didn't know that my husband is my attorney. Right now, it doesn't look like there's much we can do for Devin's family. Or for me."

"We're here for you, Christine," Penny said, reaching for the counselor's hand. "If there's anything...anything at all...."

The counselor's lips curved into a wan smile. "Can't think of what that might be." She shrugged. "Unless you do both Mr. Giovani and me a favor and...kill that witch."

The statement was completely contrary to the usually level-headed counselor Rose had come to know.

****

The PTO ladies had provided a sumptuous buffet lunch for Teacher Appreciation Day at Harding High, an annual event the faculty looked forward to. Aware of the brevity of the staff lunch "hour," they replenished fresh items for the spread throughout the school day so that all could partake at their leisure, combining their planning period with the meal if they liked.

With a full agenda for the day, Rose was unable to hone in on the feast until late afternoon. Scooping melting-hot macaroni and cheese onto her plate from a slow-cooker, Rose encountered a parent she recognized.

"Hi, Mrs. Howard. What a yummy buffet. As the kids would say, 'You ladies rock!' "

Mrs. Howard shoveled a full measure of greens onto Rose's plate. "Here. Have some more, Ms. Lane. This is the PTO's one chance to honor our teachers and staff. You, I might add, have had to put up with all three of my rapscallions. You deserve a platter times three for that."

"Lovely kiddos, every one of them," Rose laughed. "The teachers live for this lunch, you know. I'm sure you've had a constant stream of hungry educators all day long."

Mrs. Howard surveyed the tables. "There's still plenty of food left." She frowned. "We've all been kind of wondering, though. We always make it clear that any and all staff members are welcome to partake. We've had the librarians, director of guidance, counselors, and secretaries, but no one's seen the principal, Ms. Storme. Is she out of the building today, by any chance?"

Rose tilted her head. "How odd. I did see her earlier in the day. It's not like her to miss out on free food."

Mrs. Howard made a face. "I admit she's not my favorite person. I've had a few…um…call them run-ins with the principal. Truth to tell, I've never met a single parent who likes the woman." She lifted her shoulders in a dismissive shrug. "I probably shouldn't be telling you this. It's just that she's so different from Mr. Thompson, the former principal. He was always willing to work out any problems between kids and teachers, coaches, whoever."

Rose was aware that other PTO members were kibitzing on their conversation. "Ms. Storme brings a different vibe to Harding High. I'll say that. We're all still trying to adjust." What she didn't say was that Ms. Storme really did not care for teachers any more than she did for students. Parents were not high on her list either. Rose could see her making no effort to support a teacher-appreciation event. It was entirely within her character.

The door opened and the principal breezed into the room. "Sorry so late, PTO members. Lunch today with the Assistant Superintendent, Dr. Nelson. You don't turn down an invitation like that. But I'm up for dessert, if there's any left."

Rose cringed. Only Wendy could manage a rude apology.

One of the servers hastily prepared a plate and brought it to Wendy. "Here you are, Ms. Storme. Cookies, brownies and fudge."

Wendy picked up a cookie and eyed it suspiciously. "Is this peanut butter?"

"Why, yes. My own peanut butter cookies. Home-made from a secret family recipe," the woman said proudly. "There are only a few left."

Wendy dropped the cookie to the plate, which she pushed away. "I'm allergic to peanuts. All nuts. Looks like the brownies have nuts in them. Fudge, too."

A look of chagrin passed over the woman's features. "Sorry. I didn't know."

"You really should label all foods at an affair like this." Wendy's tone clearly showed her irritation. "Food allergies are prevalent and can be lethal." She turned away. "I've lost my appetite," she said as she headed for the door. "And now I need to apply hand sanitizer."

Rose curbed the urge to apologize for the principal.

Mrs. Howard rolled her eyes. "I'm heading up the high school position on the pyramid this year."

"The pyramid. Each district school has a representative on the pyramid, right? That would be eight elementary and four middle schools, with Harding High at the top. You have an important position, Mrs. Howard."

"Yes. I take the responsibility seriously," the woman said. "When I meet with the other pyramid chairs, every single one expresses concern about Principal Storme. All the way down to the primary grades. Everyone is hoping she will move on out, somewhere she can't do so much damage." She hesitated. "We're seriously considering taking our concerns to the central office. Maybe the Superintendent can make some adjustments." Mrs. Howard looked hopefully at Rose. "Do you think that would work?"

Rose twisted her lips. "I wish you luck, Mrs. Howard." *We all wish you luck.*

Leaving the event, Rose encountered Penny in the hallway. Wendy was talking to her. "Since you're here full-time, I've decided to give you a permanent IPR, a chance to pull your weight."

Penny struggled for an answer. "IPR?"

"Individual Professional Responsibility," Wendy barked. "All the teachers are expected to participate. Now, for the rest of the year, you're assigned to bus duty. Checking buses in and out, seeing that students leave and enter in an orderly fashion, etc."

"Did you say permanent? For the rest of the year? Mornings and afternoons, too?"

Rose moved in quickly. "Uh, Ms. Storme, I don't believe that's appropriate for Penny. In the first place, she's here as an intern to learn how to teach. Yes, she could serve an IPR like the regular teachers but surely not for the rest of the year. The normal IPR duration is only for six weeks, you know."

Penny straightened. "My university program would not allow me to do a 'permanent' Individual Professional Responsibility, Ms. Storme. It sounds, well, it sounds too *unprofessional*, to tell the truth."

"Humpf!" Wendy snorted, spun and barreled down the hallway to her office.

"Nice try, Ms. Storme," Rose muttered to Penny.

Chapter Thirteen

Penny sat with Brad near the top of the bleachers. With basketball season well under way she was thrilled to find Brad a willing fan, happy to attend every home game with her. Football had been a bust, she had to admit. After that one disastrous game, she and Brad had laid off the sport for the duration. Now she could display her school spirit along with Brad by showing up at home basketball games. Penny wanted to establish the fact that she was a loyal Harding Hawk supporter. It played well with the students, if nothing else.

Rose and her friend Cliff sat directly in front of Penny and Brad. Tonight was a double date with the game first and drinks afterward for the foursome. The age differences between the couples was never a problem; they all got along famously. Cliff turned out to be an expert at explaining the fine points of the game of basketball and Penny was learning to love the intrigue as well as the skill involved. Even Brad seemed impressed at Cliff's insight.

"Sunitra just scored again," Rose stood, clapping and cheering. "The lady basketball star is also a stand-out in my AP Literature class; she reads and analyzes lit on the same high level as she reads and analyzes her opponents on the court." Rose chuckled. "And she's involved in great extra-curricular activities. In addition, she writes for the school newspaper. Now, how often does that happen? Sunitra Benson is the ultimate scholar athlete."

"The girl sure utilizes her height," Cliff added. "A fiend for rebounds. One that tall is rarely so quick. She's over six feet and hasn't missed one yet. The lanky lass is always in position ahead of the opponent. Look! She just snagged another one!"

"Sunitra has been shooting baskets ever since she could hold onto the ball with two hands, according to her mother. Over the years I've taught Sunitra I've gotten to know the parent. A single mother with an only child. Those two are focused like you wouldn't believe," Rose said. "Look, Mrs. Benson is sitting right behind the bench. Her favorite spot to cheer for the team. She's the one shaking the pompoms."

"What I've noticed? The student has such a sweet disposition," Penny added. "No swelled head. No prima donna acts. Just a huge drive to succeed."

"Looking for a big college scholarship, I'd imagine," Cliff speculated. "I've read about her in the sports section of the local paper. Do you think there might be some college scouts here tonight?"

"No doubt," Brad interjected. "I might recognize some of them. They're pretty easy to spot." He moved his head from side to side then pointed to a tall, athletic-looking woman wearing a rain coat and standing near the door to the gym. "Right there, for instance. Bet you anything she's a scout. See how she's trying to hide that little notebook she just took out of her pocket."

"The woman is taking notes, all right," Penny said.

"Sunitra, and her mother, I might add, have their hopes set on University of Tennessee which has a reputation for highly-ranked women's basketball.

'Might as well shoot for a school at the top,' is the way both mother and daughter put it." Rose shifted to view the supposed scout.

"If she keeps up the season like this, I'd say Sunitra has a good chance to make her dream come true. Whoops! She just sank a three-pointer!" Brad stood and yelled, "Go, Hawks!"

"I know money for college is an issue. A scholarship, a full-ride, is a must." Rose shook her head. "Sunitra and her mother have their hearts set on UT. It worries me to think how fragile dreams can be. I hope it all works out for them."

"Oh my God," Brad nudged Penny. "Look who decided to show up for a home game."

"A Storme sighting," Penny breathed. "She actually made time in her busy schedule to support a school competition. Do you think she's suddenly developed a latent interest in high school sports?"

"More likely, she's trying to impress someone in the central office with her school spirit." Rose struggled to keep a straight face.

Cliff looked around. "Isn't that the Assistant Superintendent? Dr. Esther Nelson?"

"Sure enough. I believe you're right. What a coincidence," Rose sniffed. "Who says storms are unpredictable?"

"Look at that Cheshire Cat smile on Storme's face," Brad murmured. "A face begging for a fist."

Penny watched as the principal made her way to a seat beside the county official. "I didn't realize the Assistant Superintendent is a woman," she commented.

****

Lyn Leeson was due to return to school and Penny

couldn't wait. Every day she checked with Rose; every day she stood in the hall and peered in through the glass part of the door to Lyn's room. Farcus remained put, his smarmy troll face swiveling on his skinny neck as he tried to quell the chaos. You could hear him yelling even with the door firmly shut. "Quiet! I said quiet! Sit down this minute!" Oblivious to his demands, the students roamed and chatted and sometimes romped in the corners. One couple was rather openly kissing today as Penny observed from the hall.

"What's the hold up?" Penny muttered to herself. Lyn was more than ready to get back to work if their almost-daily conversations held true. She admitted she needed a cane for getting around school. And she would not be able to stand all day while teaching as she used to, but mentally, psychologically, and, yes, socially, she wanted to be back at work. Not to mention her leave of absence was running out; her salary would soon dissolve into nothing unless she was reinstated.

Passing Penny standing outside Farcus' door, Rose beckoned the intern aside. "Bad news. The worst."

"What? Not about Lyn, I hope."

"I'm afraid so. I just had a 'talk' with Wendy. It seems she thinks Farcus is doing an outstanding job. She's leveraging with the central office to have him finish out the year for Lyn."

"Oh, dear Lord, no," Penny breathed. "Why? How?" She gulped. "What about Lyn? Where does that leave her?"

"In the lurch I'd say. Storme wants Lyn to apply for a long-term sub position elsewhere in the county." Rose fidgeted with her glasses. "Of course, that involves a salary well below that of a fully-vetted teacher. And she would have to wait for an opening. Not to mention subs are not eligible for benefits like health insurance and retirement."

"The principal is allowed to do that? Doesn't the county have regulations about leave of absence and return for teachers?" Penny was incredulous. "I mean, surely they aren't allowed to screw a teacher out of her job like that."

"Seems there's an arcane rule saying if a long-term substitute with more county experience is hired they have preference over the teacher on leave."

Penny thought a moment. "Wait a minute. Farcus had NO teaching experience before he filled in for Lyn. Right?"

"No *teaching* experience. However, he's been employed in the county longer while working in some off-site office position. Along with Wendy Storme, I might add."

"I can't believe Storme would do that to Lyn. It's so unfair. So unprofessional. And Farcus is a disaster. Hasn't she listened to the parent complaints about him? Why, why, why would she do this?"

Rose raised her shoulders and lowered them with a sigh. "First of all, Wendy Storme prefers weak teachers; she's threatened by strong ones because they're more knowledgeable than she is about education. Second, she's itching to climb up the career ladder to the central office and no doubt thinks her move to instate a long-time county official in Lyn's place will look good on her resume. Fairness has never been Wendy Storme's strong suit. As we all know."

"Well that sucks," Penny said. "Does Lyn know? Can't she contest it or something?"

"Lyn and her husband have gone to the top to try to get her reinstated at Harding as a full-time teacher. The Superintendent is taking his sweet time dealing with it." Rose shook her head. "Adding to the stress, Lyn's husband just lost his job. Every middle management position evaporated in a merger at his company."

Penny shook her head. "I feel so bad for them. For Lyn, her family. The students. Wendy Storme ought to be grateful for a dedicated professional like Lyn. She should be fighting for her, not against her. What a crock."

They had walked the hall to the English workroom. "By the way, how's the teaching going in Burt Boyd's English Eleven?" Rose pulled up a chair by her desk for Penny.

"You know, Burt's a great guy, Rose. He's affable, has a wicked sense of humor, can throw a pun a minute if you encourage him. The kids think he's one of them half the time. Make that most of the kids. The non-academic ones, I'd say. The others, knowing they have to have some background for English their senior year? They're actually angry. As per their request, I'm teaching an after-school class several days a week. So far five or six kid have showed up. More keep ambling in as word has gotten out, I expect. We're working on writing essays and critiques and analyzing the literature that Burt has blithely skimmed over or avoided altogether. As one of them said yesterday, 'We stay busy in Mr. Boyd's class but we don't really learn anything.'" Penny tapped the desk. "I'd have to agree with that assessment. Burt runs off worksheets and has them writing ditties which there is no need to grade. It's like every day is a lesson plan for a sub who will only be teaching that one day." She frowned. "There's no *scope and sequence* which we learned about in my Principles and Practices of Education class at the university."

"Penny, you've just given Burt an evaluation that exactly corroborates my own. Sounds like you're ready to move on to another teacher for your classroom experience."

"I've come to that conclusion myself. But, I'd still like to keep up my little after-school tutorial. We call ourselves 'The Grammar Club.' " Penny smiled.

Rose heaved herself out of her chair and gave a sigh of resolution. "Well, I'm off to speak to our fearless leader again. About Lyn Leeson. I will not give up until justice is served. 'Once more, into the breach,' as the Bard would say."

Penny watched her leave with a heavy heart. Lyn did not deserve this treatment. She wished there was something she could do, but, no matter how hard she tried, nothing surfaced. Nothing. She sat at Rose's desk grading papers. Lost in thought. She jumped when Rose returned, looking wan.

"You look grim, Rose. Were you able to get through to Ms. Storme? That was a quick meeting."

Rose grimaced. "Not only did I strike out concerning Lyn Leeson, Wendy just blew me down with her latest proposal."

"Here. Have a seat. You look about to faint." Penny pushed her papers aside and made room for Rose in the tiny carrel. "So, what happened?"

Rose flexed her fingers, clinching and unclenching them. "Wendy is going full tilt for keeping Farcus in Lyn's position. She blithely assured me she'd find placement for Lyn in another school, what with all her *connections* at central." Rose fanned herself. "There's more. Against all my protests, Wendy plans to give Burt Boyd a student teacher for the last quarter."

"Oh dear. Poor student teacher."

"There's even more. Hold onto your seat, Penny. This one is, possibly, the worst. She also intends to place not one but two honors English Eleven classes with Burt next year. The classes that track to AP Literature their senior year."

"But...but they won't know anything. They'll miss out on an entire year of reading, writing, critiquing...the whole academic year under Burt."

"And guess who'll be picking up the slack? Talk about your Grammar Club. Barb Zander and I will be doing after-school tutorials every day of the week trying to catch these kids up for the national exam when we get them as seniors. Good God." Rose slumped back in her chair.

Penny looked confused. "I thought Ms. Storme was so concerned about test scores. Won't Burt's lame eleven year bring down the AP Lit exam numbers the following year?"

"Perhaps she's willing to weigh the consequences so that she can bribe Burt and get him to do something for her against his will." Rose thought for a moment. "On the other hand, Storme's concept of good teaching is so tenuous, it's possible she sees no difference between solid instruction and flim-flam."

Just then Burt Boyd opened the door to the workroom, a big grin on his face. "Guess what, Rose. Penny? Wendy just gave me the good news."

It was all the two could do not to groan.

Chapter Fourteen

Rose reflected on her latest confrontation with the human tornado. As she tried to talk sense to the principal about Lyn Leeson and Burt Boyd, Rose could not help noticing the accumulation of new paraphernalia on the principal's office coffee bar. A fancy coffee maker, bean grinder, bottles of brightly-labeled flavorings with a pump, to name a few. Wendy cradled a new mug in her hand, an earth-tone ceramic job with the word Boss painted in shiny black letters on the exterior.

"Would you like a latte?" Wendy gravitated to the bar. "I'm hooked on this new latte maker. And look at all these flavors. Raspberry, French vanilla, salted caramel, mocha." Grabbing the pump, she pushed a squirt into her Boss mug. "Ummmm. White chocolate just might be my favorite." She turned to Rose.

"No, thanks." Who could think of coffee at a time like this? Rose's stomach had tied itself in knots over Wendy's latest "executive orders." The woman appeared to have absolutely no compunctions about how her decisions affected the faculty, students, and parents. The entire community, it seemed. From the credit union to the pyramid. The sports arena to the Advanced Placement program. Why was she allowed to continue her inept bungling? How much more damage would she do before she was canned? Could anyone or anything stop her? Was there such a thing as impeachment for a principal? Another knot gripped Rose's gut. She thought for a moment she would vomit right in Wendy's trashcan. Her knuckles had turned white from her tight fists. She was going to have to find another way to hold herself together during confrontations if she wanted to preserve her hands for further use.

Leaving the office in a daze, Rose passed Clementine's desk. "Hey, Rose. You all right, sugar?" A shadow passed over the secretary's pretty features. "Want to sit and rest a minute?" She reached in a desk drawer and pulled out a religious tract. "If you read this, you might feel better."

Prayers for Healing was the title of the little booklet. Rose handed it back. "Thanks. I'll be okay directly." She inhaled and exhaled deeply a few times. "How do you do it, Clementine? Stay so calm with...with that...cyclone swirling around you all day?" She swiveled her head toward the principal's office.

"Oh, I just work on ways to help Ms. Storme stay contented. Like a cow in clover, as my Granny used to say."

"Helping Ms. Storme stay contented could be a fulltime job, from what I have observed."

"She likes to send me out on little errands on my lunch hour. I pick up her dry cleanin', refill her prescriptions, grab a bag of chips and some dip. I don't mind doing the little chores 'cause it gets me out of the office and I can run by Jamba Juice and grab me a smoothie."

"You are a miracle, Clementine."

"Only God can be called a miracle. But, I will say takin' care of Ms. Storme does require a bit of magic."

Rose looked confused. "Magic?"

Clementine's laugh was a pealing bell. "Magic beans, of course. Coffee beans, that is." She indicated her computer. "Amazon delivers. I've ordered special Kona coffee from Hawaii, the latte maker and pump and all those yummy flavored syrups from World Market where they specialize in authentic ingredients, absolutely *no* extracts. Real vanilla beans in the French vanilla, for example. Why, the variety of flavorin's is endless."

Rose raised her brows. "That works? Keeps her from tearing you a new…"

Another peal of laughter. "I always say, a good attitude is like kudzu. It spreads quickly and never quits growin'." Clementine threw a coy look at Rose. "The Boss mug didn't hurt, either."

"However you manage it, you've far outlasted all her other secretaries. I congratulate you on that. You always seem able to keep a smile on your face."

"Be strong as an oak; sweet as honeysuckle," that's what my Granny taught me."

Darling Clementine, Rose thought. Did she give lessons?

"Have a blessed day," the secretary chimed.

A familiar line intruded itself into Rose's thoughts: *Kill her with kindness.* A perfect fit, considering it came from the Shakespeare's *The Taming of the Shrew.*

****

The agitation in the room was thick enough to churn butter. Mumbling, grumbling, actual hissing emitted from the Faculty Advisory Council members.

The Language Department rep was up in arms about Storme's determination to eliminate Latin from the curricular offerings for next year. "We have the best Latin teacher in the state. Why would Storme want to kick her and the course out? Practically every kid who sticks out Latin for four years gets a huge college scholarship." The Science Department representative wanted to bring up, again, the need for another chemistry lab, or at least an update for the existing one. The principal could not seem to find money in her budget for it. No problem financing new office furniture, but science equipment was out the question? Everybody was on edge about Lyn Leeson's status. Farcus' lack of control naturally spilled over into other disciplines all day long, affecting student behavior and morale and eliciting repeated emails to teachers from angry parents. Harding High, so used to smooth operating, was now stumbling along like a used Chevy clunker with blown head gaskets. And here they were, waiting again for Principal Storme's appearance. It was like one of those Town Hall meetings where the lax legislator refuses to show up because he knows he will be blasted from all sides for not doing his job.

While they waited, simmering into a boil, Ashante Mabana, the director of the English as a Second Language program, approached Rose. "Can you step outside for a moment?" She darted a glance around the room. "It doesn't look like the Voodoo queen is going to show on time. If at all. I have something to run by you. I value your opinion."

Rose considered Ashante to be a genius. Not only could she speak Spanish and Farsi as well as English, but she was also fluent in Swahili and multiple African

139

dialects so necessary to the immigrant population, which was rather high at Harding. Right now the school was less than 50% Christian, as well, something Ashante took in with a large measure of understanding and respect. A brilliant scholar, Ashante had worked for years at a large, multi-national corporation. She had long ago told Rose that some sort of scandal on the part of the CEO had prompted her to leave the lucrative position; she could not abide corruption, especially from top management. Now, she considered teaching to be her true calling. As ESL director, Ashante could control everything that went on with a good portion of Harding's most vulnerable students. Straight and narrow. Fair and unbiased, the woman held ironclad ethics. Big-boned, Ashante carried herself like a Masai warrior. Her smooth ebony skin highlighted elevated cheek bones and contrasted dazzling white teeth in her frequent smiles.

The two retreated to a niche in the hall outside the FAC room, where they could easily see the approach of the principal, should she decide to grace them with her presence. "What's up, Ashante?"

"I am in need of your excellent insight, Rose. I could never conduct the business of ESL without your contributions and support. Your establishment of the transitional English class was brilliant. And the way you make sure our kids submit their creations to the literary magazine and the county writing contests. It means a lot to them and to us, their instructors."

"So nice of you to say that, Ashante. You indicated you want to run something by me?"

"A matter of serious concern has arisen." The ESL teacher spoke in an undertone. "It's been brewing for some time. In fact, Storme set the stage quite early in the year. Now she's pressing her point and I do not know what to do." Ashante paused. "Let me rephrase that. I know what I want to do and what I should do, but I cannot seem to get Ms. Storme to understand my position in the matter."

"Go on. What is it, Ashante?"

"The principal is highly concerned about spring testing. Specifically, the scores. She feels our ESL students bring down the scores for Harding overall. And she is correct. They do. There's some adjustment for a large ESL population, but as we all know, the tests skew to the native language-learner. We've been working hard, all year, really, with extra after-school remediation, PTO mentors, peer advisors, you name it. And we're making progress. Definite progress."

"Wendy is not happy with that? What's her beef?"

"Evidently, she wants to impress the upper county officials with Harding's test scores. Wants to be called the leader of the highest achieving school, or something. As a way to move on with her vaunted administrative ambitions, I suppose."

"So..."

"So, Wendy Storme keeps hinting that she has a 'foolproof' way to improve our ESL test scores."

Rose drew in her breath. "What? How? Foolproof test scores is an oxymoron in my book, at least when it comes to my students and the AP exam."

"Exactly. I am certain our principal plans to do something...well, something I could not condone. Something we could all go to jail for, perhaps. Will Wendy find a way to mark excused absences for certain ESL students during the testing period? Temporarily eliminate our students from the roles? Or will she somehow get the exam questions ahead of time? Share them with us and have us pump the kids with correct answers. As for now, she will only say that she wants my compliance with her scheme, though she has not come right out and said what the scheme is. Nevertheless, Wendy wants me to bring in every teacher in the department to participate." Ashante shook her head. "Never in my career have I considered a questionable tactic of any sort to artificially improve test results. I feel I should resist and threaten to resign if Storme insists on cheating."

Rose looked thoughtful. Horrible as the scenario was, it might be the only way to get rid of Wendy Storme for good if Ashante alerted the authorities to some illegal scheme. Wendy was cagey enough not to reveal details, until, possibly, it would be too late to do anything about it. What a tragedy, though, to lose a gem like Ashante Mabana over some scheme of Storme's. As she pondered her next response, Wendy Storme cycled into view.

"Let's get on with this meeting." She gripped her Boss mug firmly in her fingers.

Rose and Ashante followed the principal into the meeting. "Notice how she sucks all the oxygen from the room?" Rose whispered to her friend.

****

Dear Ms. Lane:

I am writing to you because we are not allowed to email at JDC. We can only use computers under supervision and if I violate the Internet Usage Contract, I will lose computer privileges for at least 30 days.

Here we are called "residents" and are addressed

as Mr. or Miss. We attend school and the teachers are pretty good, but it's nothing like your class, Ms. Lane. Everything is so strict. There is no roaming freely. When we move from one location to another in the building we walk single file, hands down by our sides, eyes to the front in COMPLETE silence. There's a counselor at the front of the line and one at the end. We aren't allowed to look at the girls in the female unit or anyone else. When we line up the counselors remind us with "QUIET TIME."

If we violate quiet time, we get automatic "Early Bedtime," or EBT. This means a resident goes to bed one hour earlier than designated bedtime. Since I'm a "new intake," my bedtime is already the earliest.

Any resident who wants to get out of their seat must ask the counselor or teacher for permission, including in the classroom, on the unit, in the cafeteria, nurse's office and multi-purpose room. Court yard or gym time we can move around freely, thank God.

During non-school days or times residents can go to the multi-purpose room for programs, book groups, group therapy or family visitations. Nobody in my family has visited yet. I don't know where my sister Gabby is. My dad is so pissed off about everything he's been in a depression, I think. I wish somebody would come visit me and let me know about my family, such as it is.

I sent a letter to Ms. Yamada, my guidance counselor at Harding. I addressed it to the school, but it came back to me as not-delivered. I am worried she's left Harding because of me. She is the best counselor I ever had. It makes me sad to think it would be my fault if she lost her job.

I sure miss my freedom which I never realized I had until it was gone. I miss everything about life at Harding High. I worry about Gabby. Now I don't know if we'll ever get back with our mom. When I left for juvie, my dad was mad enough to do something really violent. I can't spell it out here, but you can probably imagine his mood.

I don't know if you are allowed to visit since you are not family, Ms. Lane, but I am going crazy here not knowing about Gabby. And Dad and Mom. I also do not know when they'll let me out. It may depend on several things, like my behavior and the length of sentencing for drug dealing, even though I am innocent of that.

Thanks for all your help and Miss Bright's, too. Can anybody find out what's happened to Gabby and let me know? I am desperate.

Your former student,

Devin Giovani

Rose shared the letter with Penny. "Those poor children, Devin and Gabby. If Wendy had only let Christine carry out her plan for foster care just think how differently things might have turned out for the entire family. I'll do all I can to find out how Gabby is doing and get back to Devin."

"Have you heard any more about Christine Yamada? Has she been able to find another counseling job?"

"We talk frequently. In fact, I want to ask Christine if it's okay to give Devin her home address so that I can pass it on to him. Right now our former counselor is too embroiled in legal action to go job-hunting."

Penny blinked. "Legal action? What do you mean?"

Rose shoved her glasses to the top of her head. "She's taking Wendy to court for breaching counselor-student confidentiality. And for editing her taped 'proof' of Christine's so-called unprofessional behavior. She's hired a whiz-bang lawyer to defend her civil case against Wendy Storme. That's her very own husband, Mikel Yamada." Rose slipped Devin's letter back into the envelope. "Christine is cautiously confident she can win her case."

Penny's eyes widened. "That's convenient, eh? Being married to a whiz-bang lawyer."

"Maybe. Maybe not. Christine's husband could be an asset, but also, possibly a liability."

"Really? How so?"

Rose weighed her words. "To hear Christine tell it, Mikel is so put out with Wendy's behavior, the unfairness of her attack on Christine and her unethical efforts to compromise Christine's exemplary career that he's having trouble being objective enough to represent her, his own wife. Too close to avoid personal feelings. It could be a problem, I suppose."

"I know nothing about the law," Penny said.

"Not the law, necessarily. It has something to do with the Asian concept of saving face. Maintaining honor when you've been wronged. Understandably, there's a lot of anger involved."

Penny thought for a moment. "Well, Christine is ever the counselor. She'd certainly be sensitive to the psychological aspects of her husband's pride and anger over an injustice done to her."

"A land-mine waiting to be detonated." Rose fingered Devin's letter. "Wendy's rash actions have impacted Devin, his father and sister. Christine and

Mikel Yamada. Multiple land minds as I see it."

"I hope Christine wins her court case."

Rose threw up her hands. "Maybe that will calm Mr. Yamada down, vindicate his family's honor."

"Next thing you know, Wendy's going to have to add a personal body guard. One used to dealing with Samurai swords," Penny murmured. She was only half-kidding.

Chapter Fifteen

Penny cuddled into the crescent of Brad's warm body. Though they weren't actually living together, Brad managed to spend many nights in Penny's bed and not just on weekends. He'd taken to hiding his car in a nearby mall lot, moving from slot to slot, so the students wouldn't pick up on their relationship any more than they already had. Knowing smiles and nudges, whispers and pointed fingers abounded whenever the two of them appeared together at a school function. It was like third grade on the playground with the kids chanting, "Brad loves Penny" about romance involving a couple of nine-year-olds.

Not that Penny minded. She was falling in love with the math teacher, happier now that his mood swings occurred less and less often. No more yelling out because of nightmares. No more brooding. His wonderful sense of humor was contagious. Rose had noticed, too, and gave Penny more credit for the turn-around than she deserved.

Brad rolled over and opened his eyes. "Friday already! I swear, when we're working on AP exam prep the days fly by at warp speed. Never enough time to get the kids ready. Especially for calculus."

"The calc exam and the one for AP Literature are considered the toughest," Penny stretched. "According to Rose."

Brad slid off his side of the bed. "Big game tonight. Are Rose and Cliff going to double date with us?"

Penny answered from her closet. "Oh yeah. Rose and I are thinking dinner at the Meat Shak before the game. Afterward, Rose has invited us all to go to her house. She wants us to meet Margo, her daughter. She's home from college on a long weekend. Okay with you, Brad?"

"Sure. Sounds like a full evening. And I know the game will be exciting. We play in tandem the top two teams in contention with Harding. One tonight and one next Friday, setting the stage for district champs, I expect."

"It's all about the competition," Penny said. "I'm beginning to get it, like you men do. I used to be happy just watching the cheerleaders."

Brad laughed. "Hey, don't hand me any of that sexist stuff. Sunitra Benson? Y' think competitive spirit is limited to the male gender? Sunitra is the poster child for Title IX."

"Not to mention the other girls on the team. And Sunitra's mother," Penny admitted. "I'm just saying I've become a fan myself." She pressed toothpaste onto her toothbrush.

Brad slid his arms around her from behind. "Gotta leave early. I have some work to do before school." He squeezed her shoulders. "I'll stop at Ground to Please for coffee and a muffin on the way."

Penny completed her brushing and turned to give him a minty kiss. "Don't tell me you've papers to grade. You math teachers and your calculators don't have a clue about *real* paper grading like us English-teacher types."

Brad kissed her cheek. "My dear bright Penny, you're right. No papers and no calculator, either. I have a meeting, but I can't tell you anything about it…it's a secret."

Penny's brows elevated. "Oh, a secret? I can't imagine."

"It might involve our exceptional principal." He winked. "Then, again, it might not. As I said, it's a secret."

She loved the new, mellow Brad. The results of all that family counseling over winter break? That was a start, maybe, but there was more going on behind the scenes with Brad. He kept hinting at a "plot" of some sort. And now, a secret meeting. A way to get back at Wendy Storme? Penny closed her eyes tight and shook her head. Should she be worried about the type of retribution Brad might be cooking up? Messing with Wendy Storme could be dangerous, even if it did seem to be improving Brad's frame of mind.

Penny hummed through the rest of her morning routine. Rose had suggested she observe and then teach in the English as a Second Language department under Ashante Mabana. "The woman is a genius," Rose had told her. "I've already set the stage for your participation with Ashante."

So, she would have the opportunity to experience another fascinating wrinkle in the fabric of a big, diverse public high school. Penny was psyched. Still, she had not missed the hesitation in Rose's recommendation. What was that all about, anyway?

****

As the buzzer sounded for half time, the score was

tied thirty-four to thirty-four. The rival teams filed into their respective locker rooms, leaving a boiling, bubbling cauldron of fans in the gym not unlike Macbeth's sorceresses. The mood was a kind of magic with the stakes so high for both top-ranked teams. Rose signaled across the seats to Carter Thompson, the principal who had opened Harding High. She also spotted Garrett Barnes, the assistant principal who sneaked out in the middle of the night as well as some teachers who had flown the coop. She gave each a wave and a thumb's up. "There's an affection that lingers long after the fact when you launch a new school," she said. "They are no longer at Harding High, but these folks have come home to roost." She pointed out several to Penny while Brad spotted others. It was a festive crowd; everyone, it seemed, appeared high on adrenalin. Needless to say, Wendy Storme was in absentia.

The second half of the game the scoreboard seesawed from tie to tie. Two points up for Harding. Two for the opponent. A Foul shot, and another for Harding. A balancing two-point basket for the foe. Back and forth it went with heart-clutching speed. Sunitra Benson provided a steady hand for Harding, her baskets and rebounds rising and falling with gratifying regularity. With ten seconds left in the game, Harding was down by two points. Time out called by the Harding coach left the fans on both sides of the gym chewing on their white knuckles. Back on the court, with perfect ease, Sunitra arced a long-shot outside the paint for three points and a boisterous win for Harding. As the buzzer rang, the gym exploded. Players, coach, cheerleaders, parents, and fans hugged, screamed, and cried. "H-A-R-D-I-N-G, Harding, Harding Harding!"

Mrs. Benson had shaken her pompoms to shreds. As the jubilant players exited the gym, she approached Rose and Penny's foursome. "It's official! A coach from the University of Tennessee called earlier today. She said she's planning to send a scout to next week's game to observe my girl."

"That's wonderful!" Rose exclaimed.

"How I wish the scout had been here tonight. Sunitra played her best game ever." Mrs. Benson looked at her tattered pompom, showering flakes of crepe paper like colorful snow. "The coach from Tennessee has been following Sunitra for several years in a row. Now that she's a senior..." The woman shivered with delight. "Sunni has rejected offers from several colleges just waiting for a chance with UT. Oh, my daughter's dream, and mine. So close now we can almost touch it and believe it's real."

"We're very proud of her, Mrs. Benson," Penny offered. "She's an outstanding athlete."

"An excellent student," Rose added. "And a genuinely caring kid. She's a role model for other students and an ideal representation of what we're about here at Harding."

The mother's expression showed mixed pride and disbelief. "Sunni will be the first in our family to attend college."

"I've watched your daughter's progress for four years and I am confident that Sunitra will absolutely blossom in college." Rose waved a 'We're-coming' sign to Cliff and Brad hovering outside the conversation then turned back to Mrs. Benson. "We're so happy for both of you."

****

Margo greeted them in the foyer of her and Rose's home, smiling her welcome and shaking hands with Penny and Brad, whom she had never met. "Goodness! I've heard so much about you both. I feel I already know you!"

Penny held her response in check; Rose had long ago informed her that she'd once held out hope for a romance between Margo and Brad but that the opportunity to introduce them to each other had never arisen. "And now, it looks like it's too late!" her mentor had commented with a laugh. Rose was candid about the fact she approved Penny's romance with Brad, so an alliance with Margo was no longer important.

Margo moved in for a brief hug with Cliff. "I've chilled the white and decanted the red," she chirped. "Made my famous 'college dip,' the kind with ingredients depending on whatever's in the fridge at the time." She led them to the living room. "Here, let me take your coats."

"You're looking exceptionally perky, Margo." Rose handed her wrap off to her daughter. "You haven't been sampling the whites…or reds, have you?"

Margo's cheeks were flushed and her eyes looked bright and round as marbles. "I expect it's the fresh air, Mom. Had a nice walk with Clementine. She filled me in on her job, the school, just about every 'li'l ol' thing.' That girl truly exudes Southern charm, doesn't she?"

The three Harding teachers reacted at once with affirmative nods and grins. "I'm glad you and Clementine were able to get together," Rose said. "Her schedule and mine don't ever seem to jibe enough for us to walk at the same time. I've yet to see her on my weekend forays."

"You know she goes back home to South Carolina every weekend she can get away. To visit her 'G-Pop.' She says 'his body is failin' but his mind's a mile-a-minute,' to quote." Margo giggled. "I'm sure there's genuine devotion involved, but I think darlin' Clementine has her eyes set on G-Pop's fortune, too."

"Yes, she's driven to stay the course. I'll hand her that. The televangelist fortune her grandfather accumulated? It's to go to Clementine, the only *righteous* offspring," Rose explained to Cliff. She lifted a crystal stem glass from the side table before sitting down. "Stay with Clementine long enough and you'll get a sermonette, a religious tract and a blessing." She poured chardonnay into the glass.

"Not sure how she's done it, but Little Miss Sunshine has evidently diverted our bad weather system formerly hovering like a black cloud over the secretary's desk." Brad sniffed. "I wish she could do the same for the rest of the school."

"I believe it's the 'charm that disarms,'" Penny offered. "I've been keeping a little mental record of Clem's sayings. Know what she said to me when I asked her how she's managed to co-exist with such an evil presence as our principal? She gave me a lecture on women's intuition. Evidently Southern women, more than all other females in the universe, have learned to spot a manipulative person while taking care of their own interests. Heighten your senses, listen, and pay attention, spot the characteristics of the manipulator. 'better buy a roll of Tums: someone wicked this way comes.'"

The others laughed. "Manipulator? Me thinks our sweet little secretary is a bit of a manipulator herself," Rose observed. "She can allude to Shakespeare with her 'wicked this way comes.' Well, I can quote the Bard as well: 'Smooth runs the water where the brook is deep.' I do believe that applies to the Southern belle who occupies the desk in the main office."

Cliff sipped his wine. "This chick sounds like a character out of *Steel Magnolias.* When do I get to meet her? Does she have a guy-friend by any chance?" He smiled. "You know I'm teasing."

Penny slanted a glance at Brad before answering Cliff. "According to our colleague, Burt Boyd, every male on the staff and half the upper classmen would like to get to know her. She's quite the looker."

Brad loosened his collar and squirmed. "I'll take the Fifth Amendment on that."

"Clem keeps that particular part of her personal life close to her chest," Rose said. "I know, I know. And it's *some* chest."

It was all in good fun. The Harding staff, by and large, appreciated what Clementine Young had done for morale. At least there was one person in the building who didn't dive for the corners every time an ill wind blew in.

****

Penny's first two days with English as a Second Language classes happened to fall on the director's meeting dates with county officials. "The other three instructors will orient you, Penny. I'd suggest you observe each level, that includes A, B, and C, decide where you might want to teach. My meeting today begins at nine, so I must dash off. Tomorrow I will be attending a county-wide workshop and I'll be out all day again. I'll see you Wednesday. You're in good hands until then with our excellent instructors." Ashante gathered some files and folders and jammed them into her brief case, then headed out the door.

Absorbed in a lesson for Level-A students, those right off the boat, as the instructor called it, Penny was surprised when she turned to see Wendy Storme handing a binder to another teacher who sat working on lesson plans at the desk in the back of the room.

"Of course, I have spoken to Ms. Mabana about this," Storme told the teacher. "We want you to begin immediately. So, when she gets back from her county meetings, everything will be in place. We do have a critical timeline, you understand." The principal's jowls quivered with intensity as she spoke.

The teacher blinked in surprise. "But...Ashante has said nothing about this, Ms. Storme. I really think we should wait until...."

"I said *now!*" the principal snapped, causing her listener to jump. "Timing is crucial. We cannot afford to wait another minute if we're to raise ESL test scores." All of the *s's* in the last words hissed through the principal's front teeth. She blew out the door with a huff.

The stunned instructor beckoned the Level-A teacher and Penny to her desk. "Principal says these are copies of standardized tests used in the county. We're to...for lack of a better term...she expects us to 'teach to the test.' Says all three of us teachers and Ashante must be involved in the task." She thumbed through the binder. "I assume these are old tests used in past years."

Penny drew closer. "They look brand new to me."

She sifted through a stack clipped together. "And they're all the same."

The Level-A teacher picked up another stack. "Multiple copies of another test. Look! These are still encased in plastic. They look like they've never been opened."

The three educators looked at one another with puzzled expressions. "I know I'm only an intern, but I feel we should wait for Ashante's approval before we get involved with this," Penny suggested.

"You heard what the principal said. '*Now!*' She makes it sound like we can't afford to waste two days waiting for Ashante to return," the teacher said. "I'm going to text Ashante about this. In the meantime, let's put these aside until we know what we're getting into."

Penny couldn't wait until the class was over so she could apprise Rose of this turn of events. To put it mildly, the whole thing stunk like week-old garbage. Why had Principal Storme waited for Ashante Mabana to be out of the building for two days to initiate her plan to elevate test scores?

"I'm glad you and the ESL teachers decided not to use the suspicious tests, Penny," Rose said. "Ashante was afraid of this, or something like this. Wendy Storme is not above cheating to achieve her goals."

Penny nodded. "I'd say it's the perfect scenario for dredging up *Hamlet*."

"Y' think there's something rotten in Denmark?" Rose replied.

Chapter Sixteen

Rose had not seen Jose Mendoza, the custodian, since Wendy Storme unfairly fired him. She missed her early morning and after-school talks with the personable young man, a former student from years back. She also missed Jose's extra handling of custodial problems for her when they unexpectedly arose. The remaining janitors were conscientious enough most of the time, though Rose still was angry about the young fellow who cut up a favorite poster to cover the glass in the door of one of her classrooms. Seems he wanted to watch a sporting event on the television without being spotted while on night duty. Jose would have taken care of the matter in a trice.

But last night there was an email from Jose. A desperate-sounding one, at that. "I am in big trouble, Ms. Lane. Can I come by to see you early tomorrow morning? I need help. I don't know what to do."

Rose bit her lip and puttered around her desk in the workroom sorting out papers to be graded from those already marked. She looked up at the sound of the workroom door opening. It was Jose, or a sad degeneration of him. Hollow-eyed and thin, he walked with a stooped dejection. She rose to meet him at the work table.

"Jose. Oh my. Whatever is going on, dear man? You look positively exhausted."

157

Jose sank into a chair, his head in his hands. "It is the worst, Ms. Lane. The worst that could ever happen to me…my family."

"Tell me about it. Please. I'll certainly be of help if there's anything I can do." Rose wanted to wrap her arms around the poor wretch.

"I look and look for another custodian job." He shook his head. "But Ms. Storme, she refuse to write me a recommendation. So all I can get is piece work, you know, day labor. Stand in line at the gas station every morning and hope somebody pick me up and take me to a job for a day or two. They don't pay nothing these jobs."

Rose nodded. She had seen such queues on her way to work but had never realized Jose might be standing in one of them. "Go on. Please."

"There is never enough money. My wife, she try to find work, too, but only able to go where she can take baby along, you know? Day care costs much more than she can ever make herself. She don't speak good English, either."

"I understand, Jose. It's been rough financially for you and your family. I'm so sorry."

"So, one day, I just snap. My hungry baby crying. No food in the house and no money to buy any." He lifted his eyes to Rose. "So, I walk in the grocery store and steal some jars of baby food. Put them in my pockets. But as I leave, a guard stop me. They call the cops and arrest me." Jose blinked. "You remember that book we study in our English class you taught? *Les Miserables.* I never forget the title. I feel like that guy in the book. You know? I steal because my family is hungry."

Rose took a deep breath. "And, like Jean Val Jean, you had to pay for your crime." It was a statement, rather than a question.

"Not just a few nights in jail." The man's eyes clouded. "They say, now I may be deported. Being accused of crime puts me at the top of deportation list." Tears spilled over his cheeks. "Then what will my wife and baby do?"

"I imagine there will be a hearing with Immigration Services. I could testify in your behalf, Jose. I'd be happy to do that, if you like."

"Oh yes. If you think it would help to keep me here. There is nothing for me in my own country. So poor. All my old family gone." He wiped his eyes. "What I really need is a job. If you hear of anything— anything I can do to earn enough for my family to live on…"

Rose considered Jose's situation. "Know what? I saw Carter Thompson at the basketball game the other night. I'm going to give him a call. He may have something for you. Carter valued your employment at Harding when he was principal and he knows you're honest and hard-working. He's well-known about town. Even if Carter has no work for you, he may know someone who needs a good, steady handyman."

A gleam of hope appeared in Jose's eyes. "Thank you, thank you, Ms. Lane. You are a true friend."

"You've been treated unfairly. I'm sure Carter Thompson will see that side of the situation."

His features hardened then. "I never ever hate anyone before. But now? I hate that woman. She ruin my life and she don't care." He pounded a fist on the table. "I tell you, if they deport me, maybe then I have to kill that *Bruja*. Give them a real good reason to kick me out of the country." Standing abruptly, Jose let himself out.

Rose immediately moved to the workroom computer and dashed off an email to Carter Thompson concerning Jose's circumstances, pleading for the former principal's immediate efforts to find employment for Jose that could provide a living wage. What a sorry state of affairs Wendy Storme had created with her blithe disregard for an honest, hard-working underling. Rose could certainly empathize with Jose Mendoza's anger and understand his vow of revenge. Did the principal ever do anything that did not directly benefit herself? Wendy Storme would not think twice about lying if Jose Mendoza ended up facing deportation proceedings. Poor Jose. "Shit, shit, shit," she muttered as she typed.

She hit *send* as the workroom door opened again. Burt Boyd hailed her with his usual gee-whiz enthusiasm. "Hey, Rose. Wanna hear about the 'best teacher' bash? You remember? It was a while back, but I never had a chance to fill you in afterward."

Though not in the mood, Rose forced herself to appear interested. She'd had a snoot-full of Wendy Storme and it wasn't even seven o'clock yet. "Sure. How'd it go?"

Burt slung a leg over the chair and propped his chin on his hand. "She's definitely gathering her posse with these little soirees. Glibly behooving each of us to let her know about any trash talk among our comrades, especially if it's directly aimed at *her*, of course." Burt chuckled. "Know what she said? She claimed we are her 'best teachers' and she needs us to be her eyes and ears. 'So I can do my job. Keep the staff happy. Whatever they're upset about and afraid to tell me or the FAC, that's where you come in.' " Burt mimicked Wendy's lisp perfectly. "She thinks she's got me where she wants me by giving me a student teacher and smart kids next year, but my heart's not in it. Other than my music, I find nothing else important enough to get emotionally involved."

Burt had correctly assessed his own character and personality. Wendy Storme would not plant her snitch in the English department with Burt. "Thanks for sharing. This corroborates my suspicions as to what Wendy is about with these little 'best teacher' affairs." Rose pushed away from the computer table.

"Oh, wait," Burt said. "There's one other thing. I don't believe this has anything to do with Wendy's scheming, and I didn't notice it at her first gathering, but it was obvious at the second one." Frown lines formed between Burt's eyes. "Wendy's married, did you know that? To a dean at the university. 'My husband, Dean Storme,' was how she introduced him."

"Yes, I did know. I heard it from a friend who teaches at the university, actually. What about Dean Storme?"

"He was blatantly ogling the nubile female faculty at the party. Making lewd comments on the sly, from what I observed. A couple of the sweet young things seemed downright offended. Turned off. Wendy, apparently, was oblivious."

"Maybe she's used to it," Rose said, leaving Burt with a puzzled look on his face.

"Well, I've just picked up my third invitation to a 'best teacher' gig. A barbeque at the Storme residence, this weekend. Would you believe it? Wendy must not have given up on me. Yet." Burt grinned. "For this one she's invited somebody from the central office. She's hinting it's a very big bigwig. Y' think it's Sparky the Superintendent himself? I, for one, could not care less."

"Keep your eyes and ears functioning, Burt. Just as Ms. Storme asked."

"Be careful what you wish for, eh?" Burt cackled.

****

Dear Ms. Lane:

I am trying hard to adjust to life here at JDC but it's not easy. Some of the residents have picked me out. Maybe because I'm short or maybe because I look different. Something about my hair? They stare me down whenever the counselors or teachers are not observing closely. They call it "me-mugging." It does feel like somebody punched you in the face. I sure don't fit in here but I know "good behavior" counts in my favor so I try to follow all the insane rules.

My Dad has visited a couple of times. Thanks for getting him to come see me. He told me you urged him to show some support for his son. When Dad works at it, he can seem normal. Level-headed. But when he's mad about something, watch out. I am glad Gabby is out of the house, especially without me there to protect her when Dad's going off about something. Is Gabby happy where she's at now? I wish she could come see me, but maybe it's not a good idea.

Ms. Yamada wrote me a letter. She says she is doing fine and not to ever feel it is my fault she no longer works at Harding High. I read her letter over and over because she encourages me to be true to myself. Follow orders and be polite so I can get out of juvie as soon as possible. She has confidence things will work out for me and Gabby. All the support from Ms. Yamada and you and Miss Bright is the only reason I can keep myself from going crazy in this awful place.

Here's the thing, Ms. Lane. I'm worried about my dad. When he visits he tries to act rational and all, but he keeps saying weird stuff. Like, he asked if the guys here, the residents, have given me any ideas about how to get even. When I ask what he means, he says, "You know. If somebody does you wrong, how to get back at them, say, without the cops fingering you." It's like he's planning to hire someone to settle a score for him, a hit man, or something. I'm pretty sure he's talking about Ms. Storme. He's really pissed about what she did to me. To him. The whole family.

Please, you and Miss Bright, keep writing to me. It's something to look forward to when there's not much else here for me.

Devin

Rose handed the letter to Penny. "Poor kid." Not only does he have his own miserable existence to deal with, he's got a father who's unstable and a little sister he feels he can no longer protect. I'm not about to let Devin know Gabby, too, is supremely unhappy having been moved to a new school with her foster home placement. Christine Yamada told me about it. My heart breaks for all of them."

"What do you think about that paragraph referring to Devin's father?" Penny pulled up a chair and sat beside Rose at her desk in the workroom. "Sounds like Mr. Giovani might be plotting revenge against our fearless leader."

Rose's lips twitched. "The man seems

psychologically unstable. Who knows? He could go off half-cocked, do something he might live to regret." She shuffled some papers on the desk. "I must say, I would prefer less...less physical efforts to deal with Wendy Storme. I know the Yamadas are planning to sue. Though Christine says her husband is mad enough to pulverize the woman."

"By the way, have you heard anything from Lyn Leeson? Getting her rightful job back from that poacher Farcus?" Penny asked. "Last I knew she's waiting to hear from the central office."

"Normally, this would be a no-brainer." Rose chewed on her marking pen. "Lyn would have returned to Harding, cleaned up Farcus' mess and gotten the kids back up to speed. There's been a sea change, Penny. Wendy Storme has churned up our placid pond here with hurricane force." She looked at her intern. "I'm convinced there must be a reason. A reason why she's been allowed to perpetuate her travesty of just and fair leadership."

Penny blinked. "Like what?"

"I'm betting it has a thing or two to do with the central office. The tip-top school admin in the county. Parents, pyramid leaders and teachers have all taken valid cases to the Superintendent's office. And all have come up with zero action. There's something fishy going on. I'm willing to bet on it. She's got the goods on somebody. 'It smells to heaven,' as our friend Shakespeare put it." Rose nodded "Wendy Storme has her spies. Two can play this game. I am going to get to the bottom of this. If it kills me."

****

Penny arrived at Rose's hideout in the library

research room; she was out of breath. "I got your text, Rose. I scrambled down here as soon as I was able to hurry the kids out of the after-school Grammar Club. What's…Oh, hi, Lyn. I didn't realize you were sitting there." Lyn Leeson looked as if she had aged years since Penny last saw her, though it had only been weeks. A cane rested beside her chair.

"I've told Lyn you and I were just speaking of her, wondering how her case against Storme was faring." Rose pulled out another chair for her intern. "Sit down. Lyn's here to talk to both of us, to let us know what's going on."

"I'm afraid there's nothing positive to report. So much to consider, things that never crossed my mind before, when I knew I was safely employed. You have to worry when you have kids, of course. Our daughter's been complaining she doesn't feel well. She's pale, feverish. The doctor is doing some tests, which are expensive but necessary." Lyn swallowed hard. "My husband's insurance was canceled when he lost his job. And mine runs out in a matter of weeks, unless I can get my job back. Or find another position somewhere. It would have to be full-time; neither short nor long-term subs receive any benefits, you know. It's scary to think we'll be without health insurance."

Rose and Penny both clucked their sympathy.

"We may not be able to keep the house, either. There's nothing fancy about our home; when I was getting my full salary, we could keep up with the mortgage, taxes, and insurance. Now, with the possibility looming of reduced money or no money from me…" She sighed. "My husband is trying to renegotiate the mortgage loan with the bank, but so far it does not look hopeful." Lyn lowered her chin, a picture of dejection. "We're both staying awake nights wondering how we're going to weather this storm." A wan smile flickered on her lips. "In better times I'd be laughing at such a pun."

"That teaching position is rightfully yours, Lyn. Here at Harding. You and I know it." Rose darted a glance at Penny. "Penny knows it, too, as well as every other teacher in the building."

"Of course Wendy Storme knows the position is rightfully mine. She's just trying to string me out, force me to take another job somewhere that I won't be able to get out of for the rest of the school year, figuring we're strapped for cash. Hoping to keep her precious Farcus teaching my classes."

"Wendy Storme is a female Voldemort," Penny breathed. "Evil through and through."

"We could use Harry Potter's magic wand right now," Rose said.

Lyn grasped her cane and rose slowly. "Thanks for taking time to hear me out. Without the support of you and my other colleagues at Harding, I'd be completely lost. Right now, my husband and I...we could cheerfully do away with Wendy Storme. It's all her fault."

Chapter Seventeen

"Rose has requested that I teach in one of Barbara Zander's AP Literature classes as well as one of Rose's for a few weeks." She puffed up her cheeks. "Man! That's a lot of prep for little ole me. But, there's way too much dissention going on in ESL for me to continue there."

"Dissention? About what?" Brad put down the book he was reading and gave Penny his full attention.

"Wendy is obsessed with ESL test scores. You know how she wants to *look* good without necessarily *being* good?" Penny watched for Brad's confirmation.

"Ashante met with Rose and me yesterday." Penny narrowed her eyes. "Can you keep your mouth shut if I tell you the details? She asked us to keep it on the down-low."

Brad pantomimed locking his lips. "Let's hear it then."

"While I was teaching and Ashante was gone for two days of meetings, Wendy Storme blew into ESL and demanded the teachers use tests she provided to help the kids practice. The teachers naturally assumed these were old tests, but they wanted to wait for Ashante's return. Storme insisted they get to it immediately. The tests appeared to be brand new and unused and the teachers suspected they were the actual tests to be administered this spring. They made the

167

unanimous decision to defy Wendy's orders. They refused to administer the tests until they could confer with Ashante."

Brad whistled. "Whoa! So, Wendy Storme expects the ESL teachers to cheat on tests? I'll bet Ashante was enraged at the idea."

"Our friend Ashante was actually stiff with fury, to put it mildly. She refuses to work under a corrupt leader, which ultimately causes systemic corruption. She should know since that's why she left her former job with big business."

"So what's Ashante planning to do? Stick around and fight Wendy over it? I'd like to see that match-up: Tornado Woman versus a walled fortress."

Penny sighed. "Ashante resigned on the spot. It's a terrible loss for Harding. The news will get out soon, I'm sure."

"What about the three ESL teachers?"

"Ashante knows none of them can afford to up and quit like she's doing. She's advised them to stand strong and refuse to cheat in any way. And she's promised them she will fight for them through an organization she's involved with: *Justice for All*. It's a grassroots community outreach for any sort of shady goings on, especially with municipal issues. Oh, and she's already landed a job with the World Bank."

"*Justice for All*?" Brad asked. "I've never heard of that group."

Penny looked thoughtful "Ashante didn't talk much about the organization. I believe it's made up of other minority Americans who are interested in looking out for each other when society aims too many 'slings and arrows of outrageous fortune' at them." She chuckled. "I've been around Rose too long. She's always throwing Shakespearean quotes into everyday conversations." She sipped her coffee. "I've only come to know Ashante in a very limited capacity with my ESL experience. But Rose corroborates my impression that the woman is fierce in her convictions. Something to do with ancient tribal honor, honesty and morality, Rose says. Wendy acquired a formidable foe when she set out to compromise Ashante Mabana's ethical parameters." Penny paused. "I'll tell you, Brad. The whole time she talked to Rose and me I expected fire to flame from her nostrils."

Brad was thinking. "How do you suppose Wendy got her hands on the not-yet released tests, the ones to be administered all over the county this spring?" His chin lifted suddenly. "Oh, wait! Didn't Storme formerly work with an off-site ESL administrative office? Before she came to Harding to replace Carter Thompson, I mean?"

"I believe so. You think she could have used pull to get ahold of the new tests? Or, maybe she simply knew how to acquire them in advance of the testing period."

Brad slung an arm around Penny. "Looks suspicious, eh?" He pressed her shoulder. Hopefully you'll get another chance with ESL. In the meantime, working in Rose's and Barb Zander's AP classes? You know you'll benefit teaching at that level. After all, it's college material. And we AP teachers have to make the programs especially challenging. One, so the kids can pass the AP exam with at least a score of three, preferably a four or five, which the most competitive colleges look for." Brad snorted. "A lot of colleges and universities think we can't teach to their level in a high school setting. How little they know; so many of our students come back after a semester of college and tell us how much harder our courses are than those they are enrolled in at the freshman level."

"It's rigorous all right. I've done enough observing in both the AP Lit classes to know that. I'll have to bust a gut to keep up with the kids," Penny laughed.

"Say, isn't Sunitra Benson in Rose's AP Lit class?" Brad's brows shot up. "I don't see how the kid can concentrate on stuff like Camus and postmodernism with her whole college future on the line. The game Friday promises to be a nail-biter. I'll bet the stands are going to overflow. We'd better get there early."

"Cool." Penny swooped up her coffee mug. "Well, I'm off. Gotta get to school early, make sure I'm ready to teach oppressive literature. Southern writers. All that guilt and angst requires massive teacher prep. See you tonight for dinner?"

Brad gave her a distracted look. "I might be late. A senior class meeting after school today. I'm class advisor, you know. Big plans afoot. It may go on into the wee hours. I'll shoot you a text. Okay?"

She leaned in for a kiss. "Sure. I may just pick up some Chinese carry-out." She hurried out the door.

****

Penny felt the class was moving along fairly well, especially considering she was nervously aware of Ms. Zander's sharp tongue. Best to avoid any gaffe that would stir up a sarcastic remark from the veteran teacher which might be directed either at her or the kids.

Penny was wrapping up an all-class discussion of symbolism in Hurston's *Their Eyes Were Watching*

God, when, without notice, the door banged open and Ms. Storme blazed in with two armfuls of toilet tissue. "Here you are, Ms. Zander," the principal simpered, looking full-on at the class. "I believe you were the one who requested sufficient paper products for the teacher's bathroom."

If Storme expected either the teacher or students to find her actions humorous, she was sadly mistaken. They were as appalled as Penny, staring open-mouthed at the spectacle until the woman realized her tasteless practical joke had fallen flat.

Barbara Zander glared at the principal. "I hardly think this was necessary." Her voice could have sliced granite. "Or appropriate. You know where the teacher's bathroom is. I suggest you deposit your...provisions there." She pointed in the direction of the English workroom down the hall. "Where they might be more appreciated. And useful."

Hardly had the door closed on Principal Storme's back, when Ms. Zander muttered just loud enough for all to hear, "May you eat dirt and die."

Mercifully, the bell toned for class to end. As the students made their way out, Penny waited to hear Barbara's take on the rude intrusion.

"I have always maintained that woman is nothing but a bad bathroom joke. Today she proved it." She gently pushed Penny toward the door. "I understand tomorrow morning you'll be teaching in Rose's AP Lit class. Whatever transpires, surely it cannot top today's spectacle." She gave Penny an approving look. "I appreciate your calm, collected manner throughout. A strong façade is an absolute necessity for the skillful teacher."

Penny gulped. "Holy cannoli! Am I wrong? Or was that more like something an eighth grade boy would try to pull?" She gathered her teaching materials. "I hope you're right, Ms. Zander, about Rose's class being...less dramatic."

The next morning found Rose out of sorts. It was bad enough she had to rent three different rooms all over the school for her classes. Today she arrived at her first AP classroom to discover a note on the door saying the room was to be used for some special testing and that she and the students were to report to the lecture hall for class.

"The lecture hall!" Rose sniffed. "I cannot think of a worse venue for a large, active class of seniors prepping for the AP exam. I most certainly will not be lecturing them and neither will you, Penny. This is so typical of an administrator who has zero sensitivity to the exigencies of the classroom."

"How will they get into groups in a tiered lecture hall with fixed seats?" Penny wondered. "And we're going over *As I Lay Dying* the first half of class. I just can't picture the scenario for a discussion in the lecture hall."

"Insanity," Rose muttered. "Why don't they do their special testing in the lecture hall and let me have my rented classroom for teaching, for pity sake."

Between the two of them they gathered the necessary materials and took the elevator down to the first floor lecture hall. Penny pulled on the door to the room. "Locked."

"Shit," Rose said. "There. I've blown my goal again—not to curse before the first class of the day." She dropped the heavy book bag to the floor with a thud. "Can you text the office? Tell them to send someone with a master key to let us in before the kids come barreling along?" She grunted. "And tell them to hurry it up. Please." Under her breath she muttered, "As I lay dying, indeed. Faulkner must have known what my day would be like."

Clementine arrived minutes later, waving a key and smiling an apology. "I only got notice of your room change myself when I came in this mornin.' I'm so sorry. This must be terribly inconvenient for you."

It was hard to stay angry for long under Clementine's angelic aura. Unlocking the door and activating the lights in the cavernous room, the secretary shivered. "Whoa! It's absolutely frigid in here. Let me see if I can get a custodian to check out the heatin' system." She handed the key to Rose. "Now, don't go makin' copies of this key. It lets you into every room of the school. Includin' the principal's office," she cautioned in a playful tone. "Now, I need to get back to my desk. Mornin' is my busiest time of the day. Ya'll have a blessed day."

The students meandered in, looking confused. "Where do we sit," some grumbled. "Who's lecturing?" another wondered. "What the hell?" was the dominant question.

Rose and Penny did their best to steer the students into the front rows. How else would Penny facilitate a full-class discussion? Some hold-outs migrated to the top tier so as to be completely out of touch. Probably the unprepared kids, Penny surmised. It made for an awkward dynamic, to say the least. To top it off, the heat never did emerge from the ducts and everyone kept on coats and even hats and gloves. Some enjoyed exaggerating their chattering teeth. Others became fascinated with blowing their breath in puffs. No one, it seemed, was paying much attention to the discussion Penny was trying so hard to facilitate. Rose observed the disaster unfolding before her.

Halfway into the lesson, the door to the lecture hall swung open, revealing Wendy Storme and another woman. The principal's expression quickly turned from smug smile to startled frown. Watching from the sidelines as Penny taught, Rose realized Wendy must be leading her companion on a tour of Harding High, no doubt waxing eloquent about the up-to-date, state-of-the-art facilities. Bragging about her domain. The person with her was none other than the Assistant Superintendent, Dr. Esther Nelson.

The woman was neither attractive nor unattractive. She reminded Rose of a colorless square: square-cut hair of a nondescript color, square body shape exaggerated by a boxy blazer and straight gray skirt.

Wendy straightened, her jowls quivering with indignation. "Ms. Lane! Do you have permission to use the lecture hall? You can't just decide to move in and take over, you know. Teachers are required to sign up in the office ahead of time. We do have a protocol for these things."

Rose stood slowly and deliberately to her full height. "Thank you for that information, Ms. Storme. Actually, I am well aware of the regulation for using this facility." She cocked her head. "You do realize I was told via an administrative notice on my classroom door this morning that I was to hold class here today. Short notice at that. The room was locked, and, as you see, the heat has yet to be turned on." Rose waved a hand to indicate the winter-clad students. She smiled. "Really, Ms. Storme. Does the right hand know what the left is doing?"

Every eye in the lecture hall was trained on the interaction. No one appeared to be breathing.

The Assistant Superintendent held out both hands, palms up and looked from one to another. "Evidently not." The upward curve of her lips told everyone she, at least, harbored a sense of humor.

Wendy Storme? Not so much. She could try to pull off her own warped idea of a joke, but could not see subtle humor when it hit her in the face. "Let's move on," she hissed, steering her companion out the door, her visage like stone.

The entire class erupted into hoots and hollers of laughter. "You told her, Ms. Lane. Put her in her place." The comments ranged from funny to profane. The students made no effort to hide their disdain for the principal.

"Okay, kids. Let's get back to the fate of the Bundren family and Addie's dead body," Penny roared. Her voice had already gone hoarse from having to project in this huge pit of a room. The acoustics were terrible, like trying to talk to people on the opposite lake shore. During a storm. She rolled her eyes at Rose. Just let this class be over. Soon, her expression said.

****

"Send Sunitra Benson to the office immediately." The announcement interrupted AP Literature class so abruptly and unexpectedly that everyone jumped. Principal Storme's tone was not unlike a drill sergeant yelling, "Do you know my *name?*" to the raw recruits.

Looking bewildered, Sunitra raised her eyes to

Penny, who was conducting a timed writing practice for the open-ended essay question on the upcoming AP exam. "What? Now?" the student gulped. Penny nodded, thinking what bad timing this was on Storme's part. Not that she would care about depriving a student of an important class activity. As Sunitra exited the room, the students collectively bent their heads to their writing.

The students groaned at the sound of the bell tone signaling the end of class. While they handed in their papers, comments of, "I never proved my thesis," or, "I only had time for one quote from the text," or, "How will I ever get it all down on the exam?" followed them out the door. As Penny and Rose collected the essays and stacked them, Sunitra Benson walked in, a dazed expression on her young face.

"Okay if I sit down for a few minutes?" She all but collapsed her six-foot plus frame into a desk chair.

Penny was first to reach her. "Is everything all right, Sunitra? Something happen at home?" Looking at the student's distraught face, Penny's first thought was some kind of family crisis.

"I was afraid of that, too. Why else would the principal call me out of class? But, no. Everything is all right at home." Sunitra took a couple of deep breaths. "It is about a piece I wrote for the school newspaper. Ms. Storme didn't like it. I guess she just couldn't wait until after class to tell me so." The student frowned. "I stopped by my locker after I left her office. Picked up my copy of the latest issue of the newspaper to see if I could make sense of the whole thing." She placed the copy on the desk top and opened it to a page near the back. "Here it is. The article I did for the '*Senior*

Spot.' " She drew a finger down the columns. "Would you mind listening to this? I...I need another opinion, I think. The newspaper advisor never said there was anything wrong with my article."

Rose moved closer. "Of course. Miss Bright and I would be happy to listen. Go ahead. Read it, whatever it is that's caused such concern."

Sunitra drew another breath, before she read: "'The senior class plans an end-of-year outing to Discovery Park with a cookout, swimming, and games. Even Ms. Storme approved the plan.'" She looked up.

"That's it?" Penny was nonplussed.

"Ms. Storme was really mad. Furious. Yelling and all red in the face. '*Even*?' she said. 'What do you mean, *even* Ms. Storme approved? I can't believe your advisor allowed such a derogatory comment to be published in the school paper.' She told me it was completely out of line. Unacceptable."

"What did you say to her?" Rose's voice was subdued as she tried to take in the import of the situation.

"I...I just looked at her like she was crazy. I couldn't get what it was that so offended her, made her yank me out of class and talk trash like that. What did I do wrong, anyway?"

"Ms. Storme feels your use of the word '*even*' portrays her as unreasonable about student events. Student concerns," Rose said. "Her reaction does seem petty, though. Overblown."

Penny had to bite her tongue to keep from saying, "It's the truth. Storme doesn't care jack shit about student events. Unless they aggrandize *her* somehow."

"Ms. Storme kept on and on about how unsuitable

my article was." The girl put her head in her hands. "All I want to do right now is concentrate on my game. With the scout coming Friday. It's my one chance for a full-ride to Tennessee. I'm sorry, Ms. Lane. Miss Bright. I can't focus on anything else. Not timed writings. Not the AP exams. And, for sure, not the principal's criticism. I hope you understand." Standing, she ran out of the room, leaving the student newspaper behind.

Chapter Eighteen

HAPPY BIRTHDAY ROSE!

The banner swung over the white board at the entrance to the English workroom. Rose's colleagues gathered in a semi-circle around the coffee pot where a loaf of banana bread, blueberry muffins and a bowl of fruit had been placed. Balloons bubbled festively all over the room.

"Well! What a surprise!" Rose clapped her hands. "Who told you all it's my birthday?" Her eyes set on her intern. "Penny…it was you, wasn't it?"

Penny laughed. "Guilty as charged. The way things have been going, we all thought we needed a little party to cheer us up, so your birthday was a good excuse." She gave her mentor a smart salute.

"Corina! Your banana bread! You know it's my favorite breakfast food," Rose enthused.

Her friend nodded. "That is why you get the first slice, Mama Rose. I've had to fight off a few who did not feel the need to await the appearance of the birthday girl." She shot a scalding look at Burt Boyd.

"Here's a little present from all of us." Burt handed over a small, square box gift-wrapped and tied with a bow. "And a card signed by everyone in the department, including Lyn Leeson."

"Poor Lyn," Corina said. "She wanted to be here to celebrate with us, but she had a doctor's appointment for her daughter early this morning." She shook her head. "Lyn and her family have had more than their share of bad luck."

"For now, we're having a party," Burt reminded. "Don't worry! Be happy! Check out your gift, Rose. There's a lot of sentiment behind it."

Rose opened the box and pulled out a coffee mug with a picture of a cow cheerfully chewing its cud and the words Crazy Old Woman painted on it. Rose chuckled. It was a joke she and her colleagues shared, based on a ditty one of her students had written and presented to her. Affectionately humorous, the poem had become a code word for when Rose was feeling cranky. "Come on now, you crazy old woman, you C-O-W," her friends liked to tease. Someone had tacked the poem to the workroom bulletin board for all to read.

Enjoying a few moments of camaraderie before the onslaught of students, the teachers mingled, drinking coffee, and downing the goodies, talking among themselves. It was all good fun, but the shadow of their compatriot Lyn Leeson and the sudden departure of Ashante Mabana cast a pall over everyone. It was impossible to escape the foul weather of Wendy Storme simmering over Harding High.

Corina Collins approached Rose and Burt Boyd. As usual, Corina was impeccably dressed and coiffed. She could have just stepped out of a fashion magazine. "You will both be interested in the latest communique from our vaunted principal." Corina gazed around the room. "Barbara Zander will want to hear this as well."

"Did I hear my name?" The diminutive, cotton-haired woman made her way to the other three.

"Ah, both AP Literature teachers," Corina said.

"And Mr. Boyd. Here is the latest from the Storme center."

Rose loved the Jamaican lilt that underlay Corina's speech. "Oh God. What now?" Rose wrinkled her nose as if a bad smell had fouled the air.

"Ms. Storme has assigned the creative writing, speech and drama electives to me for next year." Corina nibbled at a piece of banana bread all the while keeping her eyes fixed on the others.

"What? You mean my classes?" Burt opened his eyes in surprise.

"Oh, yes. As well as your, what do you call them? The boneheads who always show up in English Eleven." Corina lifted her shoulders in a shrug.

"Doesn't Wendy know you majored in classical studies, Corina? British Studies and World Literature are your forte." Barbara tilted her head toward Rose. "I don't suppose the principal asked for your input? She does acknowledge you're the department head, doesn't she?"

"Heaven forbid," Rose sputtered. "She would never stoop to consult a mere teacher for advice."

Corina broke into peals of laughter. "Burt, Mama Rose, Ms. Zander... Don't you get it? Ms. Storme looks at my skin tone and thinks most of the boneheads are the same color I am. She no doubt sees it as the perfect pairing."

Rose hunched her shoulders and let them down with a burst of breath. "You know what, guys? We have to get rid of that menace, that tornado. There must be a way..."

Primly dusting her palms of bread crumbs, Corina commented, "Like this?"

Barbara slapped her hands together with more force. "No! Like this."

Even as they laughed, the nebulous of an idea formed itself in Rose's subconscious mind. This would take some nurturing, but it might work. Eventually. *Though this be madness, yet there is method in it.* Ahhh, Shakespeare. How right you are.

****

Rose stopped short of her driveway when she recognized Max's car. Her ex-husband sat behind the wheel, evidently listening to music as he waited. He moved his fingers on the steering wheel in some rhythm.

Slamming the car door, Rose strode quickly to the vehicle, tapping on the driver's window. "Max. Max. What are you doing here?"

Reaching to turn off the radio, he slid out of the seat, grabbing a bouquet of flowers before he exited the car. "I remembered it's your birthday, Rose. I brought you some flowers. Roses for my...Roses for Rose."

Rose accepted the bundle wrapped in green floral paper. "That's very sweet of you, Max. But..."

"I know. I know. It's not necessary for the ex to come bearing gifts." He glanced at the front door. "Are you going to invite me in?"

Sighing, Rose ushered him up the steps. "You're here now. You might as well come in." She unlocked the door. "No begging forgiveness or anything. Okay?"

Max stepped inside, removing his coat. "To the living room? My old chair all right with you?"

Rose nodded. "Sure. Why not." She removed her coat and placed the bouquet on a side table.

"Margo told me you have a significant other. Name

of Cliff, I believe?"

"We've been seeing each other for some time. As of now, I'd say our relationship is at the level of…committed friends."

"Yes. Well, Margo seems to like the guy. That's the best recommendation I could have, I suppose."

"It's important that we both remain fully supportive parents to Margo, even though she is all grown up and on top of her game right now." Shifting items on the shelf beneath the bouquet, Rose settled on a vase for the flowers.

"We agree on that." Max was silent for a moment. "You know, Margo is worried about your concerns as to the climate at Harding. She sees you as unduly stressed. Her very words: unduly stressed."

"Well, I've made no effort to hide anything from Margo. Maybe it's all those psychology courses she's taking, but she's a great listener."

"So the new principal is still wreaking havoc?"

"I'd say we've gone from bad to worse. From a tornado watch to tornado warnings anywhere you look." Rose carried the vase of flowers to the coffee table and sat facing Max. "It seems like every day she precipitates another crisis. The entire school is in constant alert mode. The community is up in arms." Rose kicked off her shoes. "Nobody can understand why the central office, the Superintendent himself, hasn't done something to rein her in. It's like he's afraid of her or, more likely, she's got something on him. Holding it over him."

Max steepled his fingers. "Hmmmm. Of course, I join Margo in worrying about your welfare." He gave her a sharp glance. "I mean that and I'm not groveling,

I promise." He cleared his throat. "I tell you, I'm more involved in school issues than you might realize."

Rose looked at him with interest. "I remember you told Margo and me about the credit union customers, the teachers and club sponsors and such who utilize your bank's services for school purposes, how they bitch and moan about Wendy Storme all the time."

Max stretched out his long legs. "Well, it's more than that." He chewed on his thumb nail. "I don't know how much I can say. If I tell you...you've got to keep this strictly under wraps. You cannot tell a soul. I could lose my job."

Rose sat up straighter. "As you know, I am good at keeping a secret. I can promise you that much. But, I'm thinking if it's something crucial enough to get yourself fired, maybe you shouldn't share such information with me or anybody else."

For a moment, he deliberated. "I still care about you, Rose. I know, I know, I promised not to come begging, but my conscience tells me you need to know this. You are such a pillar at Harding High." He gave her a piercing look. "If my intuition holds after all our years of marriage, I'm guessing you're working hard to find ways to clean up the mess that's going on right now."

Rose flinched.

"Ah, I've hit a nerve! This is information you might be able to build on. You'll just have to do so anonymously. And keep me out of it."

Her interest piqued, Rose shrugged away her concerns. "Okay, Max. Go for it. I admit I'm curious."

Clearing his throat, Max began. "A while back, I was called in by my boss at the branch where I work.

Seems the auditors at the main office of the credit union are making inquiries into a county account connected to the Superintendent's office."

"So…this is significant because…"

"You just told me folks can't believe the Superintendent's office appears so hands-off with your principal's unacceptable behavior. And now his finances are being audited for irregularities. If nothing else, maybe the man is distracted because of the possibility of an investigation."

Rose cast a skeptical look at Max. "Maybe I'm not grasping the import of an audit. What might it entail?"

"There are several possible scenarios. The first thing that comes to mind, of course, is fraud." Max paused. "They're involving me because Superintendent Milton Sparkman has his own account with our branch of the credit union. I'm his personal banker."

Rose mulled over Max's words for some moments. "Thanks, Max. Your information may, indeed, be pertinent to my efforts to clean up the mess, as you put it. Don't worry. I won't implicate you in any way. If it comes to a showdown, I'm ready to fall on the sword myself." She stood. "Let me get you a cup of tea. That's the least I can do."

"I won't mention the most you could do, Rose. I promised," Max grunted.

Rose was aware that Max may have simply been trying to ingratiate himself back into her life by revealing this obviously confidential information. She could certainly dismiss it as irrelevant. On the other hand, the Superintendent's situation could, indeed, have a direct bearing on the puzzle of Wendy Storme's power. This could be a valuable piece of information.

She would have to think about it and explore the possibilities. Shakespeare had the perfect line: *Sweet are the uses of adversity.*

****

Rose greeted Clementine, smiling as usual, behind her big desk. Spread over the surface were a few artfully placed personal items: a cut-glass candy jar, a flowering plant sprouting from a ceramic pot, a set of old world bookends holding five or six leather-bound volumes and, of course, her Bible. Amazing how the secretary could make something as sterile as an office desk appear homey and comforting. It was clear that the secretary was a neat freak. She'd once confided that, unable to stand the disarray of the principal's desk and office, she regularly neatened it up for Ms. Storme, neither expecting nor receiving recognition for the task.

"Morning, Clementine." Rose sailed past the secretary and into the teacher's mailroom to check her box. The usual stuff of a teacher's day cluttered the small cubicle. Attendance forms, memos and reminders about PTA meetings, student interim grades, and a Faculty Advisory meeting after school tomorrow. As she turned to head to the English workroom down the hall, she heard a beep on her phone. Who would be calling before 7 a.m.? Placing her mail and book bag on the mailroom table, Rose fished her cell phone out of her purse. "Hello?"

"Rose! It's Lyn Leeson here. Sorry to call so early. I just wanted to warn you about something. My husband is on his way to Harding. To talk to Wendy Storme." Lyn's voice shook. "Our daughter is in the hospital. Diagnosed with meningitis. She's very sick but doctors say she'll recover with round-the-clock medical care."

"I'm so sorry, Lyn. But it sounds like she's in good hands."

"Thanks, Rose. Actually, right now I'm more worried about my husband. Our daughter's diagnosis was the proverbial straw. Broke the camel's back. What with my health insurance running out and all. He barreled off to school to demand Wendy Storme give me back my job and be quick about it. Rob is a low-key guy most of the time, but Storme's withholding my position has agitated him to a frenzy. I don't believe I've ever seen him so angry. He's ready to kill her."

Rose gulped. "What do you want me to do, Lyn?"

"If you can, stop him before he gets to her office. Try to talk sense to him, get him to calm down. He'll respect you. I know he will. He was so thankful for the way you and the other teachers helped us out when I was laid up after my accident."

"I'll see what I can do," Rose answered. "Call you back."

Rose did not relish the task her colleague had dropped on her; confrontation was always her last resort at problem-solving. She quickly gathered her things and headed back into the main office. Oh dear. Was she too late? She could see the back of a man waving his arms wildly at Clementine and shouting, "No! I don't have an appointment! I demand to speak with the principal right this minute!"

Despite the secretary's insistence, the man jerked past her and strode down the hall, flinging open the door to Wendy Storme's office before Rose could reach him. Rose recognized him; it was Rob Leeson all right. He'd plowed ahead like a bulldozer. There was no stopping him. With a backward wave to Clementine, Rose hurried after him, fists held tightly at her sides.

"What? How dare you?" Wendy sputtered, spitting coffee as she spoke, stepping away from the coffee bar. "You can't just barge into my office like this. Who are you anyway? I'm calling security. I expect my secretary has already done so." Her eyes darted to Rose. "And what are *you* doing here, Ms. Lane?"

"This is Rob Leeson, Ms. Storme. Lyn Leeson's husband…"

Holding out a hand for Rose to stop, Rob interrupted. "I'm here to demand you reinstate my wife immediately. You have no legal grounds for denying her return after a county-approved leave of absence and you know it."

"Rob. Please. Sit down and talk calmly to Ms. Storme about this. I'm sure she's willing to hear you out."

Rose had no such conviction about Wendy Storme, but she was desperate to prevent any further conflict as Lyn had asked her to.

"It is already settled." Wendy's tone was icy. "Legally. Mr. Farcus' county experience supersedes your wife's."

"The hell you say! That's complete bullshit, which you invented." Rob Leeson advanced toward Wendy, arm raised.

The door crashed open and a uniformed security guard dashed in, grasping Rob's upraised arm and pulling it behind him along with his other arm. He clamped on handcuffs. "Let's go," the guard rasped. He looked at Wendy and then Rose. "You two okay?"

Numbly, Rose nodded. "Get him out of here,"

Wendy snarled. She held her Boss cup tightly in her hand.

Shaking, Rose forced her jelly-legs to propel her to Clementine's desk. "Whew!"

Clementine scooted back her chair and came around her desk. "Sit down, Rose. Let me get you a glass of water. You're pale as paper."

"Oh, I'll be all right. I find confrontations upsetting." She blinked. "You called security, I take it."

Clementine returned to her seat. "Sure I did. Can't have folks bargin' in like that. An angry parent, I assume. We see a lot of them, I'm afraid."

"I suppose you did the right thing. Who knows what the guy might have done. But Mr. Leeson is not an angry parent. Not a parent at all. He's Lyn Leeson's husband. You know, the ninth grade teacher who was on medical leave because of an auto accident."

"I heard about that," the secretary said.

"Ms. Storme's decision to keep the long-term sub in Lyn's place is causing terribly harsh consequences for the Leeson family." Rose gave the secretary a shrewd look. "I don't suppose you have any pull with the principal? Try to get her to see the right thing…the Christian thing to do, maybe. Reinstate Lyn as a full-time teacher."

"I'm afraid that would be beyond my reach. I do know my place, Rose." Clementine fumbled in her desk drawer and drew out a tract. *What to do When Bad Things Happen to Good People* was the title. She handed it to Rose.

"Maybe you should give Ms. Storme a tract. Do you have one entitled *Do Unto Others*?"

This morning's events had solidified Rose's

resolve. She would take a step in her evolving scheme to banish Wendy Storme from Harding High for good. Step number one: Contact. Ashante Mabana at her first opportunity today. *Justice for All.* It had exactly the right ring.

* * * *

Wendy Storme was late to the FAC meeting. No surprises there. In fact, it worked to Rose's advantage. She stood at the podium asking for the group's attention. Chatter was at a high decibel with talk of the latest dirty deal and the exiting of Ashante Mabana. It took a few moments to quiet the committee members.

Clearing her throat, Rose began by asking a question. "How many of you are aware of the Superintendent's Advisory Committee?"

A number of hands shot up, several heads nodded and the rest looked at her with blank faces.

"Those of us who have been members of the FAC for a few years know that once every spring the Superintendent meets with a committee made up of one volunteer from each county Faculty Advisory Council, that's one representative from every school in the county. Did one of you attend last year?"

"I did," Brad McIver piped up.

"Brad, can you tell the folks here about the event? Was it helpful?"

Brad stood and joined Rose at the front of the room. "First, I have to say, I didn't actually *volunteer* to represent Harding. I was kind of…pushed into it." He nudged Rose with his elbow. "By Rose Lane, here."

The group tittered.

"I prefer to avoid colluding with the Dark Side and stay as far away from upper management as possible,"

Brad continued.

More laughter.

"I volunteered you because I knew you'd bring us an unbiased, unvarnished accounting," Rose nudged him back.

"Unvarnished? It was mostly bullshit. The proverbial rubber stamp, to prove they care about the little peons who support their upside down pyramid style of management. With us as the broad "base" at the top and the Superintendent at the tiny point at the bottom." Brad held his fingers in the shape to show his meaning. "I believe management is supposed to work in the opposite way. Management is supposed to support us, the teachers, not the other way around."

"However, as I recall, Brad did bring back some information pertinent to all of us. Changes in teacher evaluations and tenure. Contract concerns, salary schedules and the school calendar for the next school year." Rose ticked them off on her fingers.

"All of which could easily have been covered by an email, I might add." Brad grasped the podium with two hands and leaned on it, speaking with emphasis on each word: "A waste of my time."

Rose cocked her head. "Brad, you are not helping my case here. We need a volunteer for the Superintendent's Advisory Committee meeting, which is coming up soon. Yes, it's after school hours and on your own unpaid time. Despite some negativity on Brad's part, I feel we must be represented. And this year I think we'd all agree: It's crucial." Rose gave him the stink eye.

"Turn-about is fair play," Brad pounded a fist on the podium, looking triumphant. "I volunteer Rose

Lane to attend this spring's Superintendent's Advisory Committee. Bringing us her own unbiased and unvarnished observations." He looked at the FAC members. "What say you?"

A cheer rose from the group. Chants of, "Go, Rose, Go Rose!" broke out. The reps were punchy.

Brad slung a long arm around Rose. "It's unanimous. Have fun!" As he moved back to his seat, he made a secret gesture to Rose, unseen by the audience. It was the thumb and finger OK sign, silently signaling, "We pulled it off."

Rose and Brad returned to their seats as Wendy Storme churned into the room. Offering no apology, she blurted, "All right. Who's first with a complaint? Which department?" For some reason, she looked directly at Rose.

Chapter Nineteen

Brad was in rare form; his morose and negative moods had, over time, cleared like storm clouds after a hard rain. Today he was as sunny as Penny had ever seen him, humming as he went about getting ready for school, chattering about his role as senior advisor and, above all, savoring the excitement building around tonight's basketball game with a tough rival.

"I talked to Sunitra at our senior class meeting, Penny. She is so psyched for tonight's game. Literally quivering with energy. 'My nerves are like guitar strings wound so tight they shiver,' she says. 'You are a finely-tuned instrument,' I told her. 'Just relax and let it play.' "

"She said, 'You don't understand, Mr. McIver. Mom and I got a call. A coach from University of Tennessee is going to be at the game.' " Brad mimicked the girl's high-pitched voice. "'I have to be at my best. On my game. My whole college career could depend on it.'"

Penny leaned in for a kiss. "You're pretty wound up yourself."

He rubbed his palms together. "Well, I'm stoked for Sunitra. And there's nothing better than tense competition with a tough opponent. In the long run, tonight's game has the potential to prove Harding High's sports mettle, despite the setbacks caused by the current administration."

"I'm sure there's a whole crowd of teachers, parents, students and community backers who will be there tonight." Penny wrapped her arms around him. "All looking to get over the disappointments of the football season, eh?"

Brad snorted. "You're right, of course." In a lower tone, "Not that I will ever get over it myself."

Penny was sorry she had rubbed against the old scab. She sought to change the subject. "So, where do you want to meet for dinner? With Rose and Cliff, you know. Our usual double date."

"There's going to be a huge crowd tonight. Fire marshals to control the size, I imagine. They could actually turn away folks if the gym reaches capacity." Brad gave her a sly look. "For a girls' game, no less."

Penny flattened her lips. "You think the world is finally changing? Has Title IX achieved that leveling of the field for athletes regardless of gender?"

"There's been plenty of progress. Athletes like Sunitra are the catalyst for change. With her height and ball skills she can execute an inside-outside game."

"Meaning?"

"Look, the girl can play guard or forward." He paused. "But the other team is loaded with talent, too. The sports section of the newspaper calls tonight's game a tossup. Sunitra always rises to the challenge; she'll be a contender, for sure." Brad nodded vigorously. "And I want a good seat. Hey, how about we get to the game early, go out to eat afterward? I myself will be too revved up to have any appetite beforehand anyway."

"Fine. I'll let Rose know. She can text Cliff."

Penny gave Brad a sidelong look. "Have you noticed the vibe between those two? They seem to mirror and complement each other perfectly. I wonder....?"

Brad danced her around the room. "Oh, you ladies! I love you, Penny, but who can consider romance at a time like this? There's a game tonight! That's all I can focus on."

You and Sunitra was Penny's thought. With a lurch, she realized something else. Brad had said, "I love you, Penny." Welcome words she had never before heard him utter.

****

Penny watched the crowd collect in the bleachers around them, filling rapidly as Brad had figured. Managing to save enough room for Rose and Cliff, she and Brad relished their position at center court just up from the scorer's table where parents and the most rabid fans liked to collect. Sunitra's mother perched one row in front of them, new pompoms at the ready. The atmosphere was electric with guy wires of energy zapping from tier to tier. The opponent side of the gym maintained its own momentum, quickly closing the blank spaces until the rows of bleachers were packed solid. The fire marshals were, indeed, perusing the premises, ready to close the doors on further fans.

Rose and Cliff arrived just in time. "Whew! Trouble finding a parking space." Cliff slid into his sliver of space and pulled Rose down beside him. "Looks like we made it just in time." Their eyes traveled to the uniformed marshals closing the doors and standing guard.

Informing them that college scouts often wear their school colors when observing high school games, Brad looked around. "The place is packed. I don't know if I'll be able to spot the Tennessee rep." He craned his neck. "Oh, wait! Look!" He pointed to a tall woman dressed in dazzling, soda-pop orange. "Bet that's her in her Tennessee colors." The woman's neon-bright sweat shirt stood out even in the mass of bodies around her. And when she turned, they could see that UT blazed from the front.

It was obvious to Penny that Sunitra's mother had also located the scout. Did she lift her pompoms in a little salute? Hard to tell. As the girls from each team streamed into the gym from the locker room, both stands exploded with cheers, yells and stomping feet. The Harding team circled the gym once, as was their custom then began some practice dribbles, passes and shots as the opposing team took charge of the other half of the court doing the same.

Something was not right. Soon, every Harding fan noticed that their star player, Sunitra Benson, was not on the court with the rest of the team. She sat on the bench talking to the coach. Mrs. Benson had stepped over the seats and joined them, leaving her pompoms in her place. What was going on? It was impossible to hear the three-way conversation, but the body language and facial expressions told a frightening tale. As the teams filed back to their respective benches and readied themselves for the start of the game, a rumble of disbelief rose from the Harding bench. Looking shocked themselves, the starting five gathered in a circle, bent over their stacked hands, and, standing, gave a weak collective cheer. The game was on. Sunitra Benson remained on the bench.

At first, the crowd was numbly silent. Mumbles

and grumbles of, "What's going on? Why isn't Sunitra starting? Where's our top player?" gathered momentum and rolled into a roar. The Harding girls were doing their best to keep up their spirit, but in rapid fire, the opposing team shot, rebounded and shot twice more for six points to Harding's zero. The coach worked hard to motivate the team, yelling encouragement and calling for critical time-outs. But by the end of the first quarter Harding was woefully behind. Sunitra slumped on the bench, her eyes on the floor.

The crowd remained incensed but cautious. Collectively they recognized the necessity of cheering for the girls on the court while at the same time opposing the decision to bench Sunitra Benson. "What could have happened?" Penny looked to her companions for answers.

With a stab of comprehension, Rose knew. "Remember when Wendy Storme called Sunitra out of my class? That little peccadillo about her article in the student newspaper? That's what this is about. I can't believe it, but that has to be what's happened. Storme has forced the coach to bench Sunitra. For punishment."

Brad's nostrils flared; his breathing audible. "Typical Storme. Could not care less about sports or how important this game is to the student. To the school. All to prove that she, Principal Storme, is in control and calls the shots." Abruptly he stood. "I've got to get out of here. Before I completely lose my cool." He shot a sympathetic glance at the bench, not only for Sunitra but also for the coach, whose hands Wendy had tied, he was quite sure. One look at Mrs. Benson painted a portrait in disbelief. Fury. Frustration. She clutched her tufts of crepe paper as if her life depended on them.

By halftime, the crowd had begun to thin out, word having traveled that Sunitra would be sidelined for the entire game. Principal's orders. Harding was down by fourteen points. Without their top player, there was little chance they could regain lost ground. The other Harding players wore signs of loss in their tight jaws. With shoulders slumped and her face deflated, Mrs. Benson looked toward the Tennessee scout. Defeat snatched from the jaws of victory.

"Oh my God, Rose. This is awful. I still can't believe it." Penny inclined her head toward the orange-clad scout. "Looks like she's leaving, too, not even waiting for the game to end. Poor Sunitra. It's just tragic."

Brad rejoined them, holding his hands to his head as if sheltering from a rock slide. "I milled around the hall outside, listening. The crowd? They're disgusted, mad, pissed. Everyone's cussing Wendy Storme, wondering about Sunitra, even blaming the coach." He gestured around the perimeter of the gym. "No surprise, Principal Storme chose to stay away tonight. I daresay the hometown folks might have booed her out of the building if she'd showed her face."

"Coward," Rose muttered. "Bloody, stinking coward."

Cliff had been listening. "Evaluation and observation are crucial in deciding whether to offer a scholarship to a prospective college player. That's universal. I hate to say it, but it looks as if your star has lost her chance with the University of Tennessee. Coaches and scouts are scheduled out. Even assuming the principal allows the girl to play after tonight, there's not much hope the scout would return for another look."

Brad suddenly brightened. "This cinches it. I've been kind of resisting the kids' wishes for the senior prank." He zeroed in on Penny. "You may not know this, but every year the seniors plan a little mischievous trick aimed at making fun of teachers, administrators, the school itself. It's harmless and expected."

"Sarcastic bulletin boards, for example," Rose put in. "One year the seniors filched all the wooden hall passes from each room and lined them up on the roof so that they were visible from the parking lot, proving they could get in, confiscate them and wrestle them up to the top. A stupendous senior practical joke!"

"It's been a real struggle with the prank this year." Brad curled his lip. "The kids so dislike Wendy Storme, they have plotted murder a dozen different ways and only half in jest, I fear." He sniffed. "I've insisted we stop short of that, unfortunately. Tonight…what Storme's done…it's led me to a decision."

Penny flinched. "Not murder, I hope."

Brad flashed a cagey smile. "If not murder, just short of it."

****

Talk bounced wall-to-wall around Harding High. Students, teachers, coaches, secretaries, and custodians and most of the administrators were aghast at Wendy Storme's treatment of an honor-student athlete over a ridiculously small faux pas, which offended Wendy alone. Penny filled her Bambi cup with coffee, carrying it to Rose's carrel. Loud talk from around the coffee pot reached them across the room.

"She's outdone herself this time," Rose said. "I feel

for Sunitra and her mother, as well as the scout from the University of Tennessee. Just one ugly scenario for everyone."

"Don't forget the home team fans." Penny waved her hand over her cup to cool it down. "If Brad's observations were correct, they were in a mutinous mood at the game last night."

Rose lowered her voice. "Believe it or not, it's all playing into our hands. I have a gut feeling we're going to come out on top. Every one of us who've been uprooted and thrown to the wind by Wendy Storme's wrath."

Penny tapped her cup. "You've been hinting at a plan. Are you gonna stop all the cloak and dagger and tell me what you've cooked up? Or not?"

Rose sipped her coffee, eyes catching Penny over the rim of her cow mug. "A few more details to cover, dear girl. Only one or two elements need to fall into place. Crucial elements, I might add. But I have every hope for success."

Just then Burt Boyd hove into view. "Morning, ladies. I see the whole school is abuzz with news about the game. Evidently everybody's heard about Sunitra's article in the paper. Wendy's deplorable action." He gestured toward the hall outside the workroom. "It's a virtual keg of firecrackers just waiting for a torch."

"You seem awfully cheerful about it, Burt." Rose set down her drink and fumbled through a stack of folders. "Damn. I can't seem to locate those timed writings I graded. Where are they?" She pushed a pile of papers aside. "They were routinely awful, so awful I was tempted to throw them away."

"How can I restrain my cheer when I've had the

extraordinary experience of attending my third 'best teacher' gig at the home of our awesome principal?"

Penny laughed. "You're the master of sarcasm, Burt."

"Actually, I have some rather pertinent information to relay." He glanced in the direction of the crowd at the coffee pot still talking loud enough for cover. "You want it now, or later, Rose?"

Rose pounced on the folder of graded papers. "Here it is!" She surveyed the rubble atop the desk. "I really must organize this junk. I've already infected two other carrels with my worldly possessions, but I obviously need space in another one." She looked at Burt. "I'm sure these little parties of Storme's eat into your personal time for your band-playing. I just want you to know how much I appreciate your willingness..."

"Say no more! It's the least I can do for the 'Cause.' Let's face it, I am the only one Wendy will ever invite from the English Department, which she considers to be a hotbed of resistance. She thinks she's got me in the palm of her hand. I admit I'm rather enjoying the role of double agent! She's picking my brain for info and I'm funneling her strategic moves right back to the English Department!"

"Well, then, let's hear it." Rose folded her arms atop the littered desk. "What gives?"

Burt pulled up a chair between Penny and Rose and lowered his voice. "It seems Wendy is using her little get-togethers to line up plum appointments for next year. You know, the protected positions not threatened by transfers or pink slips if enrollment declines or something."

Penny cast a puzzled look at Rose.

"That would be sponsors for year book and literary magazine, newspaper, debate—you understand. Teachers who assume leadership for those extra-curricular activities are in a protected position, highly desirable, especially for young, new teachers who are usually the last hired and first fired." Rose pointed a finger at her intern. "Like you, Penny."

"Yeah, well, Storme's making promises left and right to these wide-eyed innocents she lures in with her 'best teacher' label." Burt snorted. "In exchange for anything their virgin ears pick up in the teacher workrooms. Storme is so egotistical and paranoid, I might add, that she's gotta know what people are saying about her." He leaned closer to the two women. "I doubt the 'best teachers' know what a liar Wendy Storme is. She'd think nothing of reneging on a promised protected position for any one of them."

"I can't say I'm surprised. She might be lying to the latest hires, but, then again, she's unlikely to give a second thought to demoting a current sponsor to be replaced by a newbie if it suited her purpose," Rose said. "Protected position, or not."

"Like the current newspaper sponsor, you mean? The one who let Sunitra get away with that terrible diatribe against our principal?" Burt managed to keep a poker face at his own exaggeration. "Oh yeah. She's gone with the wind, sure to be on Storme's chopping block."

Penny shook her head. "Why is Ms. Storme so...so controlling? Surely most principals are decent, caring, more in touch with the student vibe."

Rose worked her glasses to the top of her head.

"I've studied the situation, Penny. And I think I've come up with an explanation. You know, in my many years of teaching, I've worked with some excellent principals, some good. Some so-so. I have to say Wendy Storme is my one and only truly evil, incompetent, and, yes, insecure principal. Here's the rationale: Strong principals have achieved the apex of their careers; what they want most is to do a good job, keep the talented teachers on board and satisfy students and parents with a smooth-running ship. A positive climate for all makes their job easier and more rewarding. They take pride in their schools. That said, what does Wendy want?"

"To move on up the career ladder. Rose, you've hit the nail on the head. Wendy sees us teachers as rungs on her ladder." Burt blinked rapidly. "She hates us, you know. We're good for only one thing: her climbing apparatus. The students? So unimportant as to be insignificant, irritating little ants crawling from one short hill to another. Easy enough to step on and crush."

The three sat in silence for a moment. At length Rose spoke. "Thanks, Burt. This helps fill in the psychological profile. Was there anything else you picked up at the Storme abode?"

"What about Dean Storme? At the last party he was trying to make time with the pretty young chicks," Penny put in.

Burt rubbed his hands together eagerly. "Oh. Now for the *real* dirt. To answer your question, Penny, no the Dean was not present. But the Assistant Superintendent, Esther Nelson, was. While everybody had gathered outside on the patio, I noticed Wendy and Dr. Nelson were missing. Relishing my role as an espionage agent, I surreptitiously made my way into the house and peeked into the kitchen, taking pains to keep out of their sight in the butler's pantry. The two women stood close together, facing each other, talking in low tones. I had to strain to hear what they were saying to each other. Then, Wendy lifted a hand and stroked Esther's cheek." Burt imitated. "A very tender gesture."

Penny drew back in shock. "What? No!"

"Most emphatically, *yes!*" Burt's features went tight with seriousness. "And Wendy says, 'Oh, Esther. What terrible news. Is Sparky serious? You think it's a problem for us?' "

"What does it mean?" Penny made a wipe-that-out gesture with her hands. "I know, I know. There's some kind of relationship between Wendy and Dr. Nelson. But what she said about Sparky, Superintendent Sparkman...."

A light flickered in Rose's eyes. "OMG! It's perfect!" She threw her arms around Burt's neck and hugged him. "Exactly the intel I need. Oh, oh, oh! We're on the way, dear friends. We are going to nail this. Nail *her*." She blew a kiss at Burt. "You're the best damn spy since James Bond."

****

Wendy Storme was not amused. Not that Brad expected her to have a sense of humor. If she had been President of the United States, Wendy would be the type to skip the correspondents' roast. She was way too thin-skinned to be able to laugh at herself. Nothing worse than an insecure egomaniac. That was what made it all so delicious, Brad told Penny.

"She turned purple! Kid you not. Spotters stationed all over the faculty parking lot agree. There she was, sitting in her big, fancy SUV ready to pull into the principal's privileged parking space right in front of the school entrance and she couldn't move forward. Not an inch into the slot."

Penny handed over the moo shoo pork and watched Brad help himself from the small white container. "Want a pancake? How about some plum sauce to go with that?"

Brad shook his head and grasped his chopsticks. "So, she climbs out of the car and stands there looking at the parking space and she's rigid as a fireplace poker. At least, that's the way one of the students described it." He lifted a bite of pork and noodles in his chopsticks.

"God! Will you get to the point? I'm dying to know. Just what was this senior prank all about, anyway?" She grabbed the container of fried rice and pulled it to her. "You get no more food until you describe every step, every detail. What did they do to the principal's parking space, anyway?"

Brad threw back his head and howled. "They buried her there. That's what!" He guffawed for some minutes, finally wiping at tears of laughter with his napkin. "Neatly outlined burial plot, artificial grass spread over a mound of dirt, mind you. A realistic tombstone made of cardboard engraved with *Here Lies Principal Storme, RIP. Now Harding High Can RIP, too*. They left a shovel and some work gloves, ostensibly belonging to the grave-diggers."

"You know, I saw people standing around the principal's parking space this morning. But I didn't pick up on it. And I was so busy at school all day I didn't hear the talk that must have gone on, among the seniors at least." Penny spooned fried rice from the container to her plate.

"Oh, Storme rounded up some seniors, demanded they dismantle the 'gravesite' immediately. Each one denying any knowledge of the prank, needless to say." He tipped back the kitchen chair, a satisfied look on his face. "What she doesn't know is the class plans to bury her every night, with a different tombstone elegy. I've heard some of them and they are hilarious. *She died on a broken broomstick* was one suggestion I heard. *Trampled by Harding Sports Fans* was another."

Penny slid the fried rice container across the table. "Thus satisfying the desire of most of the senior class, I imagine." She darted a piercing look at her companion. "Not to mention their advisor, Brad McIver. Right?"

"Those little 'secret meetings' I attended before school? The kids and I were planning the senior prank. And, you know, I actually thought burying the witch was maybe a step over the line...until Storme destroyed Sunitra's hopes out of pure spite."

Brad dumped the remainder of the fried rice onto his plate. "Now I can talk to my Dad in heaven and say, 'See. I got her back, Dad. Just like you advised on your deathbed.' "

Beats the heck out of the real thing, Penny thought.

Chapter Twenty

Rose made sure nobody was sitting in the adjoining booth before she slid into the last seat at the coffee shop, the best place for conversations not to be overheard by patrons of the establishment. She had chosen a time when few customers would be in Ground to Please. One by one, the others joined her. First, Carter Thompson, original principal, then Gwen Rogers, his secretary who left Harding because of Wendy Storme's insufferable treatment of her. Last to join them was Garrett Barnes, the assistant principal who absconded in the middle of the night. The one calling Principal Storme "bat-shit crazy."

"Thank you, my friends, for agreeing to meet me." Rose picked up the menu. "Let's order. Then we can talk, if that's okay with everybody."

They made short work of it, each simply ordering the brew of the day. As the steaming cups arrived, the four wound up their small talk of family and travels and current events. With the waiter's exit, Rose began. "Perhaps you have already guessed why I asked you to join me."

Carter Thompson tilted his head. "Soon as I saw whom you invited…well, I may have guessed your purpose, Rose."

"Wendy Storme," was Garrett's succinct response. "You've had it with the witch. It was only a matter of time."

Gwen Rogers nodded. "You must be wondering, why is Ms. Storme still at the helm of Harding High? You and the rest of the staff. The community. How is she getting away with her bizarre, her damaging behavior? Where's the Superintendent? Is he deaf? Dumb? Blind?"

Rose's jaw dropped. Gwen had always been the soul of diplomacy, careful to a fault with her choice of words and scrupulously circumspect about school business. Her blunt appraisal was a complete departure. "You've nailed it, Gwen." Rose blew on her coffee. "Knowing there's community concern, I wasn't sure just how much of Storme's antics had leaked out of the high school walls." She allowed her eye contact to dwell momentarily on the two men. "We're so enmeshed in the daily quagmire that we lose all objectivity. I'm afraid."

"I've made it my duty to stay informed," Carter said. "I consider Harding High to be my legacy since I opened the school and hand-picked the entire staff." He glanced briefly at each of them around the table. "Furthermore, if they're talking about the Carter S. Thompson Stadium, I'd like that to be an *honorable* legacy."

"Besides," Garrett said. "Wendy Storme is mentally unhinged. We all know that. She damn well ruined my own career goal—to rise from assistant principal to principal. That's not something a guy forgives and forgets, you know. And, really...where's Sparky's backbone, not to mention his testicles? He should be on Wendy Storme like a sweat."

Gwen straightened. "I'm going to get down and

dirty, folks. Perhaps you were aware that Carter lured me away from Milton Sparkman's office when he was staffing Harding High." She glanced at the former principal. "I had a high-grade position in the Super's office, but Carter's vision for the new school was infectious. I wanted to be a part of it. So, I came onboard with him and I loved my job." She carefully sipped her coffee. "Being a secretary under Principal Storme was intolerable. A nightmare. Her disdain for me, my position, the teachers, and students was constant and destructive. Never a let up from one day to the next. From one hour to the next." Her eyes flickered in Garrett's direction. "I imagine you felt that, too, having to work closely under her, Garrett."

"I feel your pain," he grimaced. "Storme is the reason you left Harding. The reason why I left. I'm sure all the others who bailed out fled for the same reason. How can professionals operate under a leader who is mentally unstable?"

"Some months after I quit on Storme, Dr. Sparkman called me and begged me to come back to the central office. Though I now serve as secretary for the entire office, the Superintendent made me his personal administrative assistant and I've been there ever since." Gwen lowered her voice. "Whatever we share here today, trust me. I will not carry any tales back to Sparky." She drummed her fingers on the table. "In fact, you might say it's for the direct opposite reason I accepted your invitation to come today, Rose. Not to garner information from you, but to dish out some."

Rose drew in her chin. "Okay. Let's have it, Gwen."

"When I originally worked for Sparkman, before Carter recruited me for Harding High, I knew the county schools were in good hands. Each cog of the wheel progressed smoothly, cranking out the policies and platforms necessary to support schools, their programs and personnel and, of course, ultimately the students, families and community." Gwen paused. "But when I went back, five years later, it was like somebody had thrown rocks into the machinery, clogging up the works of the central office. I honestly do not know when it happened, but the tension was palpable. Maybe I was more aware of trouble because I was 'fresh.' The others in the office had gradually gotten used to the climate change." Gwen grinned sheepishly. "Sorry. I know you're sensitive to weather analogies, Rose."

Carter wrinkled his forehead. "I got a sense of that myself. Each time I approached the Superintendent about Wendy Storme, I had the feeling he was walking around land mines, tiptoeing around delicate details. He had so many excuses for letting Storme off the hook. 'Give her a chance, she's new at this.' Or, 'She's basically good at heart, and she's smart—a quick study. You'll see.' " Carter sniffed. "What he was really saying was, 'Get off my back. I have no intention of doing what you and I both know should be done: firing her.' " Carter looked at Gwen. "What's your take on the situation, close as you are to it on a daily basis. I know from experience the secretary sees, hears and knows all that goes on in an office."

Gwen's lips were a straight line. "Sex." She stared at each of them. "It's all about sex." Her eyes lowered to the table. "You know, I'm no prude. I've been married, divorced, and remarried. I have at least one illegitimate niece," she exhaled. "That I know of."

"We won't judge you, Gwen," Rose promised. She reached across the table and took the secretary's hand. "Please tell us what you know. What makes you so uncomfortable."

"Things are spiraling out of hand. You know, I said the guts of the machinery have been compromised? Well, now the wheels are falling off." Gwen's lips turned down. "I...I just feel I have to say something to somebody...I can't keep silent any longer." She blinked rapidly. "I know how concerned you three are; I'm going to let you in on a couple of details."

They waited in silence as Gwen collected her words. "Dr. Sparkman's been having an affair with a woman he's keeping on the side. Evidently, Mrs. Sparkman is unaware, but her questions to me say there's some suspicion on her part. For example, 'Where is Sparky? I can't get him on his cell and he's not answering my texts.' Stuff like that." Gwen gulped. "I was uneasy keeping it under my hat, until...until Dr. Sparkman asked me to lie for him. When he was meeting the other woman, I mean. I knew then we were going on a downhill slide. By 'we' I mean anyone in the office who had a whiff of the scandal. We were all being sucked into a den of iniquity."

Garrett's eyes were bright. "Interesting. Now it makes sense. Did Wendy know about the Super's affair so he's afraid to fire her lest she tell on him?" He gulped. "I thought Sparkman was a straight arrow. Isn't he a church deacon, or something?"

Gwen nodded. "We who know are shocked. It's completely out of character, or so we thought. The latest? There's some kind of audit going on with the budget for the Superintendent's office. It may not be related to his mistress, but it doesn't look good." She twisted in her seat as if it were uncomfortable. "I've never seen Sparkman so agitated. It's like the man doesn't know which way to turn."

Rose had been closely following Gwen's revelations. The secretary's comments about the county financial audit linked up with Max's bank allegations, but she had promised to keep quiet about that. Her thoughts leaped ahead. "This leads to Wendy Storme...how? Or does it? Is Wendy involved in some way? As Garrett suggested, did Storme know about Sparkman's dalliance?"

"Well, Wendy knows about the affair, about Sparkman's infidelity. Has known, possibly, from the beginning." She flashed a glance at Garrett. "You were right in your assumption about that, Garrett."

Rose pondered how to phrase her next comments. "Gwen, there's some hard evidence that Wendy and the Assistant Superintendent, Dr. Nelson, are lovers. That has to contribute to the unsavory culture you refer to in the Super's office."

"Oh. I- I did n-not realize their affair was common knowledge," Gwen stammered. "It's certainly not anything I'd ever spread around myself."

Both Carter and Garrett flinched. "Holy shit," Garrett breathed.

Carter steepled his fingers. "This explains a lot." He paused in thought. "If Sparkman knows that Storme and Nelson are lovers, it might be hard for him to put a stop to the relationship since they also have the dirt on him." He turned to Gwen. "Spiraling out of hand sounds like a gross understatement."

"But still leaves us nowhere," Garrett blurted. "Sounds like they're all covering for each other without a care about the consequences to Harding High."

Rose moved her gaze from one to the next. "I'm sure we agree we have to keep this meeting and everything we've learned, secret." She locked eyes with Gwen. "We can all thank you, dear friend. For your courage. Yes, courage." Rose thumped the table. "You care enough about the school to put your job and your reputation on the line."

"I still don't see...." Garrett began.

Rose interrupted. "I have a plan. With what I now know, I am more confident than ever that it will work. We are going to save Harding High. From an F-5 tornado."

"Will you need help for this plan of yours?" Gwen asked.

Rose chewed her lip. "It may 'take a village,' as the saying goes. However, I don't think any of you will be in danger." She hesitated. "Gwen, I might need your assistance. I'll get back to you." She looked at the two men. "I assume I have your moral support. That's important."

"It all sounds very mysterious," Garrett mused.

"We educators often move in mysterious ways," Rose said. She gave no voice to her real assessment: It may not be dangerous for you three, but it could mean the end of my teaching career.

****

"I'm here for a long weekend," Margo explained. "The professor for my one Monday class is giving us a bye—something about personal leave for him. Since I had no real plans or obligations, I decided to catch a

213

ride with some kids heading my way. Hope it's okay with you, Mom."

Rose pulled her daughter close and held her for a long moment. "You know I love it when you surprise me with a visit. Of course it's okay. It's wonderful." She hugged her again. "Three whole days? Here with me? You're not planning to meet with your father, or anything?" Rose tried to maintain a level expression. Though she would never admit it to Margo, she resented sharing these little oases of daughter-time with Max.

Margo eyed her mother from under downcast lashes. "Dad's...uh...he says he's busy this weekend."

"Code for spending time with a lady friend?" Rose swallowed her surprise.

"That's the way I interpreted it. Dad gave me a lift from the carpool drop-off. Didn't hint he wanted to come in like he usually does."

Rose breathed a sigh of relief. "I'd like for your dad to find others to fill his life. I know he feels a void since our breakup. And, truly, deep down Max is a good guy. I believe him when he says he's genuinely sorry about cheating on me."

"On that note, will you and Cliff be hooking up this weekend? Do I need to make myself scarce?"

"Don't be ridiculous, dear. Actually, Cliff is out of town until Sunday, at an education conference. But even if we were booked solid for the weekend, you would always be welcome to come home and feel at home. You know that."

Margo reached for the afghan on the couch and straightened it. "I took a little nap while I waited for you to get home. I texted Clementine about meeting us for a jog. A quickie before she leaves to visit with her grandfather. You game?"

"Well, I'm actually exhausted and a bit envious of that nap you enjoyed. I could snuggle right into that afghan and be out like a light."

"Mom, you know what all the health magazines say. When you're tired, the best antidote is exercise. A brisk walk will get your juices going. We'll meet Clementine, jog around the block a few times, and come back refreshed, ready to dive into dinner plans. Maybe a movie."

"All right, all right. You've talked me into it. Let me change into my running shoes." Rose looked Margo up and down. "Is that what you're wearing? Think it's warm enough for shorts, eh?"

"I'll get the water bottles. You'll see. We'll both be sweating by the time we finish."

Mother and daughter chattered companionably as they exited the house and moved down the steps and out onto the sidewalk. "We're meeting Clementine in the usual place. At the four-way stop sign." Margo sped up. "She's such a hoot! I love listening to her slur over her vowels."

Rose arrived at the designated meeting place a bit behind Margo, but there was no sign of Clementine.

Margo executed some stretches. "This is odd. Clementine said she needed to get our run in right away so she could be off on her trip down South. She wanted to try to arrive there before dark. Evidently her G-Pop's condition is deteriorating."

Rose peered up and down the street. "No sign of her. Do you think she's all right? Maybe something's happened."

"Why don't we jog on over to her house. We can check on her. Maybe she got tied up trying to leave or something." Margo took off at a trot.

"Hey! Will you wait for your old mother, please? I can't keep up with you." Rose panted with exaggeration. "Besides, I don't know the address. You'll have to lead me there."

Margo gestured for her mother to get a move on. "Just remember, Mom. We're doing this for the aerobic exercise. We gotta put some speed into it if we're gonna benefit at all."

Rose picked up the pace, but still lagged behind her daughter. At length, Margo came to a halt. Rose put her head down and rested her hands on her knees. "Are we there yet?"

The two stood facing a one-story brick bungalow. "So, this is where our friend lives," Rose said.

"The entrance to Clem's apartment is around the back, on the basement level." Margo pointed. "She invited me in after one of our runs a while back. Follow me."

As they rounded the corner of the house, they noticed a silver rental car pulling into the driveway from the opposite direction. It stopped at Clementine's door and a second later Clementine ran out to meet it. She waved and called out, "You're early! I'm meetin' some friends for a quick run. Why don't you come in and wait. I won't be long." She looked briefly in Rose and Margo's direction, but the two had instinctively pulled back out of sight. As the man emerged from the car, she ran into his arms and they clung to one another like flood survivors clutching a log.

The man was quite handsome. A head taller than

Clementine, clean shaven and dressed in an expensive-looking suit that hung elegantly on his slim, muscular frame, he looked like an aristocrat in a vodka ad extolling some exotic sipping liquor.

Mother and daughter gawked, then swiveled their heads to face one another. "You said Clementine was driving to her grandfather's. Her ailing grandfather," Rose whispered.

Margo gave her head a shake as if it might clear the scene and rearrange it. "Obviously, the guy arrived before she expected him. Still, it doesn't explain anything, does it?"

"Do you suppose Clementine was *lying*? Who'd a thought." Rose continued to speak softly, not that either of the lovers would have noticed, so engrossed in one another were they.

"Shall we crash the party?" Margo suggested with a malicious little smile.

"Sure. It's not like we planned this any more than they did." Boldly, Rose stepped into sight, followed shortly by Margo.

At the sight of her neighbors, Clementine broke away, snapping like a rubber band. "Oh! Oh my!" she stuttered. "Where did you come from? Oh my goodness."

The man appeared less flustered. "It's all right. Why don't you introduce us, Clementine?"

Recovering her composure, Clementine straightened her jogging shirt. "Rose, Penny. This is Davis Dawson. My…my friend from down home. He travels with his work and sometimes, when he's in the area, he stops in to…" She trailed off, looking embarrassed.

Rose extended her hand. "Nice to meet you, Mr. Dawson. I'm Rose Lane. This is my daughter Margo." Clementine was clearly flustered. Something was definitely wrong with this picture.

Clementine turned to her visitor. "Go on in and wait for me, Davis. I'll be back in time…for us to take off. To see my G-Pop, you know. So nice of you to stop by and offer to drive."

For a flash-second Davis Dawson blinked his surprise, but he was quick to cover it with a smooth rejoinder. "Sure. No hurry. Lots more daylight now since we've switched to daylight savings time."

Rose knew it was a lie. One look told her Margo knew, too. What's more, Clementine knew they knew. This was going to be interesting. Would she break down and tell them the truth?

Margo decided to give her friend some space. "Hey, look, Clem. Mom and I will wait for you up front. Take your time." Mother and daughter retraced their steps around the house.

"Oh my God," Rose breathed. "We just witnessed a scene we were never supposed to see." She tapped her daughter on the shoulder. "Did you notice something rather interesting, Margo, about Davis Dawson?"

"You mean his wedding ring?"

Their eyes met.

Chapter Twenty-One

Awaiting the arrival of Ashante Mabana, Penny and Rose huddled in the library research room as the elder informed her intern about what she had learned from the coffee shop meeting. "Please don't tell Brad, or anyone else. As Gwen said, it will all come out eventually anyway. For now, we need to keep mum about this." Rose pulled her glasses from her nose to her head and gave Penny a stern look. "I probably shouldn't even be telling *you*." Her features relaxed. "It's just that I've become so accustomed to our shared interests, it seems natural."

"You've suspected all along there was some influence peddling, haven't you Rose? Between Wendy Storme and the Super's office."

"Um-hm. And when Burt informed us of the...liaison between Wendy and Assistant Superintendent Nelson, I thought I had the connection. Now? Appears it goes all the way to the top of the food chain."

Penny stood up and paced around the room. "So, let me see if I've got this straight. Wendy knows the Super is having an affair, info possibly funneled through her relationship with Esther Nelson, who shares the office. Storme uses her knowledge to pressure Superintendent Sparkman into giving her the Harding High principal position in exchange for not revealing he's cheating on his wife."

"Storme also knew if she screwed up Sparkman would be afraid to mete out consequences," Rose added. "Even when parents, teachers, community leaders protested her despicable actions." She frowned. "So, let's say Wendy Storme, Esther Nelson and Milton Sparkman all have the goods on each other. A completely corrupt dynamic."

Penny digested the information. "Well, whatever the details involved, you've been hinting that you have an idea—what I assume to be a plan of action. Are you going to dish the details?" Penny resumed her seat. "Now that you have reliable information about why Wendy's been allowed to continue her wicked ways?" She propped her elbows on the table, chin in hand. "Do you honestly think you can force the hand of the Superintendent of Education?"

"Pretty high stakes I'm dealing with, eh?" Rose thought for a moment. "Look at it this way, Penny. I may be asking for the axe myself if my plan backfires. On the other hand, I may be saving a life."

Penny's brows shot up. "And whose life would that be?"

"Why, Principal Wendy Storme's life. Look, if we don't do something about her soon, somebody else will." She held up her hands and silently ticked off all ten fingers. "Do you know how many people have voiced a desire to kill her?"

"You could be right, Rose. Jeez, even the senior class has already buried her." Penny smiled. "For now, go on to your parent conference. I'll wait here for Ashante. I'd love to have a little time to talk to her myself."

No sooner had Rose left than Ashante Mabana arrived, looking magnificent in a floor-length African-print robe with matching turban. Gold earrings swung almost to her shoulders. Penny did not know whether to embrace the woman or to bow down to her. "You look wonderful, Ashante. Purple is definitely your color. You are positively glowing!"

"Thank you. It is most likely residual, a reflection of the success of my grassroots group *Justice for All*. Our numbers are swelling and I am beaming."

"Have you stayed in touch with the ESL teachers here at Harding? I know they sorely miss you."

"Absolutely. In fact, they still look to me for advice, which I freely give." Ashante flashed a perfect set of bone-white teeth. "And, I am gratified to say, they are helping to add to the numbers of our group. My teachers deal every day with the families of immigrants, you know. Our group's purpose is to empower those who feel they have been left out of the social justice system."

"Have a seat. Rose should be here shortly." Penny gestured around the room. "Welcome to Rose's hiding place, known only to the librarians and a few special friends."

Ashante gracefully guided her tall frame onto the wooden chair. "My teacher friends tell me that Ms. Storme continues to stir up trouble wherever she touches down, as they put it."

Penny settled herself across from the stately woman. "Well, Rose has something up her sleeve—an idea to ground Wendy Storme for good, so to speak. I believe you and your grassroots community are part of it."

"Ah, yes." Another display of snowy teeth. "How happy I am to be of help."

Rose hurried into the room. "Ashante! It's so good to see you." The two enfolded each other in a prolonged hug. "I heard what Penny said, and I must add that you are not just a part of the plan, you are a *vital* part. Without your help...well, my idea is just another pipe dream."

"Let us get to it, then, Rose. What do you have in mind? If it is a way to bring down a corrupt ruler, I pledge to do whatever is necessary to help the cause. I will not tolerate injustice, oppression, or inhumanity in my world."

"I know. Your sincerity and self-sacrifice are commendable. Honorable. I hope you will think this idea is worthy of consideration."

"You, Rose, are the most admirable teacher I have ever met. I would never question the integrity of your thoughts or motives."

Penny observed the back and forth of the mutual admiration society operating before her eyes. Would she ever reach a point in her career to match these two superb educators?

"I have been selected to attend the Superintendent's Advisory Committee meeting as Harding High's representative. It will occur after school hours at the administrative building two weeks from today, at four o'clock. I plan to give Superintendent Sparkman and the rest of the reps of every school in the county, an ear-full about Wendy Storme. I realize this is short notice, but could you rally your forces within *Justice for All* to participate in a protest march there?"

Ashante's features lit up. "Absolutely! We are

always ready to march for a cause and if getting the Superintendent's attention about Wendy Storme isn't a cause, I'll...I'll eat my turban!" She pointed to her headdress with a laugh.

"I'm thinking, a rally, a march around the building holding protest signs and singing chants, if possible directly under the windows to the Superintendent's office." Rose locked gazes with Ashante. "What do you say? Is this doable?"

There was no hesitation. "I will gather our leaders together and we will begin work immediately, my friend. We will make our cause for justice known."

Penny worked to keep her jaws from gaping. Of all the schemes she thought Rose might be incubating, a protest march led by Ashante Mabana and her *Justice for All* cohorts had never crossed her mind. It was a bold plan. And, yes, it could backfire and blow them all to smithereens.

Ashante pushed back her chair and rose to her full height. "You may be surprised to know who has joined our band."

"I'm guessing here, but I'd hope Jose Mendoza is on board. He's possibly in danger of deportation as a result of Storme's cheating and lying."

"Ah, yes. Mr. Mendoza is a charter member. Also, Mikel Yamada, Christine's husband. He's actually acting as our lawyer, *pro bono*. Mrs. Benson, Sunitra's mother, both Lyn Leeson and her husband, among others. Dozens of community leaders and ordinary concerned citizens. All eager to see that justice is served regarding Principal Wendy Storme and her administrative decisions at Harding High."

Rose clapped her hands. "Way to go, Ashante! I'm

psyched!"

Raising her hand for a high-five with Rose and then Ashante, Penny cheered: "Here's to justice for Harding High!"

****

Penny was struck by the changes in Devin Giovani. It began with his eyes, a bitterness that narrowed his gaze, compressing his lids, and crinkling the corners, like crow's feet in an aging face. A jaded wariness weighed on his shoulders. Projecting his torso forward as if he anticipated something dangerous might leap out from behind a corner, he maintained a jerky nervousness acquired over the months at the Juvenile Detention Center.

"They released me to an alternative school. *New Beginnings.*" The words escaped through sneering lips. "If I behave myself there for the rest of the school year I should be able to come back to Harding next fall." He shrugged. "So they say."

"Is that what you want?" Penny struggled for the right words and tone. "To attend Harding again?"

"What I want hasn't changed. Getting me and Gabby out of Dad's house, going to live with our mom. It's all I ever wanted."

"How is your sister Gabby?" Penny immediately regretted the question.

Devin's face darkened, his eyes squeezed into slits. "She hates her foster home. Says she's bullied at the new school. She misses me." He balled his hands into fists. "My dad? He's mad at everybody about everything that's happened. It's like he wants revenge and he doesn't know where to start. With me or Gabby. With Mom. With Ms. Storme. He's drinking too much."

Penny's thoughts darted in a dozen different directions trying to find something she could say that would be comforting, not patronizing. "Do you want to talk about...about your experience at JDC, Devin? I'm not a counselor, but I am a good listener." She pulled a chair to her desk. "Sit down. Tell me about it."

The boy dropped heavily into the seat. Taking a few deep breaths, he began. "Juvie is nothing more than jail for under-age offenders. They're watching every kid every minute. It's called 'constant surveillance,' and I know that because one of the teachers used the term while warning a student troublemaker. And if you're under suspicion for something, they double down like guard dogs. You can't move from Point A to Point B without asking permission." He raised his eyes to Penny. "It's like kindergarten where you have to ask permission to take a piss."

Penny waited for Devin to resume. She did not want to appear to hurry him.

"Most people have no idea how rigid that place is. Only three doors are allowed to be open at a time and if you're placed in your room or removed from it by a supervisor, the door must be locked. Bed checks? Every fifteen minutes somebody comes in to check on you through the night. They say it's for health and safety, but the residents, as we're called, we know it's just another form of absolute control over us."

Devin's breathing had evened, but his words tumbled out as if he were ridding his mouth of a vile taste. "One girl—she disrespected a teacher—the monitor marched her to her room and locked her inside. They woke her up at 4:30 the next morning as further punishment. No appeal. Another girl, they found gang graffiti marked on the back of her door. She got forty-eight hours locked in her room."

For a few minutes both the student and Penny sat in silence. "Two girls were talking smack. It was nothing really awful, just some sarcasm during courtyard recreation. Both of them were placed in the intake cell." He paused. "And if you do something they consider very, very bad, they can send you down state where it's even stricter and it's so far away it's hard for family to visit."

"I can see why you consider JDC to be a prison, Devin." Penny took a risk with her next gambit. "Do you feel it actually rehabs juvenile offenders? I mean, did it make you think, 'Boy, I'll never mess up again, get myself back in here'?"

The student gave her a curious look. "I did nothing wrong, nothing to get me into juvie in the first place. You do realize that, don't you?" He did not wait for Penny's answer. "I will say my experience at JDC accomplished one thing."

Penny waited.

Devin's eyes narrowed. "From my time in juvie I now understand my dad's anger issues. I know how he feels when everything falls apart, seems unfair, when he lashes out at the closest target."

Penny realized then what it was that had changed most with Devin. It was a subliminal fury, lurking barely below the surface of his consciousness. Anger at forces that must appear invincible, formidable, and never-ending, completely beyond his control and caused by no fault of his own.

"Now that I'm back to living with my dad, I feel

myself being sucked into the whirlpool of his rage. I don't even want to help him out of it because I'm there myself and I like the feeling of the power." He flexed his fingers then tightened them into fists again.

Flinching, Penny gasped. "Devin, that's so unhealthy. Look, Ms. Yamada has opened her own counseling clinic. Would you like me to make an appointment for you? Talk it out with her? Can you tell her what you've told me?"

The boy took a deep breath. "I don't know. I feel like it's probably too late. And my dad is...well, he's egging me on. He wants to do something to...about Ms. Storme. Wants me to help him do something."

"If you can hold on, Devin. I have it on good authority. Ms. Storme is going to be called to account for the wrongs she's inflicted." She picked up her cell phone. "Now, I'm going to call Christine Yamada. I insist you talk to her. This is your life on the line."

"Okay. I'll talk to her," he said after a moment of silence. "Might not do any good, but I'll go if you get me an appointment real soon." Standing, he prepared to leave then looked back at Penny. "Thanks, Miss Bright. You know, you're gonna be a great teacher someday."

Penny was shaking all over. Calming herself as best she could, she scrolled through her phone contacts. "Christine Yamada," she murmured to herself. "Please answer. Please be there."

After the third ring, she heard a familiar voice. "Christine Yamada, Counseling Services. How may I help you?"

Chapter Twenty-Two

Rose surveyed the room with interest. She recognized many of those present as long-time county school teachers she had met over the years, some at department chair meetings, others at workshops, one or two from graduate school. How many knew about the mess Wendy Storme had created at Harding High? Most of them, Rose decided, judging from the sympathetic looks, head shaking aimed directly at Rose, finger pointing and text messages lighting up her phone screen, "OMG. You're at *that* school!" It was hard to stifle the reputation of a tornado like Wendy Storme.

The Superintendent's office suite included a cavernous work space for him and an adjacent, slightly smaller one for the Assistant Superintendent, Esther Nelson, whom Rose could see sitting at her desk. In between the two offices was a niche for secretary Gwen Rogers. Both offices were tastefully decorated with floor to ceiling bookshelves, solid wood desks and state-of-the-art computer systems. Rose waved a finger at Gwen, who gave her a knowing look as she walked down a short hall to the conference room where the meeting for the Advisory Committee was to take place.

Palatial in size, the chamber was elaborately outfitted with cushioned chairs, a long polished conference table and a technical-looking sound system. Recessed lighting and framed oil paintings created a luxurious ambiance. All designed to put lowly teacher-types in their place Rose suspected. After all, this was where power politics presided. Several over-sized windows cast a glow of late afternoon sun around the spacious room. Ah, Rose thought. Windows. Lots of windows. Casement windows, just as Gwen had described to her at their little meeting a few days prior to the event.

Superintendent Milton Sparkman strode to the lectern with a confidence typical of fat-cat top managerial types. Pricey dark suit, silk neck tie, slick, expensive haircut, glasses with designer frames. The very picture of white-collar success. As he spoke into the microphone, his voice was well-modulated and confident, with only a hint of condescension like one driving a Tesla into a Kia dealership to ask directions.

"Welcome to the Superintendent's Advisory Committee. I thank all of you for attending." Sparkman's smile was as sincere as that of a model for an orthodontia ad. Rose expected him to ask the attendees to identify themselves and the schools they were representing, at least give everyone a moment of recognition, but he rolled right into his agenda instead. Teachers' individuality, their respective schools, were not significant enough, evidently; Sparky wanted to move along as quickly as possible for such a mundane meeting. How important could "advisors" from every school in the county possibly be to such an erudite and successful Super?

Sparkman blathered on for several minutes about the standings of standardized test scores, budget concerns that might affect salaries and benefits, and hiring practices, none of which interested a single FAC rep in the room. At length, he stopped talking and turned another florescent smile on the group. "And now for any concerns. Would someone like to begin?"

Clenching her fists at her side, Rose stood. "Superintendent Sparkman, I am Rose Lane, FAC representative from Harding High."

A low murmur rumbled through the room, then utter silence. Every eye focused on Rose standing straight, tall and assured.

"I said I represent Harding High, but it would be closer to the truth if I told you I represent the entire support community of Harding. The eight elementary schools and four middle schools. The pyramid leaders, PTA officials, parents and students, among many other community leaders." Her voice rang clear and confident, loud enough to project to every individual present without need of the technologically advanced sound system.

Superintendent Sparkman gave a slight start then quickly recovered his composure. He opened his mouth to speak, but Rose plowed on. "Sir, it is apparent to me and all those I represent, that you must be unaware of the damage Principal Wendy Storme has inflicted, not only on teachers and students, but on coaches, guidance counselors, program directors, general staff, parents and others. Because, Superintendent Sparkman, if you were aware of Ms. Storme's unprofessional, damaging actions on such a large scale, surely you would have taken action."

In the moments before the Superintendent could formulate a response, a crescendo of mixed sounds surged toward them from outside the walls. "I would like to open the windows," Rose said, moving decisively toward the casements and throwing them open one at a time. "So that we can all see what this is about." She motioned the Superintendent to her side while throwing an inclusive look at the rest of the gathering.

Growing progressively louder were the pounding of marching feet, the beating of a kettle drum and loud chants of, "Hey, hey, ho, ho, Wendy Storme must go, go, go!" on bullhorns.

As other teachers crowded about the windows, Rose noted there were dozens of marchers, perhaps over a hundred, some carrying signs that read, "Save Harding High! Replace Storme!" and "Stop Storme!" Among the protesters were those Ashante had told her about: Jose Mendoza, Lyn and Rob Leeson and Sunitra's mother, Mrs. Benson, shaking her pompoms. Garrett Barnes marched beside Carter Thompson to Rose's utter surprise, and, holding a sign that stated, "Clear the sky of Storme," was none other than Devin Giovani's father with his arm slung around his son. Leading the parade, head held high, was Ashante Mabana, wearing a red turban and dressed in a red and gold African print pants suit. On a long pole with a brass knob at the top, she carried a flag, which she pumped up and down, like a drum major, with the cadence of the march. The logo *Justice for All* furled forth with every thrust.

Superintendent Sparkman's face paled and his hands trembled. Turning slowly from the window, he pierced Rose with his glare. "Was this your idea, Ms...?"

"Lane. Rose Lane." Rose lifted her chin slightly. "Yes sir. I did help plan this protest." Her gesture indicated the marchers who continued to circulate below the windows. "I thought it might validate the intense community disapproval of the way Wendy Storme has administered Harding High, and send a message better than anything I myself could convey."

A van displaying the television logo for a local channel pulled up. Cameramen jumped out and a reporter held out a microphone to Ashante, who stopped marching long enough to speak.

Looking out the window again, the Superintendent's face darkened to purple. His jaws clenched into a grim line. "I have had enough," he growled. Facing the teacher representatives, he barked out, "This meeting is over. Please leave. You will be contacted with a make-up date."

As others gathered their things and made ready to leave, the Superintendent placed a hand on Rose's arm. "You...Ms. Lane. I will see you in my office. Immediately."

Instinctively inhaling and exhaling yoga style, Rose placed herself somewhere between euphoria and despair. Would Sparky fire her on the spot? She checked him with a swift sideways look. Though his demeanor remained stoic, his color had muddled like a marbled Easter egg. Suffused fury. The march went on, if anything, louder and more demanding than when it began. Rose fisted her hands and took another breath as she followed the Superintendent to his office.

****

"Rose. I can't believe you...you and Ashante....*Justice for All*. You pulled it off? Right under the Superintendent's nose! The lead story on the nightly news!" Penny gawked at her mentor. "I mean, it

232

was such an audacious idea. I honestly gave it zero per cent chance of working." Rose and Penny were settled in the research room facing each other across a tiny table.

"A little drama is worth a thousand words, I always say." Rose considered her next words. "Actually, we were quite lucky. Timing is key, you know. A small detail concerning the finances involving the Superintendent's office added just the right touch of pressure. Something the Super let slip."

Penny hugged herself with delight. "Will you go through it, Rose? Step by step? It's all so...delicious! I want to be able to tell Brad every detail..." Her eyes widened. "Oh! It's okay to tell him, right?"

"Well, the event is all over the news, but we'll need to keep some of the details among the three of us. I can't see the harm in that. Just be sure it goes no farther...until the details are made common knowledge. You know, you can't keep this kind of thing secret forever."

Penny nodded so hard her hair fell over her eyes.

"So, after all the teacher reps left the conference room, the Super ushered me into his big posh office and offered a chair. Gwen Rogers saluted me as we passed her desk. She'd kept up her end of the plot by texting Ashante about when to prepare her forces and begin the march." Rose caught a breath. "Gwen also notified the television station of the protest march."

Rose smiled as she thought of Gwen's compliance with the set up. Gwen had even made sure the meeting would be held in the windowed conference room so that Ashante's band of followers could be easily seen and heard. "Sparkman called in Esther Nelson, said he wanted her to be sure to hear what I had to say. I must tell you, the Assistant Superintendent looked uncomfortable, like she might be stepping into a boxing ring without any gloves."

"I can picture that," Penny chuckled. "Maybe too close a connection with Harding High, eh?"

"Whatever. Anyway, I sat down and pulled out my notes, pages and pages documenting all of Storme's major blowouts, from firing Brad to deep-sixing Sunitra's chance for a basketball scholarship at her chosen university. The longer he listened, the more agitated he got. Twitching eye, nervous tic of the lips, constant foot tapping. You get the picture." Rose paused to catch her breath. "It was something to watch the suave executive fall apart by pieces."

"What about Dr. Nelson? Any reaction from her?"

"Let's just say her eyes grew slightly bigger with every example I cited. By the end she looked positively apoplectic. It was like she was seeing, for the first time, what her lover was really all about—what evil she could be capable of."

Penny held out her hands, palms up. "So, you had them where you wanted them—right in the palms of your hands. How did it feel, Rose? To be the standard-bearer for the persecuted of Harding High? To make your point to the tip-top?"

"Bear in mind, I was still completely in the dark as to what the top two bosses in my workforce had in mind for me. I will say, though, I could tell that the protesters had achieved their and our goal. The Superintendent and Assistant were disgusted with Wendy Storme." Rose drummed her fingers on the table. "No, disgusted is too mild. They were both boiling mad. Like volcanos, hissing steam as a build-up to a full-blown eruption." She laughed. "Dr. Nelson's complexion went lava-red every time a marcher blasted something out on a bullhorn. Her face was like a weather map showing pockets of dangerous storms."

"So, Ashante and the marchers kept it up. Whew! What a scenario!"

"Gwen and I had decided she would not signal Ashante to stop until I gave her a sign. I must say, it was all very effective. Sparky announced to Dr. Nelson and me that he'd decided to call in Wendy Storme for a conference. Tell her she has to individually speak to and make amends with every single man, woman and child she has blown over, and she must do so within two weeks or she is history. He even asked me for my notes while promising not to reveal my identity as the whistle-blower, and he said he would contact Ashante to thank her and tell her *Justice for All* had been influential in his resolution of problems at Harding High. But here's the grand finale, so to speak. After he dismissed Dr. Nelson he kind of let something slide out..."

Penny leaned in.

Rose took a breath. "The Superintendent said something odd. He was talking to himself. 'Storme, Nelson. It no longer matters...what they know.' Then he looked up at me like he forgot I was sitting there. 'Damned auditors.' He stood up and shook my hand, thanked me and dismissed me—from the meeting, not from my job, that is."

"What do you make of it, Rose? His comment about the auditors?"

"Reading between the lines. I can't reveal my

sources, but I know there's a discrepancy in Sparkman's budget. My bet? He's paying off someone. Blackmail? Extortion? Who knows? Whatever or whoever is involved, if Wendy and Esther have been holding something over him they've lost all influence now that he's sure he's going to be exposed through the audit."

Penny's doe eyes brightened. "Any ideas about the possible blackmail or extortion? What Sparky might be so afraid of?"

"The only one that makes any sense." Rose slowly and deliberately bowed her head. "His wife."

****

"Rose, can you come here for a minute?" Clementine beckoned Rose to her desk.

"Sure. What's up?" Rose and Margo had not spoken to Clementine about the mysterious stranger who'd arrived at her door in a rental car. The handsome dude wearing a wedding ring and kissing Clementine with ardor. There just did not seem any graceful way to bring up the subject.

"Ms. Storme wants to schedule you for a meeting later in the week. After school. Would Thursday be all right with you?"

Rose drew back. "Oh. I...I guess that'll be okay. Uh, any idea what she wants to see me about?"

Clementine looked serious. "All I know is, she's got a list a mile long of folks to speak with, something involvin' the Superintendent. She wants to see you at the end, kinda like a train of box cars with you as the caboose. Looks like it's gonna be a busy day, for all of us." The secretary fidgeted nervously with her appointment book. "Let me tell you, Ms. Storme is not in a good mood about whatever this is." Clementine's face fell. "She's hard enough to work for, Rose, but when she's grim...." The secretary looked down at her desk and shook her head slowly side to side, covering her eyes with her hands.

Rose had never seen the young woman when she wasn't upbeat and perky. "Clementine, are you okay?" Rose moved closer to the desk.

Wiping at a tear, the secretary raised her head and smiled feebly. "Sorry, Rose. It's really silly of me. I mean, I should be happy but my emotions must be workin' overtime. I shouldn't let my job get to me when I've just heard the best news. My G-Pop's assisted living place sent me their weekly update regardin' his health. Seems the new meds are havin' a positive effect. He's in remission. They say this will give him more time." She wiped her eyes again. "What a blessin'."

"Try to get some rest, dear girl. I expect you're right about sensitivity to the rise and fall of strong, conflicting emotions. It could make anybody teary-eyed. I'm sure your faith will sustain you."

"I'm tryin', Rose," she sniffed. "I'm tryin' so hard...to be good."

The last three words were spoken in a whisper.

Chapter Twenty-Three

There was no doubt in Rose's mind: Wendy Storme was dead. Her body sprawled at Rose's feet with a finality only death can convey, as though mind, body and soul had never existed; life had been an illusion; death the only reality.

Rose's first instinct was to scream. Her second, stronger urge, was to run. Navigating on shaking limbs, she dashed out the door and into the main office where Clementine sat at her computer. "Oh my God, Clementine! Get the school nurse. Now! It's Wendy. I...I think she's...dead."

The secretary drew back, startled. "Lord, give me strength," she sputtered, picking up the desk phone and punching the button for the school clinic. "Come quick! It's Ms. Storme! In her office." Clementine held onto the phone. "I'm callin' the EMTs next," she said.

Rose and Clementine bolted to the principal's office, though neither wanted to step into the room itself, hesitating at the door and eyeing each other. Rose nodded in the direction of the corpse. "When I came in she was sitting at her desk before she slumped to the floor. That's where I left her."

Medical bag clutched in her hand, the nurse charged past them. Turning the body to lie face up on the floor, she began CPR. Though the nurse pressed and released, pressed and released Wendy's chest, the blue face remained unchanged. "I'll keep this up until the EMT squad arrives," she grunted. "It doesn't look good, though. No response whatsoever."

Minutes later, as Rose and Clementine stood like manikins on the periphery of Storme's desk, two uniformed emergency responders whizzed past them and spoke to the nurse. "Any signs of pulse?" one asked her. "Let's get the EKG monitor on her."

Despite their efforts, Wendy's body remained blue and rigid. "No electrical response," one medic said, looking around the room at the others. "She's gone."

"I'll notify the police." The other medic pulled out a beeper. "They'll want to ascertain there's no foul play or anything suspicious."

"It looks like a natural death. Possibly an allergic reaction," the nurse put in. "Ms. Storme does have some severe allergies." The nurse moved in on Wendy's desk. "She always has an Epi-pen handy, though. If she were having a reaction, surely she would have injected herself." Her eyes surveyed the desk. "Better not touch anything," she said. "With police, on the way."

While the medical personnel talked, as they awaited the authorities, Rose and Clementine spoke quietly to each other. "Lots of people in and out of the office today, right, Clementine? You told me I would be the last conference, as I recall. The caboose, I think you called it." She glanced in the direction of the body and shivered slightly. It was, for sure, the last conference. For Rose and Wendy, too. "I suppose you have a list of her appointments? The police will no doubt want to know who all Wendy came in contact with today." She paused. "I mean, if they suspect foul play."

Clementine jumped. "Sorry. I'm stuck somewhere between numb and shock. Let me go get the list of today's appointments." She backed out the door.

For the first time, Rose took in the details of the scene. The trash can beside Wendy's desk was full to the brim with used Styrofoam coffee cups. Her eyes traveled to the coffee bar on the side wall. All it lacked was a barista. Rows of flavorings in glass bottles, a pump to be inserted in the flavor of choice. Canisters marked, Kona, French roast, Columbian, and breakfast blend containing beans, most likely. An electric grinder and a state-of-the-art coffee maker completed the picture. Starbucks would be envious.

Next Rose took in the principal's desk. Not known as a neat-freak, Wendy tended to keep things in piles rather than files, according to Clementine, who claimed she had to tidy up the principal's office daily. Still, the condition of the desk now could be described as full-on disaster. Like it had been hit by a tornado. In the bottom drawer sat an opened purse, upside down, evidently dumped of its contents. All the other drawers gaped fully extended, their contents askew as if someone had frantically rifled through them...for what? An Epi-pen, perhaps?

Clementine returned with a sheet of paper in her hand. "I made a copy of today's appointments. Want to see?"

Rose adjusted her glasses, took the paper and glanced at the recorded conferences that had been set up for twenty to thirty minute intervals. Each name or couple had been checked off, indicating they showed up: Jose Mendoza; Lyn and Rob Leeson; Mrs. Benson,

Sunitra's mother; Christine and Mikel Yamada; Devin Giovani; Ashante Mabana. Her eyes scrolled down and stopped at the next-to-last name on the list. The name just before her own: Brad McIver.

A young policeman hurried into the office. He bent over Wendy's prone body then looked up at those gathered in the room. "Any ideas of the cause of death?" He paced the room, making notes on an electronic pad before addressing the medics and nurse. "Has anybody touched or moved anything?" Pulling a latex glove over his hand, he picked up the Boss cup, looked inside and sniffed the contents. "I'm taking this with me to be checked out at the lab."

"I'm guessing anaphylactic shock," the nurse offered as the policeman returned to the body. "Ms. Storme had life-threatening allergies, including peanuts. All kinds of nuts, actually. If she accidentally ingested peanuts, she would have had to use an Epi-pen immediately. Epinephrine must be administered, otherwise her throat could close up and she would choke to death." The nurse gestured toward Wendy's body. "The swollen face points to anaphylaxis."

The two medics nodded.

"Accidentally ingested," the officer murmured, as he tapped the keys on his device. He looked up. "We will begin an investigation immediately." Turning to Clementine, he asked, "You're the secretary? Do you happen to know who Ms. Storme's doctor is? We need to get him or her on board for a death certificate. Then the coroner."

Before she could answer, a beep told Clementine she had a text message. Fishing in her pocket, she pulled out her cell phone and read. "Oh no! No!" she cried. She slumped to the floor in a dead faint.

The nurse reached her first. Raising Clementine's head, she administered smelling salts, murmuring, "Come on. Come on now, Clementine. Wake up! This has all been such a shock. I know."

The secretary's eyes fluttered then opened in a blanched-white face. "Th...the hospital no...notified me...it's my...my G-Pop," she stammered. "He's dead."

****

The authorities had requested that everyone present when Wendy's death was discovered keep quiet about the situation. Obviously, they knew nothing about the Harding High grapevine. It had served the school well when an F-5 warning was afoot and it would continue to speed word along the lines of communication branching out into every corner of the building.

Harding High was electrified. The principal was dead. Ms. Storme could never again wage war on them—not the students, the teachers, the staff. While some wandered with glazed expressions of shellshock, others could not suppress their relief, if not their joy. Various theories as to the cause of death blitzed about the school, bouncing from wall to wall, but, overall, the conclusion appeared to be that good karma had prevailed at last, erased the blight and quelled the storm forever. Carter Thompson, the original principal who had so solidly established Harding, was back at the helm as interim principal until a replacement could be found for Wendy Storme.

It was clear the police now considered Ms. Storme's death suspicious. They had analyzed the spilled coffee from her mug; it contained a high concentration of peanuts. Anaphylactic shock as the nurse had diagnosed it. The questions: Who doctored the drink, at what point during the day did she drink it and what happened to the principal's Epi-pen? The problem: So many people apparently had reasons to dispose of the woman. Any way they looked at it, the conclusion was: murder.

Rose wasted no time. Using Clementine's conference list, she personally interviewed every person who met with Wendy Storme the day she died. It was a process of elimination. She realized she herself was a likely suspect. After all, hers was the last name to appear on the list of Wendy's appointments that day. But, then, who was to say the suspects must be confined to those officially named there? Many, many others had an axe to grind with Wendy Storme, from the disgruntled sports fans to the Superintendent of Schools, Milton Sparkman. Even Esther Nelson must have had her reasons. How any of these "others" could have poisoned Storme's coffee was another question, of course.

Rose considered hiring a lawyer, but she was confident she could solve the mystery, protect herself and any other innocent suspects. In fact, Rose Lane was ninety-nine percent sure she knew who the perp was. She just had to nail down the motive. Isn't that what detective fiction always pointed to as the deciding factor for who done it? Maybe if she had read more murder mysteries. But then, Shakespeare had the answer to so many of life's questions. *Truth will out*, from *The Merchant of Venice* applied perfectly here.

They called Rose in for questioning two days later. Taking an academic attitude, after all, she had never before been a murder suspect, Rose paid attention to every nuance, every tactic, every word from the detective. He was really rather good, starting off with softball questions like, "How long have you been a teacher?" and gradually working up to, "What was your relationship with Ms. Storme? How did you view her unconventional administration? How did it affect you personally? Your department?" Apparently, they had done their homework, talked to the Superintendent, the Assistant Superintendent, who knows how many others. Even the yes-men and toadies would have to admit to Storme's hammer-hard, top-down management style. They might be spineless, but why mince words? Wendy Storme was a tornado of a woman and everybody knew it. And now she was gone.

Appearing outwardly confident, Rose still harbored a kindling of inner fear. The old guilt complex involving any interaction with police. She answered every question truthfully, allowing that she had numerous reasons to dislike and distrust the principal, but pointing out amiably that she had no reason to murder her. After agreeing to a DNA test, Rose gathered her courage and asked the detective, "So, how's the investigation going, Sergeant? Have you got your man—or woman yet?"

The detective looked momentarily surprised, perhaps unused to being on the receiving end of questioning. "We...we'll let you know, Ms. Lane. Right now, we're covering all the angles, all the suspects, and we're gathering evidence."

"Good luck, then. I hope, for the sake of everyone at school, that you'll soon have your perpetrator." She pushed back her chair. "Are we finished here?"

"I always reserve the option of recalling witnesses, or anyone with possible information or insight concerning a crime." The detective stood and shook her hand. "Thank you for agreeing to come to the station today."

"I am happy to help, Sergeant."

Driving away, Rose's thoughts focused on one central idea: her own detective work. There were only a few details to be revealed before she knew, for a certainty, who the murderer was.

Rose slid into the seat at the last booth of the coffee shop where Penny and Brad were waiting.

"You're looking awfully smug for somebody who's just been grilled by the police as a murder suspect." Brad shoved a paper cup filled with coffee into her hand. "I've gotta say, I'm not looking forward to *my* interrogation tomorrow."

Penny gave Brad a sympathetic look. "You're innocent. You've nothing to fear."

"You say. You're not on Storme's damned appointment list." Brad scowled.

Rose sipped her coffee. "Look, Brad. Consider this: When you met with Wendy Storme the day she died, she offered to dump Sparkman's nephew, the guy she hired, and give you back your job as head football coach. That's what you told me. Right?"

Brad nodded. "She absolutely guaranteed me the position. I said I'd think about it."

"That's fair. No sense in acting needy or anything." Rose's sarcasm was evident.

Penny chuckled and Brad gave a grudging upward turn to his lips.

"Here's the point. With that offer from Storme, you

had no reason to kill her. Am I right again?" Rose said.

"I see where you're going with this, Rose. I admit it does bolster my confidence a notch. I hadn't thought it through, I guess." He tipped his coffee cup against hers in a toast.

Checking her watch, Rose stood abruptly. "You two enjoy the drinks. I'm meeting someone. I have to dash."

Penny's brows shot up. "Cliff?"

Rose hesitated. "No. Actually, I'm going for a jog."

Chapter Twenty-Four

"This jog was a great idea, Rose." Clementine maneuvered some stretches, pushing her feet against the curb. "I can't think of a better way to work out the kinks, physical or mental, than a good run. With a good friend."

Was the last comment an afterthought? Or was it a plea for vindication? "I find a good brisk walk is the perfect venue for conversation." Rose bent over and touched her toes several times, limbering up. "And I do want to talk to you, Clementine."

"Well, I've been dyin' to talk to you, too." She gulped. "Oh, my. Bad choice of words."

Rose groaned.

"So, do you mind if I ask...how did your police...interrogation go?" Clementine retied her walking shoes. "I suppose interrogation is the correct term." She straightened. "Was it a real grillin'? You know, glarin' lights, a lie detector test. Were you handcuffed? Did they make you swear on a Bible?"

Rose snorted. "I believe they save the Bible oath for the trial." She recovered quickly. "If there is one, of course." Did Clementine's flushed cheeks just pale a shade or two?

Rose kept a sharp eye on the young woman's body language. It seemed she tried to hide her shaking voice with repeated, unnecessary stretching and deep breathing. "You've been asked to go to the police station tomorrow, I believe."

"Um hmm. I'm just wonderin' what to expect, you know. Never talked to the police before, except for a speedin' violation one time." Clementine gave a weak smile. "I talked the cop out of a ticket by invitin' him to a revival service at my G-Pop's church. Told him they always needed security there and that I'd put in a good word for him if he wanted a high-payin' second job."

Rose began to jog in place for her warm up. "I was a little nervous myself. But the detective I talked to seemed like an okay guy. He never pressured me into saying something I didn't mean and he didn't try to put words in my mouth." She smiled. "No lights, polygraph or handcuffs. They did ask for a DNA sample, however."

"It all sounds standard. Do you ever watch those law and order television shows where they try to trick people to make their case?" Clementine shivered. "I'd hate for that to happen to me."

"I experienced none of that. Not that I was worried. I have nothing to hide, you know." Rose fiddled with her visor hat in order to avoid eye contact with Clementine. "Have you figured out what you'll say? Your defense?"

"Defense?" The younger woman stiffened. "What do you mean?"

Rose took off, walking at a slow pace. "I think you know what I mean." As Clementine pulled aside her, Rose continued. "See, I googled your G-Pop's megachurch. It wasn't hard to find due to its size and success. There, right on the home page is a lovely, cozy picture of none other than your friend Davis Dawson, he of the rental car. Your hometown friend you were passionately kissing outside your house. The one wearing a wedding ring. Only, the photo shows an adoring wife, who is very pretty, I might add. And three irresistible children." Rose glanced sideways at her companion. "Evidently, Davis Dawson stands way up in the management of the church. An evangelical leader of the highest caliber, according to the website, who was hired a decade ago by your very own G-Pop himself."

Clementine did not break stride. "I know it looks bad, but there's another side to every story."

"That's why you moved here, right? It wasn't about losing your job. It was about carrying on an affair with your hometown lover far away from his wife and kids," Rose said. "Far away from your judgmental G-Pop, I might add. The one from whom you were to inherit millions, so long as you walked the straight and narrow moral road."

Clementine slowed to a stop. "We're in love. Davis' marriage is a sham and his wife is a shrew. He's plannin' to divorce her. We're goin' to move somewhere no one can judge us. An island in the Pacific or a mountain top out West where we can be ourselves, share our love. Not be criticized by anyone."

"I imagine your inherited millions might make that plan much more possible." Rose halted. "It didn't work out the way you hoped, though, did it?"

Clementine blinked rapidly. "Wendy found out early on. She held it over me. Threatened to tell my G-Pop and ruin everything."

"She forced you to take her bullying, swallow it with a smile of Southern sugar and Christian compassion, do her bidding, tidy up her messes and cow-tow to her every whim, no matter how petty or self-serving. She dared you to quit on her like all the other secretaries did. Or else she'd tell your G-Pop the one thing you did not want him to know." Rose smacked her hand to her forehead at the realization. "That explains it. Everyone wondered how you endured the proximity to Wendy Storme day after day maintaining a smile and a positive attitude. You should have won an Academy Award for best actress."

"When I discovered her affair with the Assistant Superintendent, I had something to counter her extortion with." Clementine's smile faded. "Word of the affair got out anyway and then the Superintendent himself told them to knock it off. So I was back to ground zero with Wendy the Storm."

Rose fixed the younger woman's shoulders with her hands. "How did Wendy find out about your love affair with Davis Dawson?" Rose strongly suspected that Clementine's affair was a piece of the murder puzzle.

Clementine hesitated, breathing shallow breaths, her lips pressed into a tight line. "Nobody knows about the private side of my life, Rose. As you intuited, that's why I moved away from my beloved-but-nosy home town. To protect us. When you and Margo caught us kissin', that was the first crack in the dam. Provin' I wasn't as clever as I thought."

"How did Wendy find out?" Rose repeated, her voice firm.

"Well, that was the second crack and it was entirely my fault. I hadn't been workin' very long at Harding High. I knew Ms. Storme was difficult, but she had not yet shown her true nature. At least not to me. I dropped my vigilance, I guess you'd say."

"Go on," Rose prompted.

She gulped and continued. "Storme found letters. In my desk drawer where I keep my religious tracts. I should never have left them there but I didn't think she would go near my faith materials, faith bein' something so overtly counter to her own moral mindset of 'lookin' out for number one.' This was before I knew how wicked she really was."

"Letters? From…?"

"One from G-Pop, in which he reiterated his requirement for my lily-white reputation as the inheritor of his fortune. And the other from Davis, of course, the direct counterpoint to G-Pop's requirement. Davis, professin' his love for me and describin' how he planned to leave his wife. Both men always communicated with me via letters; G-Pop was not comfortable usin' email and Davis feared an electronic record." Clementine frowned. "I couldn't bear to destroy them, though I should have. I know that now. They were the two most influential people in my life."

"So Wendy finds the damning letters. Then what? Did she keep them?"

"She made copies. Flashed them in my face, mind you. Every chance she got for months. And when the Superintendent directed her to do penance and absolution for her crimes after Ashante Mabana's protest march, Storme told me as soon as she wrapped it up she was going to rat me out to G-Pop. The Superintendent had forced Storme to eat crow and make nice with everybody she'd wronged, so she intended to vent her anger on me. I had served her purpose and she was all too ready to do away with me. That's how mean-spirited the witch was."

Rose tapped her foot. "I suppose you searched her office for the copies. I believe you have the master key."

"Oh yes. I tried to find those damning letters— more than once. Includin' the day of the...the day of Wendy's death."

"But you never found them. Is that why the desk was in such disarray? You were taking one last look for the evidence of your affair with Davis Dawson?"

Clementine's lips were clamped shut, her eyes hard. "I never found them," she finally muttered.

Rose pondered how to phrase her next question. "We thought the messy desk resulted from Wendy frantically looking for her Epi-pen." Rose cast a shrewd look at her companion. "What about the Epi-pen, Clementine? You must have known where Wendy kept it, familiar as you were with her office."

"Why, Ms. Storme always kept two Epi-pens. One in the center drawer of her desk and one in her purse. She locked her purse in the bottom left drawer and she kept the key on her key chain."

"Then, how did the pens go missing just when the principal needed them to...save her life?" Rose emphasized her last three words.

The secretary looked defensive, but she responded quickly, as though she had readied an answer to that very question. "They had expired. Ms. Storme brought both of them to me and demanded I get them refilled immediately. Which I did. I was going to pick them up at the pharmacy that same afternoon...the day she died."

"Clementine, I'm going to ask you something else. Something I am quite sure the police will want to question you about. How was it that Wendy Storme ingested peanuts mixed into her coffee mug when she was so careful to avoid the deadly allergens?"

"Do the police know the coffee was to blame? Maybe one of the many people in and out of her office that day offered her food containin' nuts. Or maybe a person who didn't know about her allergy had given her a homemade brownie. If you grind up peanuts real fine and cook them in brownies, you couldn't taste them at all." Clementine looked hopeful. "Or, maybe with all the coffee consumed that day, maybe somebody slipped peanut-flavored syrup into her cup. If Wendy's coffee already contained a strong flavor, say Irish cream, and there was peanut butter syrup added to the mug, she wouldn't know—wouldn't be able to taste it."

Rose twisted her lips. "Have you considered hiring a lawyer? You're going to need one." Especially if you can't come up with a better answer than the one you just gave me was a thought Rose left unsaid. She remembered a long-ago conversation with the secretary in which she boasted about the authentic ingredients in the coffee flavoring she bought for the principal. No artificial flavors from the World Market. Only the real stuff. Real peanuts in the peanut-butter flavoring, for example?

Clementine's eyes suddenly clouded with tears. "It's so hard. Just so hard. I...I've tried to talk to Davis about the whole situation. I desperately need his support, but it's like he's driftin' away. He's not even answerin' my texts or emails." A wistful look crossed her face. "We Southern women have a philosophy, you know. Men are like peaches. We salvage the good and make peach pie out of the bad." She sniffed. "I thought I had a real peach in Davis Dawson. Maybe I was wrong."

The woman looked so pathetic Rose had to force herself not to offer a comforting gesture. Instead she modulated her tone. "It's good we had this talk. I have to warn you, the detective indicated he might recall me to testify." She squirmed. "If there's a trial, my hope is that I will have a chance to let the judge and jury know how truly terrible Wendy Storme was. I will be happy to enumerate her every despicable deed."

"Thanks, Rose." Clementine wiped her eyes. "What if I need a character witness?"

"You can count on me."

Back at their starting place, the two women touched hands. Pulling away, Clementine wagged her head from side to side. "It was just two hours afterward. Two hours. Two hours after Ms. Storme died my G-Pop went to heaven." She raised soulful eyes to Rose. "Thirty million dollars."

Epilogue

They sat around Rose's living room, drinking iced tea and snacking on chips and guacamole. Cliff, Penny and Brad, Margo, and Max, who had insisted on joining them because he was privy to certain details they might not know about.

"So, there's to be a murder trial?" Margo asked. "Wow! I can't believe we've been friends with someone capable of murder."

"It's obvious you never met Wendy Storme," Brad joked.

Penny socked his arm. "For a while, there, I thought you might actually be capable of the deed yourself."

Brad pulled Penny closer and whispered in her ear, "You helped me dig myself out of the dark, sweetheart."

The others smiled at the two of them snuggling on the couch.

"You knew, didn't you, Rose?" Cliff put in. "Tell us, Miss Marple: How did you figure out who the real killer was?"

Rose shoved a chip in her mouth and drank from the sweating tea glass, taking her time to answer. "Before the cops got to them, I spoke to every single person on Wendy's appointment list that day." She directed her gaze at Brad. "Remember, Brad, you told me Wendy had offered you the head football coaching position?"

Brad nodded. "We met at the coffee shop. Right after you talked to the police."

Penny agreed. "Yes. And it was obvious Brad was totally stoked with her proposal. Willing to forgive and forget, I remember it clearly."

Rose cocked her head. "Which leads to my point. Brad wouldn't murder somebody who had just restored a broken dream." She returned to Cliff. "As for the others? Remember my talking about Jose Mendoza, the custodian the principal conned into building her home coffee bar with county materials? She falsely accused him when the officials came calling about the fake work order? She had him wreck the office furniture so she could buy more and then accused him of vandalism? The poor guy had to steal food for his starving family and was on his way to deportation. Well, Storme not only got him removed from the criminal alien list, she also restored his job at Harding High and made him head of the night custodial staff, doubling Jose's hourly wage. Now the man is one happy camper. Right?"

Cliff's smile creased his cheeks. "Strike another one from the suspect pool, Detective!"

"Ready for strike three?" Rose replaced her glass on the coaster. "Lyn Leeson, de-staffed by Wendy's lame long-term sub, Ralph Farcus. Storme landed Lyn a job with curriculum in the county office. Recognition for Lyn's superb credentials and a hefty salary increase. With benefits galore."

"Another possible suspect with no motive for murder, eh?" Cliff was impressed.

"Christine Yamada, the counselor Storme turned in for protecting Devin Giovani's bogus drug charge? She and her lawyer husband opened a private counseling firm. Well, our late principal managed to secure a contract with Social Services for troubled students to be referred to the Yamada clinic. That's for all county schools. A move sure to supply the Yamadas with a solid client base." She paused. "Christine says she and her husband are settling out of court on their lawsuit against Wendy."

"I see your line of thinking, Mom," Margo said.

"There's more. Devin Giovani wanted only to take his little sister Gabby out of the abusive home with their father and link up with the mother. On Storme's advisement, Christine's clinic was able to facilitate the move for the kids. Mr. Giovani, acknowledging his anger issues knew it was best. Christine is working with him, as well."

"That's awesome." Penny flashed a satisfied look at Rose. "Wendy Storme must have been very busy those last two weeks of her life."

"Ashante Mabana will be returning to Harding as ESL director. She told me Storme contributed a personal check for a substantial amount to fund the operations of *Justice for All*." Rose settled back in her chair.

Brad leaned forward. "You say Storme donated money to Ashante's grassroots group? You mean there was actually an altruistic bone in Wendy's body?"

"It would be nice to think so, Brad, but we'll most likely never know. It's certainly possible that her contribution to Ashante's civic organization was what it took to get the woman back on board as ESL director,"

Rose said.

Cliff spoke up. "What about the basketball player Storme benched so that she missed the scout and the scholarship? I was actual witness to that debacle."

"Oh, this one's my favorite, folks." Rose snapped up another chip and dragged it in the guacamole, chewing and swallowing it in two bites. "Wendy somehow nudged the Superintendent into naming Sunitra Benson for the Superintendent's Scholarship to the college or university of the student's choice. Along with a partial basketball scholarship from Tennessee, Sunitra will have her full ride." She wiped her hands together. "Mission accomplished. Mother and daughter couldn't be happier."

Penny had followed Rose's comments closely. "What do you suppose Wendy planned to say to you that day, Rose?"

"I've thought a good deal about that. I honestly believe that our dear departed principal intended to demote me from English Department chair and urge me to transfer. Wendy Storme was many things, but she was no fool. She likely had concluded who ratted her out to the Superintendent, even though I believed him when he said he would not reveal my role."

Max had thus far kept silent. "Rose, you are an amazing woman. Your process of elimination left the only other person in and out of Wendy Storme's office all day, the only person the principal had not smoothed over with apology and promise. The one person she planned to cheerfully toss to the wolves. The perp: the secretary, in the office, with the peanut butter." He chuckled. "Well, it sounds like the game of Clue until you get to the murder weapon, eh?"

Rose laughed with the others before growing sober. "It will all come to light in the trial, every sordid detail, I'm afraid, about Clementine's illicit affair and her grandfather's requirements for his inheritance. I won't elaborate, but it appears to be an almost airtight case. There was virtually no way anyone other than one of Wendy's appointments that day could have invaded her office and spiked her coffee." She leaned back and crossed her arms. "I've had a long talk with Clementine and know she has a ready defense, but parts of it just won't fly with a jury."

"I guess it looks pretty bad for her," Margo sighed. "It's a shame. She was becoming a good friend and jogging companion."

"You know Clementine—ever the philosopher. 'I started off as a peacock and ended up a feather duster,' was how she put it." Rose shook her head and then turned to Max. "You say you have a detail to share?" She drew her brows together. "I hope this won't compromise your job, Max."

"It has to do with the Superintendent and a condensed version has actually been in the papers. So I think I'm safe speaking here. I've been told by a reliable source that Sparkman has supplied the details to the auditors." Max turned to Rose. "Remember, Rose, when I told you, in confidence, about the audit regarding the Super's personal account at the Credit Union where I work?"

Sipping her tea, Rose nodded.

Max continued. "The Superintendent has a discretionary fund, which is just that, a fund for whatever county use he deems necessary. That fund is with the main branch of the CU. I became involved when, as his personal banker, I realized an uncharacteristic withdrawal and deposit pattern with Sparkman's own checking account. Large amounts out and then, shortly thereafter, back in. At the same time, the main branch had observed a similar pattern with the discretionary fund. The two red flags led to an audit."

"Sparkman alluded to that at our conference after the Advisory Committee meeting. Ashante's protest march around the administration building freaked him out, rattled him so that he let it out. 'Damned auditors,' were his exact words," Rose reflected.

"Oh, I remember!" Penny chimed in. "I asked you what you thought the audit was all about and you came up with blackmail. And his wife."

Max whistled. "Rose, you've just been elevated from Detective Poirot to Sherlock Holmes. That's at the core of the audit findings."

All eyes were trained on Max.

"Sparkman acquired a mistress some three years ago. Evidently a few folks in the office knew about it, since it is hard to hide such a thing." He shrugged and slanted a sideways look at Rose. "I can attest to that."

"Well, I knew about the affair," Rose put in. "Gwen Rogers, Sparkman's secretary told Carter Thompson, Garrett Barnes and me about it. She called the office a den of iniquity. And she hated the whole sex scandal atmosphere there."

Max gave her a congratulatory look. "The Assistant Superintendent also knew, but Sparkman was able to keep it quiet because he had discovered Esther Nelson and Wendy Storme's lesbian affair. They were guarding each other's nasty secrets."

"So, Sparkman was filtering money from his

personal bank account to the discretionary fund..."

"To be laundered in a shell company for paying off the mistress who was blackmailing him, threatening to tell Sparkman's wife." Max crossed his arms. "Looks like Sparkman may be going to jail, too."

For a few moments, they sat in silence, each lost in their own thoughts. At length, Rose spoke. "You know, there was no confession during my talk with Clementine. If I have to testify and I'm asked about that I can honestly say, 'No. She did not confess to the murder.'" Rose shifted uncomfortably. "I suppose that's the least I can do for my friend—my desperate friend."

"Still, it looks like murder one. Premeditation is written all over this crime," Cliff said.

Rose looked thoughtful. "You know, you read about those horribly abused women who finally snap. They can't take it anymore and they murder their abuser. Maybe it could be considered a crime of passion."

Brad nodded. "I've thought the same thing. Clementine took Storme's abuses day after day, all the while acting the part of Rebecca of Sunnybrook Farm."

"It was bound to break her down." Rose shook her head slowly. "Then, when Wendy vowed to out her to her G-Pop...it doused all hope."

"She was desperate," Penny said. "She had to save her inheritance."

Rose sighed. "There you have it. The greed factor—the one element the jury can never dismiss, no matter how awful the situation might have been."

"The irony? If Clem had just waited a few hours, she would have known about her G-Pop's death. She wouldn't have had to…" Margo trailed off.

Penny opened her arms wide. "Which leads us all to wonder: What happens to those thirty million dollars?"

Brad gave them a wry look. "That's the super jackpot question."

After a silent moment, Rose spoke. "Not saying I'm sure about this, but last time I talked to Clementine she hinted at an answer to that question, Penny. And Brad."

"Don't keep us hanging, Mom," Margo urged.

"You know that cheater, Davis Dawson? Cheated on his wife and then dumped Clementine when it looked like she was in trouble."

All eyes rested on Rose. "If she actually gets the money, Clementine is thinking about buying her G-Pop's mega-church."

Max's eyebrows shot up. "You can do that? Buy a church?"

"Clem seems to think so. It's nondenominational and independent. The grounds and buildings are extensive. The television show is under an extended contract."

Brad knitted his brows. "Why in the world would Clementine want to do that?"

Margo laughed. "Let me guess. She buys the church and then she fires Davis Dawson."

Rose took a deep breath. "Wouldn't Shakespeare have loved this plot? He already has the perfect line: *O what may woman within her hide, though angel on the outward side.*"

A word about the author...

Susan Coryell is a member of Authors Guild, Virginia Writers, and Smith Mountain Lake Writers. She has a BA degree from Carson-Newman College and a Masters from George Mason University, and is listed in several volumes of *Who's Who in Education* and *Who's Who in Teaching*. One of her favorite activities is to talk with budding writers at schools, writers' conferences, and workshops.

Susan has always been interested in Southern concerns about culture and society, as hard-felt, long-held feelings battle with modern ideas. She was able to explore these themes in her cozy mystery/Southern Gothic series the Overhome Trilogy: *A Red, Red Rose*, *Beneath the Stones*, and *Nobody Knows*, with fictional settings based on Smith Mountain Lake in Southern Virginia. The ghosts slipped in, to her surprise.

A Murder of Principle grew from her thirty years as a career educator.

Susan is also the author of an award-winning young adult novel.

When she is not writing, the author enjoys boating, kayaking, golf, and yoga. She and her husband love to travel, especially when grandchildren are involved.

http://www.susancoryellauthor.com

Made in the USA
Middletown, DE
17 March 2018